SMOKE IN BERLIN

Oriana Ramunno (Melfi, 1980) lives in Berlin with her husband and three kids. Following a number of prize-winning crime novellas and short stories in various magazines, she started writing her debut thriller *Ashes in the Snow*, inspired by the story of her great-uncle, who was detained in the Flossenbürg concentration camp.

Also by Oriana Ramunno

Ashes in the Snow

SMOKE
IN
BERLIN

ORIANA RAMUNNO

Translated from the Italian by Antony Shugaar

HEMLOCK
PRESS

Hemlock Press an imprint of
HarperCollins*Publishers* Ltd
1 London Bridge Street,
London SE1 9GF

www.harpercollins.co.uk

HarperCollins*Publishers*
Macken House, 39/40 Mayor Street Upper
Dublin 1, D01 C9W8, Ireland

Published by HarperCollins*Publishers* 2025
1
Copyright © Oriana Ramunno 2025
English translation © Antony Shugaar 2025

Oriana Ramunno asserts the moral right to be identified as the author of this work

Antony Shugaar asserts the moral right to be identified as the author of the
translation

A catalogue record for this book is available from the British Library

ISBN: 978-0-00-866892-1 (HB)
ISBN: 978-0-00-866893-8 (TPB)

Set in Sabon LT Std by HarperCollins*Publishers* India

Printed and bound in the UK using 100% Renewable
Electricity at CPI Group (UK) Ltd

For Sebastian

Prologue

22 June 1944

Underneath Berlin

With the bombs came darkness.

Whenever they landed uncomfortably close by, the naked light bulb dangling from the ceiling swayed back and forth. Occasionally, it would go out entirely, and then they were cast adrift in that lack of light, which felt strangely like death. The plaster would crumble and drop in a noisy drizzle from overhead. Before settling in heaps on the floor, it kicked up puffs of dust in the air, getting into her nostrils and making them itch. Tears would stream down her cheeks, not just tears of fright, but tears of dusty irritation.

The bombs brought darkness, and Duda hadn't seen sunlight in such a long time.

'It hardly matters. You're not missing much, girlie.'

The man who brought her food informed her that the sun no longer shone over Berlin any more; there were just long drawn-out twilights. The sky was constantly obscured by the thick smoke billowing up out of the city's blazing neighbourhoods. Actually, it was a good thing that nothing could be seen. That way, *those people* just went flying back without dropping their loads of bombs. She was lucky, really, that she already lived underground, because *up top*, every time the air raid sirens blared, people were forced to scramble out of bed in the middle of the night, rush downstairs, run for their lives in the crush of the crowds, and cram their way into already packed shelters. And if there were firebombs, buildings burst into flame, windows shattered, and burning beams fell from above. The air heated up until it was scorching hot and sucked everything into its maelstrom. Then, when they returned to the surface, they all seemed like so many ghosts. Silent, hunched, grey with dust and ash.

So that's why she wasn't really missing a thing by staying down there, underground, day and night, for months on end, the food man explained, and Frau Frya nodded behind him. Or had it been a year already? Time changed underground, crumpling up and stretching out. Sometimes she seemed unable to remember anything from before – nothing, not even her own name. She knew only that she had dark eyes, just like her mother and her grandmother before her had had. Just like the walls of Berlin after the flames died down, said the food man, adding that you could scrape the charred black from the bombs off the stone with your finger and use it to write with.

'The backs of the books stand in rows.' Duda read aloud for everyone in the room, to help kill time, though underground time was damned hard to kill.

She followed along, keeping her place with the tip of her

finger. The edges of the book's pages were singed. Frau Frya said that it was a miracle the book had even survived. All the other books, carefully arranged on the bookshelves or stacked in tall piles, nearly teetering, had also escaped both Nazi bonfires and enemy bombs. They, too, lay hidden underground, but not like dead bodies. More like seeds. Seeds lie underground through the whole winter, as if they aren't even there, but all the while, they're nourishing themselves, growing stronger, protecting themselves against the freezing temperatures, and then, when spring finally comes, they break through the ground and reach up to the sun, like some miracle.

Who could say whether the same thing would happen for them.

'I know them all still, I remember arranging them in order.' The light from the lamp was dim at best, and she was forced to strain to make out the letters as she uttered each syllable. 'I implore them with my eyes: "Speak to me – take me up – take me, Life of my Youth – you who are carefree, beautiful – receive me again."'

She stopped reading.

'What's the matter?' the food man asked. 'Are you tired of reading? Here, let me take over.'

She shook her head. She wrapped herself tighter in the shawl embroidered with red roses.

'No, it's just that I can't remember any more what life was like before.'

'Before all this, you mean?'

She nodded. But it wasn't entirely true. If she tried hard enough, if she squeezed her eyes shut tight and pressed her hands over her ears, and if she held her breath to ward off the stale, dusty funk of sweat and fear, then *something* would come back to her. The sky had always seemed free and bright, *before*. She used to run barefoot on the wet grass, in front of the gypsy wagons. She remembered the colourful skirts and Grandma Rose's shawls. There were lions, there were elephants. And there was Dieter.

Chapter 1

Berlin, Nikolaiviertel Quarter

Hugo stirred his ersatz coffee.

The sound of the coffee spoon against the porcelain offered the illusion of safety, though he'd never been closer to danger than he was now. In a city that sat beneath a rain of fire, and with more than one secret to hide, he constantly felt like he was walking along the edge of a cliff. It would be so easy just to let himself fall, put an end to these sleepless nights, like the one he'd just suffered through, but all it took was a glance towards the bedroom, where little Gioele still lay sleeping, to make him remember that he still had something that made keeping his balance seem worthwhile.

He glanced out of the window and sipped his ersatz coffee. Outside, the sky looked like molten lead. A mass of metal suspended over the city, ready to flow down and over the dawn twilight. A dull light crept into the kitchen, casting everything in a benumbed blue: the table, the oven, the dishes still stacked in the sink. The house was asleep. He could feel it breathe, hear the creaking of the beams, the groaning of the bricks still intact in the midst of an almost destroyed neighbourhood. He was one of the lucky few with a roof still over his head.

He savoured that unusual silence, which was usually drowned out by the ominous sounds of air raid sirens, the roaring of planes, and the anti-aircraft fire. On the horizon, beyond the buildings and towards the suburb of Brandenburg, he could still see the column of smoke rising high into the sky. The buildings had been consumed by flames, turning into so many furnaces that blazed for hours. Now, with the fires finally under control, all that remained was that grey mass of smoke curling up into the sky. It contracted and spread out over the city, settling on buildings and in people's lungs.

Fire and ash.

He tried to draw a breath into his lungs, but once again he felt that sensation of some imitation of death that had sunk its claws into him for days now. The harder he tried to inhale, the shorter his breath. It was like trying to fill a torn bag.

'You're alive, Hugo . . . You're alive,' he told himself.

He clung to the windowsill. The fact that he could speak meant he was still getting oxygen. He didn't know why he craved air so desperately. Was multiple sclerosis stealing away his lungs, too, along with his leg? Or should he blame the sleepless nights and the constant close contact with death that had been part and parcel of their daily life in all those months of bombings?

Or maybe it's because I'm hiding a Jew.

The wind carried the stench of something burning into the living room. Hugo shut the window.

Less than a handful of months ago, during the investigation at Auschwitz, he remembered breathing in that same smell. He couldn't seem to get it off his skin, out of his nostrils. There were nights when he awakened in a pool of sweat. He had dreamed that he himself was burning in the heaps of corpses, along with the dead Jews. His body blistered and swelled upon the scorching embers, his flesh tore open, his eyes melted, and the SS guard dogs barked and licked their ravenous chops. When the air raid siren startled him awake from those nightmares, he practically sighed with relief.

Hugo placed the coffee cup on the table, grabbed his cane, and dragged himself to the bathroom.

He dropped his undershirt on the floor. He scrubbed his face and neck with the last remaining piece of soap. The mirror before him reflected a face he scarcely recognized. Who *was* he now? He was no longer a member of the Nazi Party, but hardly a soul to be blithely absolved, either. He scraped the razor over his cheeks, shaving carefully. Again and again, the same act, as if each stroke of the razor could scrape away a layer of darkness. But he wasn't trying to fool himself. The things he'd seen at Auschwitz would remain etched into his flesh forever, together with the sure knowledge that *he* had been a cog in the machine. A bar of soap and a razor would never suffice. No absolution.

Hugo patted his face dry. He donned his shirt. Knotted his tie. Combed his hair.

He opened the cabinet and hefted the box of Pervitin in one hand. It had been a long and trying night. The pain caused by the disease seemed to get worse when he was upset, and life with the Gestapo breathing down his neck combined with the fear of dying in a bomb blast strained his nerves well past breaking point. He was ready to snap at any moment. Though tempted to put the methamphetamine back in the medicine chest, at last, he simply placed the pill on his tongue and gulped it down.

He glanced into the mirror and swam into the icy reflection of his own eyes, lost. There were too many demons he had to hold at bay. He certainly couldn't do it alone. He'd never been able to.

Chapter 2

Outside, Berlin was nothing but a paltry memory of the splendid city it had once been. The night-time lights and the boisterous, jumping nightspots had been banished by curfews. Lamps and streetlights were extinguished lest they lead enemy bombers to some choice target. In parts of the city, the air was still redolent with the scent of linden trees and cool lawns; elsewhere, the twin stench of flame and blood overpowered all. Where there had once been flower-beds, now there were vegetable patches to make up for the chronic food shortages. Even Gendarmenmarkt had been stripped of its former loveliness and turned into nothing more than an open-air farm.

Hugo stepped around a fallen building cornice, shoving the debris aside with the tip of his cane. He glanced up at the window of his apartment, on the second floor of the still-intact building. The damp cardboard that stood in place of the shattered windowpane revealed nothing of the bedroom behind. Yet that did nothing to make Gioele any safer.

He checked his wristwatch. Half past six in the morning. It must be something very serious if Arthur Nebe had asked to see him urgently at such an early hour. The ringing phone had shattered the silence of his apartment. Actually, though, he hadn't been sleeping. He'd been tossing and turning in the bedsheets, so he felt some gratitude to the officer on the other end of the line for forcing him out of bed. An instant later, a hint of suspicion crept into the mix. The Kripo chief would send a police car to pick him up: was that police or Gestapo? At the thought, a chill ran down the back of his neck, even though the heat of late June, made warmer by the fires, had hovered oppressively since dawn. He loosened his shirt collar, but it didn't help. His skin burned.

'Heil, Hitler!' A young man waved his arms emphatically in his direction. The young man was clearly in a hurry.

Hugo felt relief at the sight of the green Ordnungspolizei uniform as well as the squad car parked a short distance away, occupying the only parking spot on the street free of debris. At least this wasn't Gestapo, at least not officially.

Hugo quickened his step. 'Honoured to make your acquaintance, Herr . . .?'

'Lukas Eder, sir.' The young man opened the car door for him with all the deference of a puppy. Only then did Hugo notice that he wore a black eye patch. 'It's my great honour to drive for you, Herr Fischer.' With one hand, the young man cleared the seat of file folders and brushed away the ash that had blown in through the broken window. 'You're the talk of Orpo.'

'And what do they say about me there?' Hugo took his seat, feigning blithe indifference. He tossed his cane onto the back seat and pulled the door shut. 'That I limp because of my multiple sclerosis?'

The youngster laughed, as he'd expected. No one could conceive of the idea that an Aryan like him could be suffering from a degenerative disease. If it hadn't been for Dr Meyer's complicit silence, he'd have long ago been subjected to forced euthanasia. In the best-case scenario, there would be sterilization, to ensure he had no opportunity to contaminate the precious German blood pool by siring children.

The young man shook his head with a grin and started the car.

'Everyone knows you had polio, just like Roosevelt,' he finally replied.

'And do they say that I'm concealing a Jew at home?'

'That would be rich!' The young man laughed even louder. 'A Jew . . . No, what they *do* say is that you're one of the Third Reich's finest criminologists . . . And they also comment on the brilliant manner in which you solved the Braun case at Auschwitz.'

Hugo let the subject drop, by no means flattered by all the flattery. The less said about the Braun case, the better. He'd even avoided telling Nebe more than he strictly had to. The case had been filed away, the camp Kommandant was satisfied, and that should have been it. How it had been done, and at what cost, was destined to remain a secret, burdening no one's conscience but his own.

Outside the car window, Berlin went streaming past. It resembled nothing so much as one of those dismembered corpses he so often saw in the medical examiner's office. A streetscape swathed in bruises, burns, broken bones, and people trying desperately to reassemble it all. After every bombing, people dragged bodies from under the rubble and laid them out on the street. Hundreds of men, women, and children, clothing ripped, faces filthy with blood and dust, all lined up like pieces of a shattered domino set. Perhaps this was some form of punishment for the things he'd seen at Auschwitz-Birkenau.

'What's that place like, anyway?' The young policeman went back to asking questions.

'Which place?'

'Auschwitz, the camp . . . Do they really burn Jews there?'

'Where is it we're going?' Hugo asked, trying to steer the conversation elsewhere.

'Wannsee, sir . . .'

'What is it that Nebe wants? And why Wannsee? Couldn't he just summon me to his office?'

'I have no idea. All I know is that he told me to come get you, nothing else.'

Lukas Eder shrugged indifferently. He was driving slowly through the rubble, glancing back and forth between the road and Hugo's face. The young man's face still looked utterly innocent. Even the black eye patch wasn't enough to make him seem menacing.

Hugo sighed. He leaned back, letting his head sink into the seat. He wriggled a little, trying to find a more comfortable position, and inwardly uttered thanks to the Pervitin, which was starting to take effect now. The thing that made his life so complicated was his inability to complain aloud. He had to conceal his fear that some part of his body might suddenly fail, like his lungs, for instance. He could never hope for so much as a crumb of human concern. People only noticed the dark circles under his eyes, but who didn't have bags under their eyes, after all, in a collapsing world?

Still, all he was allowed to say was that he hadn't slept well. If he had any weeping to do, he'd have to do it in the dark, in the privacy of his bedroom. Or perhaps in the living room, but early in the morning, long before sunrise. It became clear to him how deeply lonely he was.

'In any case, the answer is yes.'

'The answer to what?'

'To your question. Yes, they burn Jews.' Hugo could feel the ersatz coffee churning in his stomach. There was no sound other than that of the car lurching along Unter den Linden, steering around the rubble around the bridge. 'They gas them to death in a special chamber, then they burn the corpses in crematoriums. Is that what you wanted to know?'

Lukas burst out laughing. Hugo wasn't surprised. It was the laugh of a boy who still smacked of his days in the Hitler Youth. And yet, in Lukas's rigid posture, from his clenched jaw to his skinny fingers clutching the steering wheel, Hugo recognized a familiar tension. No doubt the young man felt anything but comfortable with those conversations.

'And that makes you laugh?'

'Forgive me, Herr Fischer. It's just that I can't help noticing how we Germans always seem to have an efficient solution for everything. You can't deny it.'

'No, it's true. We're *efficient*, if nothing else.'

Lukas ground the gears as he awkwardly shifted. Hugo decided to lean in a little harder, trying to understand just what kind of a German he was dealing with.

He waved his hand at the shattered cupola of the Berliner Dom, which stood reflected in the river Spree, no longer proudly bedecked with its gorgeous stained-glass windows. 'The fact that Berlin looks like this, we can blame it on

Jews, gypsies, and communists. They all dragged us into this war. I say, long live German *efficiency*. Am I right?'

The young man gave him the side-eye. He seemed far from stupid. If anything, he seemed shrewd, at least to judge from his one good eye, which gleamed bright blue. Lukas's grip tightened on the steering wheel, and he compressed his lips, and then sucked in his lower lip. Hugo had the impression that something was grinding away inside him, perhaps the fear that his suddenly dilated pupil might give him away. After all, there were Gestapo informants everywhere.

'Keep your eyes on the road,' Hugo warned him.

They left the Berliner Dom behind them and drove past the Friedrich Wilhelm University. The campus had been ravaged, the library had burned to embers. Every single thing, in that city where he'd grown up, was slowly crumbling to ashes or melting in the flames. This is where the Führer's psychosis had brought them. Hitler alone had been responsible for this disaster.

During the earliest bombings, the German people had poured out into the streets in support of the Third Reich, waving flags. A red river, running fast with sentiment and enthusiasm. Now, German morale was in the gutter. They'd been living under bombardment for months, in the coldest season of the year. They'd been made homeless just as snow piled up along the streets, as icy winds sliced through the rubble. Whole families had nothing left to their names, and what little remained to them could be stacked up on a handcart or carried in a valise. Flags fluttered, that was still true, but with the weary lethargy of a dying people.

Lukas slowed down to wend his way around the heaps of debris. Alongside the roadway, there were already women setting up open-air stoves. That was the sole consolation in a city that reeked of death. Soon, the smell of simmering soups would mingle with the odour of dust, and the crackling of firewood heating bricks would make them forget the raging flames of the bombing raids.

Just short of the Brandenburg Gate, which still rose, grey and imposing, against the brightening sky, a gendarme waved them to a halt.

Lukas pulled over at the checkpoint, turned off the engine, and handed over his permit and his badge. The German shepherd sniffed at the air, restrained by its leash. The gendarme lowered his rifle and peered inside the car. He scrutinized them, eyes peering out from beneath the brim of his green helmet.

'You may proceed,' he said at last.

Lukas started the car again, slipping his permit back into his breast pocket. Hugo glanced up at the rear-view mirror. The squad of military gendarmes and the shattered buildings of central Berlin grew smaller and smaller behind them, on the far side of the Brandenburg Gate's monumental columns. The grey stone of the city proper started to give way to the lush greenery of Tiergarten. They also left behind them another symbol of the birth of their great empire: the Victory Column. An empire that now lay in shambles.

For dust we are, and to dust we shall return.

'Once we've won the war, we'll fix everything good as new.' Lukas seemed to read his thoughts. 'No matter *whose* fault this all may be.'

'You can't fix the dead good as new,' Hugo retorted.

'No, you can't fix them, fair enough. Have you any children, Herr Fischer?'

'Only one,' he replied curtly.

'What about your wife, is she very beautiful?'

'I'm not married.'

'But if you have a child . . .'

'I had an affair with a Bavarian woman. She died in December, so I'm the child's only living kin. Believe me, I'm not much of a father.'

'I have no children.' Lukas smiled, his eyes looking out at the road that was taking them towards the Zehlendorf district. 'But I'll have some, once I find a good woman, that you can be sure of. My mother lost all her other sons in battle, and I want to make sure I give her plenty of grandchildren. That'll bring a smile back to her face, just like she was before the war. God, I don't even remember what things were like before the war . . .'

Hugo turned to take a look at him. His blond hair, shaved at either side of his head, was tousled by the warm wind blowing in through the broken car windows. His lips, full and prominent, his skinny neck, with the Adam's apple that almost seemed to stick out through his flesh, and his cheeks, covered with such a fine down that there was no need to shave: he was barely more than a boy, just starting out in life, but in a world that already lay sloppy dead.

Hugo wisely refrained from telling him any of that.

'You're so young. Just how old are you?'

'Twenty-four, sir.'

'And you weren't sent to the front?'

'Of course I was.' Lukas pointed up at his eye patch. 'Since all my brothers were dead already, once I got this injury, they sent me home. Once the war is over, I hope to join the Criminal Police. I'd like to become a criminologist.'

'It's not a very nice job.'

'Then why do *you* do it?'

Hugo said nothing. What *could* he say? That he understood the dead better than he did the living? That it was only among the dead that he could find the strength to cling to life and accept the disease that was devouring his brain? Or that this was his way of banishing the ghosts of the past and cleansing his conscience?

'The pay is pretty good,' he replied at last.

'All right, fair enough . . .'

The car continued on its way towards the bend in the Havel river. Lukas, now silent, turned off onto the road that ran around Lake Wannsee and pulled to a stop in front of a small villa nestled amidst the greenery, one of many overlooking the little haven that was the Alsen villa colony. No blackened, bomb-cratered walls here, or at least, not yet. No sound but the lapping of the lake water and the chirping of birds in the branches of the trees. The air was thick with the scent of blossoms. No weeds, no rubble, no shattered glass piled up at street corners. A paradise, so close to hell itself.

'We're here.' The young policeman switched off the engine. 'I'll wait here in the car. I can take you back afterwards.'

'So you're hoping to become a criminologist, are you?' Hugo grabbed his cane and got out of the car. 'Come along and maybe you'll learn something.'

'Do you mean it?'

'I'm prone to changing my mind easily, so come on, get moving.'

Lukas didn't have to be told twice. He jumped out of the Mercedes and hurried after him.

They found Arthur Nebe awaiting them at the villa's entrance. The SS insignia on his uniform gleamed in the morning light. He greeted the two of them with a nod, his eyes shadowed beneath his hat brim, his eyes glum with the burden of being here instead of somewhere else handling weightier matters.

As they approached him, Hugo glanced around at the other policemen, who were standing off to one side smoking. They were speaking in low tones and shaking their heads.

'I'm sorry I had to have you dragged out of bed at this early hour.' Nebe rested one hand on his shoulder, a familiarity he reserved only to a favoured few. 'But I had no choice.'

'I wasn't sleeping anyway. So what's going on?'

'We have a nasty situation. Herr and Frau Weidt are dead. This is a matter that demands the utmost discretion in how it's handled, if you follow me . . .'

Just then, the two coroners exited the villa. Following behind them, a group of labourers carried two heavy black body bags. Hugo unfastened his shirt collar and inwardly hoped that the Pervitin wouldn't make him any more jittery than necessary. Was this a matter requiring such discretion that he wouldn't even be allowed to view the bodies at the crime scene?

'What's the meaning of this?' he asked, exhaling. 'You summon me for an investigation and then cut me out of it?'

'What are you thinking, Fischer? Of course, I've had every detail of the scene photographed; there's nothing you won't be able to review later, at your leisure. Keller will make sure you can watch the autopsy. I just need to get this place straightened up before the press arrives. I'm sure you can understand . . .'

'That's not the way I work . . .'

Nebe forced a smile to his face, so that his nose resembled

the beak of an eagle about to strike. 'You worked at a far worse crime scene at Auschwitz, didn't you?'

'Something I'd just as soon not experience a second time.' Hugo felt his teeth clamping. He forced himself to breathe more steadily. 'Was it absolutely necessary to move the bodies before I got here?'

'I had my reasons. Believe me.'

'Are there any witnesses, at least? Who raised the alarm?'

'The children. They're with the neighbours right now . . . They're still a bit . . . *shaken up.*'

'How old are they?'

'The boy is ten, the girl fourteen. By the way, how's your son these days?'

Chapter 3

Gioele looked up.

The bomb was dropping from on high. It resembled a grey egg, descending slowly like a snowflake. At first, it was nothing but a dot, hard to distinguish from the winter sunshine that sat over Berlin like a kind of dampness, but in time it grew, dropping ever closer until, in the end, it was there, ready to open up.

When it hit the building, it sounded like a storm exploding. There was a roar of crumbling bricks, twisting iron, and windows shattering into a thousand gleaming shards. Then came flame, bursting outward, flickering tongues twisting and sweeping everything away in their path. Then the building became a dragon exhaling fire from its every orifice.

Gioele felt the heat hit him. The scorching wind sucked him in. His clothes stuck to his skin, and the shockwave slammed him against a shop window marked with a Star of David. The glass rained down on him in sharp fragments, and the dust from the explosion suffocated him. Ash fell slowly, darkening everything. As the fire consumed the city, snow began to fall. The heat of the flames gave way to a chill.

Gioele rubbed his eyes.

He looked around.

He was in Block 10 of the Stammlager at Auschwitz, in the dark hallway that led to Mengele's office. He walked slowly down the hallway, leaving Berlin behind him. The floor was freezing cold beneath his feet. The office door stood open. He pushed it aside easily and peered into the room. Outside the window, he could hear the soft sound of falling snow. A faint glow seeped in, imparting a glow to the eyes of Mengele's test subjects. They were arranged neatly, fastened to a bulletin board with large pins. Gioele recognized the eyes of his brother, his mother, and his father.

'You abandoned us.'

The sound of a voice made him turn and look. In the pitch-black tangle that occupied one corner of the room, something stirred, but he could make out nothing in the darkness.

'You abandoned us just so you could save yourself.' It was his brother. He recognized him by the way he mispronounced his R's.

'That isn't true!' he shouted, clenching both fists.

'You left here with a Nazi!'

'That isn't true!'

'Yes, you did!'

A foot emerged from the tar-black shadows. Then another, and another. Gabriele, his mother, and his father all stared out at him, their eyes so many dark, hollow, cavernous sockets. They no longer had eyes, yet they still seemed to see him.

It was true. He had abandoned them.

Gioele felt a scream pressing against his ribs.

He grabbed the blankets, trying to hold on to anything that could keep him from falling. He gasped for air, but he couldn't fill his lungs. He tried to get out of bed, but he was nailed to the mattress. All he could see was his bedroom ceiling and part of the wall on his right, with the cardboard-covered window and the drawings hanging on the wall. Again, he tried to inhale. He was dying.

'Keep calm, calm down!'

A pair of hands grabbed him firmly, forcing him to sit up.

'I can't breathe,' he gasped.

'Of course you can breathe; you're talking, aren't you?'

'I can't breathe!'

The hands shook him over and over. Only then did his body seem to remember what it was supposed to do. His lungs expanded. The air rushed in all at once, forcing a sound out of him that rang in his ears like something inhuman. A swarm of ants surged through his legs and arms. He squirmed to shake them off, but they were everywhere, under his skin, inside his muscles.

'Breathe,' the voice continued. 'Good boy. Slowly now.'

Gioele looked at the man who had come to his aid, and only then did he recognize Edmund. He stared at him through thick round glasses, his eyes like a pair of steel marbles. He smiled, and suddenly, Gioele felt safe.

'It's all right,' Edmund whispered in his smoke-coarsened voice. 'Oh, what have we here?' He ran his hand through Gioele's hair, right behind his ear, and extracted a shiny coin. 'Well, if every nightmare you have earns you a coin from behind your ear, we'll soon be rich!'

Gioele was tempted to laugh, but instead, he felt his eyes and nose fill with salt. He buried himself in Edmund's arms, unable to hold back his sobs. His chest ached from trying to push back the tears.

'Go ahead and cry, it'll cleanse your soul a bit,' Edmund murmured. 'Do you want to tell me what you dreamed about?'

'No.'

'That's all right.'

'I . . .'

Gioele stopped. He looked at the drawings on the wall. He had drawn the faces of his brother and parents before they faded entirely from his memory. The tingling in his hands returned, stronger than before.

'I hate Hugo!' he shouted. 'He took me away from Auschwitz!'

'And isn't that a good thing?' Edmund sighed. His glasses slid down to the tip of his thin nose, so that he had to push them back up with a deft motion. 'Hugo told me exactly what happens in that place . . .'

Gioele hunched his shoulders. The image of Jews crammed into the shower room made him shiver. He remembered the naked bodies pressing against him, the hands pounding on the steel door, as they begged for it to open, the screams of terror echoing off the porcelain tiles. The SS soldier who finally opened the door and let him out – Hugo Fischer as he grabbed him, wrapping him in his coat and hurrying him to safety, telling everyone he met that he was the boy's father.

Gioele felt like crying again.

'Hugo saved your life.' Edmund wiped away a tear.

'But he took only me! He'd promised to help my parents, not just me!'

'There was nothing else he could do, and you know it.'

Gioele hid beneath the blankets. He felt ungrateful. His mother had taught him to be kind and grateful, yet all he felt was anger and resentment. He was glad he hadn't died, and that made him feel even more wretched. How could he be happy when he was the only one who'd been saved? All those emotions overwhelmed him, blending into one horrible feeling. He had drawn it once: it was a dark, sooty monster, and there in the monster's belly was *him*, a tiny red dot being devoured.

'I know there was nothing he could do,' he whispered. 'Still, he only took me from one prison to another. He never lets me leave this place. He keeps me locked up like a mouse, but he's always in the outside world . . .'

'Hugo is doing his best. He just wants to keep you safe.' Edmund gently took the boy's arm. He uncovered the flesh where the number had been tattooed on him at the camp, when he first became one of Dr Mengele's children. 'You have a fake identity document, but it's not enough. This can't be erased . . . And if the Nazis ever see it . . . we're in trouble, for you, but for us, too. Do you realize what a risk we're running just to keep you safe?'

Gioele yanked his hand away. He hated that number, but then again, it was the only thing still linking him to his brother and parents, the only thing that reminded him they were still at the camp.

'Look how sweaty you are.' Edmund ran a finger around the inside of his pyjama collar. 'Let me draw you a warm bath. It'll help you relax a bit.'

He moved to take off Gioele's shirt, but Gioele recoiled, without meaning to. Being naked in someone else's presence made him tremble. His teeth started chattering, and now he couldn't stop.

'I'm sorry.' Edmund placed both hands on his thighs and heaved a sigh. 'I didn't mean to.'

'I don't know *why* it bothers me so much . . .'

Edmund smiled. 'I do. And one day, you'll be able to understand it.'

He took him by the hand and led him into the bathroom. He ran a tub of warm water, and when his bath was ready, he left the bathroom so he could bathe alone.

Gioele undressed. The air on his bare skin made him shiver. The feel of the tiles beneath his feet was almost intolerable. He climbed into the tub and curled up in the warm water, knees pulled to his chest. So many people had seen him naked in the showers at Auschwitz. That night, he remembered undressing with the other prisoners and entering the room lined with white tiles. Pressed up against each other, skin against skin, he'd felt no shame. But now, the mere thought of Edmund or Hugo seeing him without clothes on simply terrified him.

'Are you done?' After a while, Edmund's voice came from behind the door.

Gioele got out of the tub, dried off, and got dressed. He approached the fogged-up mirror, wiped it clean with one hand, and saw his eyes in the reflection. The eyes that had won him *Uncle* Mengele's attention: green, with that tiny spot of brown, only in the left iris. Heterochromia, the doctor had said.

Gioele combed his hair just like Hugo's. He even dabbed on two drops of Hugo's cologne, from the bottle that sat there on the shelf. He wondered why he even bothered to wash and groom himself, if he was only going to stay indoors, hidden away.

Edmund stood outside the door, waiting for him, arms crossed.

'Why the long face?' he sighed.

'It's nothing . . .'

'All right. Now I have an idea of something we can do.' He glanced in the mirror and smoothed back his white hair. He polished his glasses, adjusted his braces and tie, and went over to put on his jacket. 'Let's go for a nice walk.'

'Outside?'

'Of course.'

'What about Hugo?'

'There's no need to tell him anything. It'll be our little secret.'

'But what if he finds out?'

'Well, I *am* his father, aren't I?'

Chapter 4

'My son is just fine, thank you.' Hugo tightened his grip on the handle of the cane, leaning on it with his full weight as if that could also give him greater leverage over Nebe, who stood firm in his SS uniform. 'Herr Gruppenführer . . . I *need* to see the bodies. Believe me, the dead speak better than the living. You called me here to solve a case, so let me do my job.'

Nebe's small blue eyes, hidden beneath thick, dark eyebrows, scrutinized him. He clucked his tongue against the roof of his mouth and managed to put a smile on his leathery face. Hugo understood that Nebe was finally relenting.

'Listen carefully, Fischer.' He pointed his finger at him. 'A quick look, nothing more. The journalists are coming, and the last thing I want are any compromising photos.'

'It seems to me that the press hasn't been much of a problem since the Reichstag fire . . .'

'Your tongue has been getting dangerously loose lately, you know that?'

Nebe motioned to the coroners, who pulled the gurneys

towards them. Dr Keller opened each body bag with a sharp tug and then stepped aside. Hugo moved closer, motioning for Lukas to come and look as well.

'Do you have a problem looking at dead bodies?' he asked.

'No, Herr Fischer. I saw plenty of dead bodies at the front.'

Hugo pointed to Herr Weidt's corpse. A gunshot wound had blown away the right side of his skull. There wasn't much left of the cranium. He could hardly even make out the man's facial features, buried as they were under bone fragments and brain matter. Blood had poured out of his mouth, soaking his shirt and filling the air with an unpleasant, metallic odour.

'What can you tell me about him?' Hugo turned to Nebe.

'Benedict was an eye specialist at the Charité, a renowned physician.' The Gruppenführer gestured towards the other body. 'But the true star of the Party was his wife, Marlene.'

Hugo opened the other body bag. Frau Weidt looked as if she were asleep, except for all the blood that had soaked her slender neck and breasts, visible through her nightgown. He saw a gunshot wound to her chest.

'Any other signs of violence?'

'A laceration to the back of the head.' Keller dabbed at his double chin with a linen handkerchief. 'Someone must have struck her hard from behind. There doesn't seem to have been any struggle, but that's something I'll only be able to confirm after the autopsy, as I'm sure you'll understand.'

'What do you mean that she was a star of the Party?' Hugo turned back to Nebe.

'Marlene was an anthropologist; she was a collaborator of Robert Ritter's at the Racial Hygiene Research Centre. The Party held her in particularly high regard for her studies on Gypsies. They were both very important figures, as you've probably gathered by now, and I don't want the Gestapo interfering in this case. I want a swift, clean, discreet investigation.'

'Understood.' Hugo rubbed his face. If Nebe feared interference from the Gestapo, there was something fishy going on here. 'Have you come up with any idea of what might have happened?'

'It looks like a combination crime of passion and suicide. Benedict Weidt clubbed his wife on the back of the head with a marble statuette we found in the house. He finished her off with his handgun, which was legally registered, and then shot himself in the head. You can see the result.'

Hugo listened carefully. He could hardly help but smile, disrespectful though it might have seemed. He blamed the Pervitin. It felt like Nebe was feeding him only the select information he chose to provide. And who was Hugo to contradict him or search for some other version of the truth, especially if the Gestapo might stick its nose in? He thought of Gioele, and the urgent need to steer clear of any sticky or dangerous situation suddenly outweighed his instincts as a detective.

'So, you've already solved the case,' Hugo commented. 'Why bother to bring me in at all?'

'Because I want proof of the motive. I want you to find Marlene's lover.'

'You believe there was a lover?'

'There always is. And, let's just say . . . certain rumours are going around.'

'I understand. Please show me where you found the bodies.'

Nebe led the way with a military stride. Lukas followed them in silence.

Inside the villa, the large windows let morning light flood in, cascading like cool water over the pastel-coloured walls and highly polished wood floors. A series of marble statues and busts were interspersed with paintings and hanging plants. The living room looked more like an artist's studio than the home of a luminary in the field of ophthalmology. Only one painting revealed Herr Weidt's true passion: out of that large oil painting, a large black eye stared at them intently.

Hugo walked past a gold-framed mirror leaning against the wall. It reflected natural light from the windows, scattering it everywhere. It seemed impossible to think of this place as a crime scene. He imagined Benedict and Marlene having breakfast at the round table by the windows that overlooked the garden, while one of their children played the grand piano. How had they come to such an end? What resentments and demons had taken hold of them?

Nebe stopped beneath the crystal chandelier at the centre of the room and pointed at the rug between the sofa and the marble fireplace. Next to the sofa, by a pedestal with a square base, lay a statuette of the goddess Diana, broken in half – the weapon someone had used to strike Marlene in the head.

'He collapsed to the ground here,' Nebe said, pointing out the bloodstain spreading across the rug. 'He killed himself right in front of the woman he loved.'

'He had a strange way of showing it.'

'He must have lost his mind.'

Hugo felt his leg tingling more than usual. There was something about this crime scene that didn't add up. The absence of the bodies was the single most jarring feature, of course: why had Nebe excluded him from the crime scene, why had he ordered the bodies removed in such haste? Since when had the head of the Criminal Police feared the arrival of journalists who were mere puppets of the Party? He studied the rug. There were still scattered remnants of brain matter. The fabric had absorbed the blood, keeping it from puddling across the floor. There were no shoe prints, therefore. But something else *was* missing, he could feel that. He let this sense of incompleteness settle and take form. If his hunch was correct, his mind would surface it when the time came.

He turned to Nebe. 'Have you checked the gun for fingerprints?'

'The forensic technicians will do their best . . . but apparently the youngest son picked up the gun when he found the bodies.'

Hugo looked again at the empty space where the bodies had lain. 'This is the last time I collaborate with the Kripo if I'm forced to work under these conditions,' he stated.

Nebe didn't budge. He stared at him with a smug smile, fully aware of his power.

'Eder,' he called out to Lukas, who had been standing by the large mirror. 'What do they say at the department about Hugo Fischer?'

'That he's the best criminologist in the Reich, Herr Gruppenführer.'

Nebe spread his arms wide. Hugo felt he had completely been made a fool of.

'I trust your excellent skills,' Nebe concluded. 'You've

never let me down so far, so why start now? It's a simple case, almost run of the mill. Find that lover for me as soon as possible, so we can come up with a motive and solve the case to everyone's satisfaction.'

Hugo gave in. He had no desire to engage in a pointless battle of wills with a man he respected, but who was in any case still an SS officer.

'Can I *at least* speak with the victims' children?'

'Of course. But do your best not to pile more trauma atop what they've already experienced . . . Those poor kids have seen things no child should ever have to see, that's for sure.'

Chapter 5

'You've seen things that no child should ever have to see.' Edmund placed the beret on his head, then seemed to change his mind and took it off. 'No, we'll leave your eyes uncovered. Big and light coloured, who would ever expect such eyes on a Jew?'

'Do Jews look so different?' Gioele stared at him. 'My aunt had the same eyes as me, and Frau Levi from the second floor had light coloured eyes too . . .'

'Well, yes, according to my uncle Eugen, at least. Now, give me your arm.'

Gioele obeyed. Edmund wrapped his arm tightly, covering over the tattoo, turning the fabric over and over again. He finished up with a knot.

'Now, how did you hurt your arm again?' Edmund rehearsed the boy.

'By falling down the stairs while running to the air raid shelter.'

'You're sharper than other Jews, no doubt about that,' Edmund joked. 'Remember, say as little as possible and don't stare at anyone. You have no idea how much we tell people just by the way we move our bodies.'

He grabbed Gioele's head and planted a kiss on his forehead. Gioele closed his eyes. The smell of tobacco on Edmund reminded him of the room where his father would smoke with his colleagues from the university, in those spring afternoons back in Bologna.

'Do you know how often I've asked Hugo to give me grandchildren?'

Edmund rummaged through the small cabinet by the front door, searching for the keys. He opened a drawer and took out the passport Tristan Voigt had given Hugo when he'd helped him smuggle Gioele out of Auschwitz. Sometimes Gioele would open it just to look at the photo of Voigt's son, and every time he did he was astonished at how closely he resembled him. They were like two peas in a pod. His name was Bastian, only Gioele had grown up in Bologna and Voigt's son in Bavaria. Next to the name 'Bastian', Voigt had carefully scratched out the last name and meticulously added 'Fischer'. The same went for the birth year. Everything else was original. No one could mistake it for a fake because it wasn't.

Edmund put the documents back into his jacket pocket and stepped outside. They locked the door behind them and descended the still-intact staircase. There was a small breach on the ground floor that allowed a draught to get in, but the rest of the building had survived the bombings.

Gioele had to squint when they stepped outside; he wasn't used to such bright daylight any more.

'I've asked him for grandchildren hundreds of times, but his head's always somewhere else, in the clouds!' Edmund lifted his face to catch the morning sun. The wind had moved the cloud of smoke away, and the sky was starting to clear. 'All he ever thinks about is his work, never a steady relationship with a nice woman, though he's a good-looking man, well educated . . . He takes after his father, right?'

Gioele laughed. He kicked a tile, and the tip of his shoe was now completely covered with dust.

'What are you laughing at, you cheeky little rascal? When I was young, I had my share of conquests, you'd better believe it. Even at my age, there's one lovely lady who's got me head over heels . . . But Hugo, all he ever thinks about is corpses, nothing else. With corpses, you can't exactly . . . well, thank goodness there are brothels to take care of that. Can I say *brothel* in front of a kid?'

'I don't know what that even is . . .'

'Good thing. Just make sure not to repeat it in front of Hugo, please, or you'll get me in terrible trouble.'

Gioele unleashed a gale of laughter that burst from deep down in his belly. Edmund was the best thing that had happened to him here in Berlin. Edmund was always ready to pull a coin out from behind his ear when he felt sad, and he constantly bad-mouthed both Hitler and everyone like him – though only indoors, of course. As Hugo said, Gestapo informers were everywhere, even the sweet little old lady who lived on the corner.

Gioele skipped along through the rubble and climbed onto a large block of stone shaped like a horse's head – all that remained of an old equestrian statue. From up there, he could see the Spree river, as it tirelessly cut through the city. He took a deep breath of the dust-filled air, and it seemed cleaner than the air indoors in the apartment where he'd been cooped up for the last six months.

'You're so handsome when you laugh,' Edmund said contentedly.

He tried to climb up onto the broken statue beside him but had to give up the effort because of his bad back. They went on walking hand in hand along the river, listening to the sounds of the water lapping against the hulls of the docked boats. They climbed the steps to the bridge, then walked down the street to a large building whose red bricks lay scattered across the ground. It must have been a beautiful structure once.

'Look there. The Marienkirche is still standing.' Edmund pointed to the church that still rose intact.

Gioele sneezed. Everything seemed to be covered with ashes and dust. He even noticed it on their clothing, which Edmund retrieved dry but always completely grey.

'Oooh, see what a rush they're in.' Edmund gestured towards the army trucks racing past them, on a road carefully cleared of debris.

Gioele stopped to watch. The green vehicles roared past, kicking up a cloud of dust that took a while to settle. Even the swastika emblems on the sides looked faded, in this city bleached by bombs.

'They're all panicking about events in France,' Edmund whispered. 'They won't say it, but we're losing the war.'

'What's happening in France?' Gioele whispered back.

'The Allies are giving these bastards a real hard time.'

'But you're a German yourself . . .'

'A German.' Edmund raised his index finger as if about to pass a judgement, but first looked around to make sure they were alone. 'Not a Nazi pig. Can I say "Nazi pig" in front of a kid? Just don't ever repeat it, okay? I had friends who've been hanged for much less . . .'

Edmund spat a gob of saliva onto the ground. He took Gioele's hand and led him across the tram tracks. They walked to the train station and from there to the shops that lined Rosenthaler Straße. There wasn't much left on the grocery store shelves, and almost everything was rationed. That said, though, Edmund told him, there was always the black market at Alexanderplatz.

Gioele noticed a sheet of white paper fluttering on the ground outside the butcher's, as if waving to him. He bent down, picked it up, and stuffed it into the pocket of his shorts.

'Can I use it to draw on?'

'Of course.' Edmund pointed to the façade of a square building that cast its shadow over the street, offering a little relief from the summer heat. 'We've arrived.'

The big front façade bore a sign that read 'Fabrik'. They entered the narrow, dark courtyard. Enclosed by the four walls, the sky overhead was diminished to a mere rectangle. Gioele stood looking up, staring at the sky until Edmund motioned for him to follow. They stopped at a door. The worn brass plate read: 'Broom and Brush Manufactory'.

Someone opened the door just a crack after they knocked. A blue eye peered out, scrutinizing them carefully. Then the woman nodded shyly and stood aside to let them in. She led them up the stairs to the second floor. Gioele glanced around at the bare walls, bare except for a photo of a group of smiling people. The smell of glue permeated the plaster, but the place was far too quiet for a factory that was still in operation.

The woman gestured towards an office door, then turned and left.

Edmund knocked. Gioele instinctively grabbed a corner of Edmund's jacket. From behind the door a voice called out to enter.

'I hope I'm not intruding . . .' Edmund poked his head through the door.

'Fischer! You're always welcome!'

The man sitting behind the desk stood up so fast that he nearly knocked over the papers on his desk, as well as a large globe that almost toppled onto the floor. He grabbed the long cane resting in a corner and strode towards them with determined steps.

'How are you?' He was staring at an indistinct point in the room, but he was clearly addressing Edmund.

'I can't complain.' Edmund removed his hat and rubbed the back of his neck. 'My back is giving me some trouble . . . But our house is still standing. We even have a working phone line and plenty of hot water, so as long as I'm not a refugee, I won't complain pointlessly. Am I right?'

'That's what I like about you – no whining. But you didn't come alone . . .'

Gioele hunched his shoulders and clung more tightly to Edmund. This man was talking about him but wasn't looking at him. His father had once told him that a person's soul is in their eyes, and if they don't look at you, they've got something to hide.

'This is Gioele.' Edmund clearly stated his real name.

'A Jew?'

Gioele suddenly pulled away. What was going on here? Was Edmund revealing their secret to another German? Was he about to hand him over? Hugo had been very clear. If the Gestapo found out that he was here, they'd send Gioele back to the camps, and Hugo himself would be executed for betraying the Reich. Only those who turned in Jews would be spared.

He darted towards the door, but Edmund grabbed him by the collar before he could reach it, almost sending him sprawling to the ground.

'Where do you think you're going?' Edmund hissed.

Gioele tried to wriggle free, but he couldn't move. His heart was pounding in his mouth, refusing to settle back into place. It throbbed, pushing an acidic taste up his throat. He glanced back at the man with the cane, who still stubbornly refused to look at him.

'You need to calm down,' Edmund murmured. 'You're among friends here. Herr Otto Weidt is one of *us*. The workers in his factory were all blind and deaf . . . Jews.'

'But if someone won't look you in the eye, then they're lying to you!' Gioele shouted. 'And he refuses to look at me!'

'Gioele!' Edmund shot him a cold glare. 'I hope you realize what you're saying!'

'Don't worry, it's fine.' Otto Weidt reached out his hand until he finally managed to place it on Gioele's head. Gioele recoiled. 'How could he have known?'

'Known what?' Gioele cried.

'The reason I'm not looking at you is that I was very sick, and it left me blind.'

Gioele shrank in shame. A hollow feeling in the pit of his stomach made him feel small and empty, and for a moment, he wished he could just vanish.

'I . . . I didn't know . . . I'm really sorry.' This time, Gioele was the one to lower his gaze.

'The doctors did everything they could to save my sight, but there was nothing they could do. And do you know what? I thank God for it. Now, I *see* many more things than I did before. I see them clearly, with my heart, do you understand what I mean? And those who see clearly with their heart know what's right and what isn't. So you're welcome here, young friend.' Otto turned to Edmund, as if he had somehow sensed his exact location in the room. 'Have you come to leave him in my care? Frau Porschütz can't take any more in her house . . . The Gestapo raided her in June. But there's still room in the workshop . . .'

'No, no.' Edmund waved his hands in the air. 'We'll take care of him, my son and I. He's got genuine identity papers. It's a long story . . .'

Otto turned back to Gioele. 'You speak German, but Gioele is an Italian name, isn't it?'

Gioele nodded. 'My father was born in Bolzano. He taught German Language and Literature in Bologna. I grew up speaking both languages.'

'You're starting to pick up a Berlin accent, you know that?' Otto Weidt laughed before turning back to Edmund. 'So, how can I help?'

'I need more *papers* . . .' Edmund whispered. Speaking softly had become the norm, even when they were alone. 'There are more of them now, and food is scarce . . .'

'Don't worry, I'll take care of it.' Otto opened a desk drawer with the confidence of someone who had a map of the office printed in his mind. He pulled out a white envelope and handed it to Edmund, who carefully tucked it into the inner pocket of his jacket.

'Thanks for all you do, Otto.'

'It's me who should be thanking you. God sees all of us. *He* sees clearly, unlike me. But be careful – there were a lot of arrests at the black market a few months ago.'

The door to the room suddenly swung open, startling Gioele. Even Edmund tensed. A short, skinny boy, short of breath and his forehead sweaty, had burst into the office. He stared at the floor, and Gioele immediately understood that he was as blind as Otto Weidt.

'S-sir, the p-police are at the door,' the boy stammered. His lip trembled. His cane tapped nervously on the wooden floor.

'Police or Gestapo?' Otto Weidt hardly seemed fazed. He smoothed the creases of his jacket and ran a hand through his thinning hair to tidy it.

'P-police.'

'Oh, that's much better. The police are far easier to bribe.'

'It's about your c-cousin Benedict, sir, n-not about the factory . . .'

'What manner of trouble has Benedict got himself into this time?' Otto sighed and pointed in the general direction of the floor below. 'The two of you should take the back door to leave. It's best not to cross paths with the police when you're out.'

Chapter 6

The Weidt children were huddled on their neighbours' sofa, wrapped in a dark linen blanket that made their faces look even smaller and more gaunt. The little boy sat silent, seemingly unwilling to speak. His sister stroked his hair and occasionally kissed his temple affectionately. She resembled her mother, or at least what little Hugo had glimpsed of her under all that blood.

'I know it isn't easy, but I need you to tell me exactly what happened.' Hugo sat down facing them. 'I'm here to help.'

The girl nodded. Her lips trembled, ready to burst into tears.

Lukas stood silently, his face expressing the pain of someone almost overwhelmed by empathy. His gaze bounced between Hugo and the children, and he was shaking his head. Hugo thought to himself that if Lukas was going to be so sensitive, his career as an investigator would be short-lived. And yet, in the car, he'd shown no hesitation at mocking the death of others in the concentration camps. Was this what they had become? People capable of sympathy only towards those considered fully human?

'Was it you who found the bodies?' Hugo asked the girl.

Klara Weidt gulped, and Hugo saw her throat move. 'There was a loud noise, and it woke me up . . . a gunshot . . . I went downstairs and found them there, lying on the floor. There was so much blood. And Papa's gun . . .'

'Klaus, did you happen to touch the gun?' Hugo tried to catch the boy's eye, but it was no use.

'No, he touched nothing.' Klara pulled her brother close protectively.

Herr and Frau Weber both placed their hands on her shoulders, as if to shield her. Little Klaus disappeared entirely, popping under the blanket.

'They hurried to tell us immediately.' Herr Weber nervously smoothed his thick white moustache, styled in the fashion of a bygone era. Even the house's decor bespoke nostalgia for a glorious past. 'We were the ones who called the police,' he added.

'Did you see the bodies?'

'No. I couldn't bring myself to go in there.'

'Klara, how many shots did you hear?'

'I don't remember . . .' The girl shook her head, sobbing. 'One . . . Just one, I think.'

'Did you hear anything?' Hugo turned to the Webers.

'Nothing,' Herr Weber declared.

'That's not true, Peter . . .' His wife placed a hand on his arm.

'Oh, you're right.'

Hugo leaned forward. Lukas seemed to snap out of his daze.

'We heard a shot too,' Frau Weber murmured.

'*She* heard it,' Peter clarified. 'I'm a heavy sleeper.'

'Just one gunshot?' Hugo looked back and forth, from one spouse to the other.

'Only one shot.' Frau Weber began wringing her hands, her withered skin marked by vitiligo. 'But I didn't think much of it. You often hear noises of that sort, what with all the bombs . . . So I just went back to bed.'

'And have you ever noticed anything unusual around the villa? Any strange people?'

'What sort of strange people?'

'I mean to say . . .'

Hugo took a deep breath. Nebe had warned him not to add trauma to existing trauma. Surely for these children to learn that their mother had been murdered because she was having an affair would be exactly the kind of unnecessary trauma that the head of the Kripo had been talking about.

Hugo took his hat and grabbed his cane. He motioned to Lukas and the Webers.

'Could you please see us to the door for a moment?' he asked.

The couple understood immediately and discreetly left the living room. Frau Weber stood by the door, hands clasped, her eyes as sharp as if she had guessed the reason for Hugo's discretion.

'Have you ever seen a man visiting Frau Weidt?' Hugo asked directly this time.

'No,' Peter shrugged.

'Of course we have!' his wife contradicted him.

'What are you doing, spying on the neighbours now?'

Frau Weber tensed, her cheeks flushing, and Hugo feared for the poor husband's life.

'How dare you?' the woman hissed. 'I just keep an eye on the neighbourhood, especially in times like these . . .'

'And what did you notice that was so strange?' Hugo hurried to divert the argument and get to the point.

'Over the past month, there is a man who has frequently visited the Weidts. But . . .'

'But?'

'If you're thinking that he was a lover, you're wrong.' Frau Weber placed a hand over her heart. 'Benedict was always present when this man came to the house.'

'So he could hardly have been Marlene's lover . . .'

'Unless it was some peculiar sort of game, the kind you youngsters seem to enjoy . . .' Frau Weber gave Hugo a look that left him feeling uncomfortable. She laughed at his embarrassment and turned to look at Lukas. 'He looked like you, you know?'

'What?' Lukas shrugged, caught off guard.

'Relax, I didn't say it was you. He was at least ten years older than you. But he did resemble you in certain ways.'

'Thank you for the information.' Hugo was eager to save Lukas from further embarrassment. He shot a final glance at the Weidt siblings, huddled together there on the couch, before bidding farewell to the Webers. Now those children would have to be each other's family.

Chapter 7

'So what do you think?' Lukas asked.

The police cars had already left, and the villa had been sealed off, just in time to block the prying eyes of curious onlookers and the press. Hugo pulled out his cigarette case and offered one to Lukas.

'The Weidt children aren't very helpful, at least not at the moment.' Hugo closed his eyes, basking in the warmth of the June sun. 'They're too scared; they've been traumatized. Memory isn't reliable in cases like this. It would be better to wait a while before trying to question them again. I do find it strange, though, that Frau Weber only heard one shot . . .'

'Perhaps they only heard the second shot,' Lukas ventured.

'Could be. If they're heavy sleepers. The state of Dr Weidt's face suggests that he was shot at close range, with the barrel held against his body – which would be consistent with suicide. Nebe's right, it's an open-and-shut case, or close to it.'

Hugo lit his cigarette and took a drag, but he had difficulty taking a deep lungful of smoke.

'Are you all right, sir?'

'Yes . . .'

Hugo dropped the cigarette on the ground and crushed
it out with his foot. He couldn't even savour that pleasure
any more, and now good tobacco was getting harder to
find. Maybe his shortness of breath was caused by smoking – or perhaps from the pollution in Berlin's air after the
air raids. People found themselves forced to walk around
wearing pilot's goggles and gas masks, with wet scarves
over their noses.

'Come on, let's get back to the city.' He loosened his shirt
collar, hoping it would help him breathe easier.

'How will you proceed after this?' Lukas started the
engine.

Hugo settled into the passenger seat and waited while
the young officer put the car into reverse.

'The first thing I need to do is find Marlene's lover,' he
replied. 'That's what Nebe said, and that's what I'll do.'

'Do you believe there really *is* a lover?'

'It's a plausible theory.'

'May I help with the investigation? I'd really like to
learn . . .'

Hugo glanced from the road to the young man beside
him. He had learned both from his own mentor, and from
personal experience: never trust anyone. As an investigator,
you become attuned to small details, to the weight of glances and words. Trust was hard to come by.

'Did you know Benedict Weidt?' Hugo asked, just to
make sure.

'Only by reputation.'

'You've never been his patient, say, for your eye?'

Lukas laughed. 'Do you think that I . . . Oh no, Herr Fischer. I can assure you, I never met him. There's no conflict of interest. All I want is to help and learn from you.'

Hugo turned his gaze to the car window, watching the road stream past. Perhaps Lukas was just a bit overeager, but all his interest made Hugo wary.

'So, you've never been treated by him?' he pressed.

'No, Herr Fischer. My eye was beyond saving, believe me. Even someone like Weidt would have been powerless to restore my sight.'

'Not even a great medical luminary?'

The young officer lifted his eye patch and turned towards Hugo. Where his eye had once been, there was now a gaping hollow socket. It didn't look as if some piece of shrapnel had taken his sight; it seemed as if someone had actually dug into the socket and ripped out everything inside and around it.

Hugo looked away, out of modesty.

'I'm sorry.'

'It's nothing, sir.'

'Let's meet tomorrow afternoon in front of the Kripo offices, all right? Meanwhile, I'll gather all the necessary authorizations from Nebe and your superiors.'

'So you're saying I can help you?'

Hugo nodded. It was better to keep Lukas close than to have him scheming behind his back.

Hugo turned to look out the window at the last trees of Tiergarten, where the youngsters of the Hitler Youth were clearing away the remnants of bomb-damaged trees. He realized that the Charité hospital was nearby. With some luck, he might be able to catch Dr Meyer on duty. He could have his lungs checked, stock up on morphine, and also ask a few questions about Dr Weidt.

'You can drop me here,' Hugo said, pointing at the central station.

'Are you walking home?'

'I need to stop by Charité hospital.'

'Are you not feeling well?'

'I feel just fine.'

'But you said you needed the hospital . . .'

Hugo cut him off abruptly. 'Let's get one thing clear right away. If you're interested in helping me with the Weidt case, you need to ask fewer questions about my personal life, understood?'

'Understood, sir.'

The young officer pulled over to the kerb and got out to open Hugo's door. Hugo noticed the disappointed expression on Lukas's face. It almost softened his heart.

'I didn't mean to be so harsh,' Hugo apologized.

'No worries, sir.'

'Also, try to be a bit less deferential if you want to work with me.'

'All right . . . Can we use our first names instead of being so formal, then?'

'No, that's a bit too much.'

Hugo said goodbye and started walking towards the station. He allowed himself a laugh only once Lukas could no longer see him. He didn't trust the boy and yet he liked him. That one good eye was both clear and clouded by something – hard to read. That was another reason Hugo had agreed to let Lukas help. He needed more time to figure him out.

The smile faded quickly, replaced by a sudden jolt in his

heart: amidst the crowd, a flash of copper hair made him set his foot wrong, almost causing him to fall. A woman in a violet silk dress was walking briskly towards the hospital. She turned for a moment, looking around for directions, and Hugo caught sight of the delicate, fresh face of Adele Krause, the Auschwitz nurse.

Hugo wondered whether long-term use of Pervitin could eventually cause hallucinations.

'Fräulein Krause!' he shouted.

His voice was drowned out by the sudden wail of air raid sirens. The crowd began to stampede, mothers grabbing their children and rushing headlong for shelter. Hugo was shoved one way and then pushed aside. His cane slipped from his hand, and he fell trying to grab it. He hit the ground on one knee and felt his trouser leg tear.

'Herr Fischer!' Lukas grabbed him from behind and yanked him to his feet. He handed him back his cane and hurried him towards one of the nearby public bomb shelters. 'We need to get to cover!'

Hugo followed, putting up no resistance. Whoever that woman might have been, she had disappeared into the crowd along with everyone else.

Chapter 8

Babi Yar, 1 October 1941

One Day After the Massacre

The forest is silent. The tree trunks, bleached pale by the pre-dawn half-light, look like so many skeletons planted in the earth. They stand dense, slender, amidst white leaves like tiny scraps of bone. I glimpse children's skulls, dull and polished smooth, and women's femurs, but they're merely stones that Ukraine's cold winds have burnished.

The silence that has enveloped this place is unbelievable.

I look at my hands. I can't get rid of the dirt under my nails. I've tried scraping it away with a knife blade, but it persists, still there, along with the crusted blood. My fingers are trembling. I hate that: it keeps me from being able to level my rifle and makes me look like an idiot. I step out of the tent, now that no one can see me, now that everyone else is curled up fast asleep, in the barracks we've set up for the upcoming *Große Aktion*.

It's cold. I start to shiver.

I don't know if I'll ever see my mother again.

I follow the path up the hill. I loosen the collar of my uniform. My throat burns. My eyes ache. War seemed so much more beautiful in my childhood dreams, but here no loveliness attaches to it.

The air in the gorge of Babi Yar reeks of death. A rancid smell hangs over the earth, over the bare vegetation, so nauseating that it could make even the sky weep. God willing, rain will fall eventually. That rain might wash away all the blood that has darkened the river and the walls of the ravine.

I clamber up to the top of the hill, where the trees thin out. I seem to hear the sound of maggots starting to burrow into the corpses.

I look down over the cliff. I glimpse a black, shapeless mass, faintly illuminated by the moon. I know what's down there, in the ravine, in the river that runs through it, in the earth that has soaked up all the blood and shit of those poor wretches.

Obergruppenführer Jeckeln was elated at the end of the day, as he wrote up the reports to send to Berlin. He drank rum with Rasch, his chest puffed up with pride, as they counted the thirty thousand corpses at the bottom of the gorge. Who knows what glorious acclaim he'll receive from the highest ranks of the Third Reich. Maybe word of his deeds will even reach the Führer's ears.

Fuck the Führer.

Even though it is dark out, I can see them. Thirty thousand bodies packed into the bottom of the ravine, crushed one atop another, men and women, women and children, all mixed together. And among them are Miryam and Anna, still clinging to her breast. I was never supposed to know their names.

Will there ever be a way to forget?

I reach down and pick up a sharp stick from the ground.

I'll never see my mother again.

Chapter 9

24 June 1944

Berlin, Nikolaiviertel

Gioele clung to the sheets, struggling to gasp in a mouthful of air, but the bedclothes seemed to be trying to devour him. In the darkness of the night, the nightmares became real.

He tried to stand up. First sitting upright in bed, then lowering his feet to the floor. Left foot, right foot. The floor was so cold. His heart pounded against his ribs, climbing up into his throat. Gioele defied his fear of the dark and hurled himself against the wall where his drawings were hanging. He patted the wall, tore down the sheets of paper, crumpled them up in both hands. He no longer wanted to see the eyeless, cruel faces of his brother and parents.

He lay there, weeping on the floor, surrounded by scraps of paper that looked like the confetti they tossed from carnival floats at Giardini Margherita, though he'd only ever watched from a distance because they weren't allowed to celebrate that holiday. Back in ancient Roman times, his father had told him, that had been a festival that featured mass mockery of the Jews.

He wiped his dripping nose and walked out of the room and into the dark hallway. At night the house resembled a dark cave. They couldn't light lamps or candles except in rooms whose windows were boarded up with planks and cardboard, lest light leak out and offer enemy bombers luminous signals to attack.

Gioele moved along the walls, feeling his way by touch. He wondered if he had somehow wound up in the belly of a monster, whether he was actually awake or still dreaming. Perhaps he'd soon find himself in Dr Mengele's office. Instead, the bathroom door opened with a creak, and finally, the moonlight streaming through the small window restored the world's outlines, illuminating the bathtub and the washbasin.

He went in. The medicine cabinet was locked. He opened it, clicking the lock and breaking the silence of the house. He picked up the topmost little box. It was very light in his hand. So light that he wondered how it could possibly make Hugo so happy.

'Methamphetamine hydrochloride,' he read.

He had seen Hugo toss back those pills a couple of times; then his eyes turned feverish. He had learned to understand Hugo based on the tiniest gestures: when nightmares tortured him, Hugo didn't complain, but his hands turned pale and his limp certainly grew worse. Some mornings, his grey eyes would vanish into the dark circles beneath his eyes. Then he'd swallow those pills and, for a while, all would be quiet again.

Maybe they'd work for him, too. Maybe they'd bring back his parents' and his brother's eyes, transforming his nightmares into sweet dreams.

Gioele tore off the wrapper and took out a tablet, holding it between his fingers.

He turned it over in the pale moonlight.

'Put that down right this second.'

Hugo's voice made him jump. Startled, he dropped the tablet and watched as it jittered across the blue floor tiles, only to vanish into a dark corner between sink and urinal.

'What did you think you were doing?' Hugo grabbed him by the shoulders and slammed him against the cabinet. The glass doors trembled like butterfly wings.

'I . . . uh . . . nothing . . .' Gioele realized that his voice was giving him away.

Hugo snatched the box out of his hands. The loose lock of hair dangled dishevelled over his forehead, making his face look even more sharply angular.

'Do you have any idea what this *is*?' Hugo insisted.

Gioele hunched his shoulders, intimidated. 'You take them when you're sick, I mean, I thought . . .'

'This is methamphetamine! Speed!'

'But I thought . . .'

'You thought what? Why don't you kids ever think about the consequences of your actions? This could easily have killed you!'

Hugo's voice was a hiss in the stillness of the house. His face was taut, slick with sweat. Gioele didn't like it when Hugo was like that – he looked like one of the cruel guards at Auschwitz.

'I just thought it might make me feel better . . .'

'This is dangerous stuff!'

'But *you* take it . . .'

'I'm a grown-up. And I have a responsibility to keep you safe.'

'You're not even my father!' Gioele clenched his fists. A hot wave rose in his throat. He wished he could hit the cabinet, or Hugo, or anything to stifle that fire. He fought to hold back the tears, determined not to look like the brat Hugo thought he was. 'You never helped my father – you left him there at the camp. You thought only of yourself! You're bad, a bad person like every other German!'

'Don't you dare speak to me like that!'

'I hate you!'

'Cut it out!'

Hugo grabbed him by the hair. Gioele squeezed his eyes shut. He had received so many blows in Auschwitz that just one more smack in the face would make no difference. He braced for a slap, or maybe a punch or two, but Hugo's fingers slowly loosened their grip.

When he opened his eyes again, Hugo was running a hand gently over his face. The man looked even more ashen and weary than usual. His chest rose and fell quickly under his nightshirt and robe.

'I didn't mean to do that,' Hugo apologized, licking his lips. 'Let's get rid of this stuff.'

He opened the small box and poured the tablets down the drain.

'What are you doing?' Gioele stammered out.

'I'm trying to set a good example for you. Now come with me.'

Gioele followed Hugo down the hallway. The sound of Hugo's walking stick sounded like the rhythmic, regular tick-tock of a grandfather clock.

They entered the bedroom and Hugo lit candles. The glow illuminated the window shuttered against the outdoors with cardboard, the bed, the cupboard, the desk piled high with papers, and the imposing bookcase behind it. Hugo was a voracious reader, just like his father. They would have got along well, Hugo thought. He walked over to the desk. He passed a hand over the globe, spun it, and ran his finger down to the Italian boot, to the very spot where Bologna must be.

'Is that a nice city, where you come from?' Hugo stepped closer, his voice finally calm and under control.

Gioele nodded.

'What do you miss most from your hometown?'

'My friends. My family. My brother and I used to fight a lot, but we did everything together. There were two other babies born before us, but they died right after being born. It's why Mama and Papa always paid such attention to us . . . Yes, I think that must have been why.'

With a flick of his hand, Gioele sent the globe spinning and then stood staring at it until it slowed down of its own accord. He shifted his gaze over to a picture of a woman with large, liquid eyes and narrow lips. She stood smiling against a snowy background, holding a pair of skis. She looked strikingly like Hugo.

'Who's that?' Gioele asked.

'That's my mother when she was young. That *was* my mother.'

'Do you miss her?'

'Yes. Things were never the same after she was gone.'

'Why don't you have children? Why aren't you married?'

'You have a great many questions tonight . . .' Hugo sat on the edge of the bed and gestured for the boy to follow suit. Gioele settled beside him. The springs squeaked. 'Maybe because I'm no good with children. I don't like them. I'm no good with people as a general thing.'

'Because of that?' Gioele pointed at his leg.

'What about it?'

'You never complain, but I can tell when you're in pain. Maybe you're scared that other people might figure out how sick you are if you let them get too close to you? Is that it?'

Hugo tousled Gioele's hair with a quick touch, the same way his father used to do when they were still a family, when the war was still far in the future.

'Maybe so . . .'

'I don't really hate you,' Gioele whispered.

'I know that.' Hugo rested his elbows on his knees and looked down at the floor. 'And it's not true that I don't like kids. Those are just things you say in anger. But it's not like kids come with an instruction manual.'

Gioele laughed. He rubbed his nose, which was still itchy.

'But let me make one thing clear,' Hugo continued. 'If only I could have, I'd have helped your family. But this . . . it's all bigger than me. Do you understand?'

Gioele felt his hands and legs start to shake. He intertwined his fingers to calm himself down. What if his brother and parents never came back from the camp? If even Hugo couldn't help them, who ever would?

'Do you want to tell me anything about your mother?' Hugo watched him, waiting for an answer, perhaps sensing the flood of thoughts cluttering his mind.

'She makes a wonderful Torta di Riso, it's a delicious rice cake,' he whispered.

'My mother used to make apple cakes.'

'My father is really good at chess.'

'Edmund, no, not really.'

Gioele chuckled, sensing his heartbeat calming, but it wasn't enough. Memories faded day by day, slipping from his grasp as he tried to hold onto them.

'My father reads books, lots of books,' he went on. 'German books.'

'Oh, really? What's his favourite book?'

'*The Magic Mountain.*'

'I love that book, too.' Hugo laughed, the candlelight finally making his eyes sparkle. Yet in that laughter, Gioele also seemed to detect a note of unease. 'You can't find that book any more . . . The Nazis burned every last copy, even mine. It's a forbidden book.'

'Forbidden,' Gioele repeated. The word tickled his mind and made him understand that it must be a really good novel. 'Papa has a copy at home. We can give you our copy when the war is over.'

'Thank you, that's very kind of you.'

'Hugo . . .'

'Yes?'

'Can I sleep with you tonight?'

Hugo hesitated for a moment but then hugged the boy. Hugo's cologne, so reminiscent of his father's, flooded Gioele's eyes and heart with tears.

Chapter 10

'The Nazis burned every last copy.'

The cold metal cup of the stethoscope slid down his back, stopping at his lungs. It made the hairs stand up on the back of his neck.

He'd told Gioele that lie to keep from looking like a monster to his eyes. To *his own eyes*. The Nazis hadn't burned books all by themselves. They, too, he and the other students, had burned those books: they, the promising young minds of the Reich, befuddled by all those promises. He'd done it himself. He had thrown his own copy of *The Magic Mountain* into the flames. At the time, it had seemed like the right thing to do. Who wouldn't want Germany to be great and victorious again?

'We're done. You can get dressed now.' Dr Sauerbruch's voice jolted him out of those shameful memories.

'Well?' Dr Meyer, arms crossed and standing near the closed window, waited for his colleague's verdict.

Hugo took a deep breath. Outside the Berlin sky was clear, a sheet of blue that promised nothing good for the future. It was the kind of day when, as a boy, he would have run to dip his feet in the river Spree. Now, instead, he would gladly have run to hide in an air raid shelter. The dream of a great and victorious Germany was nothing but a distant mirage.

'There is some weakness.' Sauerbruch folded away his stethoscope and straightened his glasses.

'What does that mean?' Hugo first glanced questioningly at the great luminary of respiratory medicine, and then at Meyer.

'In multiple sclerosis, a transient loss of strength may present in the respiratory muscles of the chest and abdomen. You basically have to work harder to breathe in and out. Of course, the wonderful air quality these days doesn't help . . .'

'But it's *transient*, right? Temporary?'

'Certainly, but you need to take care of yourself. Do you still smoke?'

Hugo nodded. Sauerbruch shook his head, his Hitler-style moustache never budging.

'You'd better cut back on cigarettes,' he said. 'How much pain are you experiencing?'

Hugo buttoned his shirt, his gaze fixed on the door that was always carefully locked during his appointments with Meyer and Sauerbruch. 'I need more Pervitin and morphine.'

'For heaven's sake, young man!' Meyer threw his arms in the air, his coat fluttering with the abrupt motion. He was forced to push back the snow-white forelock that had tumbled over his forehead. 'I gave you a whole box just last week!'

'I threw it away.'

'Why?'

Hugo gestured as if to warn him to enquire no further.

That was the basis of their meetings: silence and reciprocal trust.

'All right, then.' Meyer rummaged around in the medicine cabinet. 'But you need to make each dose last longer.'

'I know.'

'This stuff . . .'

'Causes addiction, I know.'

Meyer shot a glance at Sauerbruch as he hefted the vials of morphine in one hand and the box of Pervitin in the other. The respiratory physician decided to weigh in.

'On a scale of one to ten, how bad is your pain?'

Hugo knotted his tie. He slipped on his jacket and adjusted the cuffs. He let out a laugh that only made both doctors frown. They still treated him as they had when he was just a young boy brought in by his father.

'On a scale of one to ten?' he finally replied, pretending to consider. 'I sleep less than four hours a night and I'm working on a case that will likely rob me of even more sleep in the coming few days. Are you going to give me *chemical* help or not?'

'Keep in mind, now, it's the methamphetamine that's causing your insomnia, not the disease,' Meyer insisted. 'The side effects of this stuff are no joke, and you're taking rather lightly the very serious risk of addiction.'

'Anxiety, cardiac arrhythmia, insomnia.' Sauerbruch came to his colleague's support. 'Moreover, it could also interfere with your cognitive abilities, Hugo. I hardly imagine that would be ideal in your line of work.'

'We don't think twice about pumping soldiers full of this junk at the front,' Hugo replied, his tone tinged with defiance. 'Anyway, there are other excellent reasons I don't sleep.'

'Air raid alarms?'

'Not that alone.'

'Would you care to tell me what's going on?'

'I have a lot to worry about on the job.' Hugo skipped over the minor detail of a Jewish child hiding inside the walls of his home.

'This only makes your condition worse, you know. You should try to rest and live a quiet life.'

Impossible demands, Hugo thought. He held out his hand and Meyer gave him the morphine and Pervitin. The doctor went and sat back down at his mahogany desk. He took out a handkerchief and wiped away the dust that had settled on the stained-glass lampshade until it shone bright green again.

'At least try to slow down your pace a little,' Meyer added.

'I can't afford to rest. I'm working on the Weidt case.' Hugo dropped this piece of information without much emphasis, waiting to gauge the reaction of each of the two doctors.

'The Weidt case?' Meyer's round glasses magnified his eyes, wide open and bulging with ill-concealed curiosity.

Hugo noted and weighed that response. He deduced from it that word of the murder-suicide had already circulated in certain circles, and that therefore the case was already presumed to have been solved. No doubt police investigations provided excellent grist for office hallway speculation.

'It was a suicide, right?' There could also be no doubt about Sauerbruch's interest.

'I can't say for sure, but I certainly wouldn't want to leave any leads untested.'

Hugo clicked open his briefcase and stowed the morphine and Pervitin safely away inside. He pulled out the notebook in which he'd jotted down all the information he'd garnered from Nebe. Absent-mindedly, he flipped through the pages. He noticed the word 'lover', underlined emphatically.

'You didn't come here to question us, did you?' Sauerbruch asked with a laugh.

'Let's just say I thought I'd mix business with business, let's just say that,' Hugo conceded. 'Did you know him very well?'

'How can you ask? Here at the Charité we all know each other well,' Meyer exclaimed. 'He was a towering genius in the field of ophthalmology.'

'And a first-rate surgeon,' Sauerbruch added. 'I've operated side by side with him more than once, on patients with multiple shrapnel wounds. A steady hand and a brilliant mind. What happened to him is just awful . . .'

'I know that professional circles like yours aren't exactly given to gossip, but . . . have either of you by any chance heard any talk about Frau Weidt having an extramarital affair?'

'She was certainly beautiful, and people love to backbite,' Sauerbruch said, slipping his hands into the pockets of his lab coat and shrugging eloquently. 'I did notice her with her husband at the hospital Christmas party, and they seemed quite intimate, truth be told.'

'Intimate is a big word to use,' Meyer commented. 'They had *very* different views of life . . .'

'What do you mean by that?' Hugo asked, focusing his gaze on Meyer.

Dr Meyer hadn't changed a bit since the first time Hugo's father had brought him to the clinic for an examination. He unfailingly sat straight-backed, but in spite of that

tensely tendoned posture, his eyes seemed to express the
attitude of a man who took life calmly in his stride. Just
how Meyer had managed to steady his nerves and pass unnoticed by the Gestapo, with all the patients afflicted with
degenerative diseases he had kept hidden from the Aktion
T4 programme, remained an unexplained miracle.

'I mean that Frau Weidt worked at the Centre for Research on Racial Hygiene,' Meyer explained. 'While Benedict, in contrast, was notorious for his arguments with Dr
Wagner.'

'Pardon me, but I'm afraid I don't quite see the
connection . . .'

'Marlene was a leading figure in the field of eugenics.
Perhaps you've heard of her. She was especially renowned
for her study of the Gypsies of Marzahn.'

'Perhaps, I vaguely recall *something* . . . but I'm *fortunate enough* to have been blessed with an uncle who became famous for those studies, so I do understand what
we're talking about.'

'Eugen Fischer, right?'

'The very same. So what does this Wagner fellow have
to do with it?'

Meyer took off his glasses, cleaning the lenses on the
hem of his lab coat. 'Thomas Wagner is quite well known
in the field of ophthalmology for his racial theories. A few
years back he had quite a heated debate with Weidt about
the morphology of the eye of the inferior races. Benedict
did not subscribe to those theories at all. And then there
was another matter: the fact that Wagner was using Marlene's gypsy subjects as a pool from which to draw children
with heterochromia and send them to Dr Mengele, a very
promising young doctor who was operating in a camp in

Poland. Weidt didn't like that much either. He exposed dangerous vulnerabilities on the issue of race and very nearly attracted the attention of the Gestapo.'

Hugo felt his throat go dry. He'd have gladly paid for a glass of water to assuage the sudden sharp sense of unease that had suddenly gripped him the moment Meyer had mentioned Mengele. He recalled the doctor's quiet smile and his grotesque collection of eyeballs at the Auschwitz Stammlager's Block 10. In all likelihood, he and Wagner had shared experimental findings. Who could say what Wagner would have given to lay his hands on Gioele's heterochromatic eyes. Hugo jotted that name down in his notebook, more for his own interest than for the investigation.

'So, Weidt really didn't share his wife's theories,' he remarked.

'Which are the official theories of the Reich . . .'

'A couple who were anything but close.'

'Precisely.' Meyer spread both arms wide. 'But they never quarrelled in public. Certain laundry is only washed at home.'

'Could it be that Dr Wagner and Marlene had a relationship . . . perhaps more intimate than merely professional, shall we say?'

'I think not. Or at least, not that I know of. The age difference between them was too great, and he was a happily married man.'

'*Was?*'

'Wagner was killed in February. A bomb landed right on his house. Him, his wife, their children. All slaughtered.'

'I'm sorry to hear that.' Hugo erased the name from his notebook with a sense of relief. 'Thank you for this little chat. I have no further questions for the moment. And thank you for your examination and for your admirable discretion.'

'You're always welcome here. And please give my regards to that old rogue Edmund.'

'I'll be sure to convey your regards, Doctor.'

Hugo left the office feeling that he was missing more than one piece of the puzzle. There was something about those few Benedict Weidt stories that painted the picture of a man who deeply respected human life: not, in short, a murderer.

He walked down the corridor which was bathed in morning light. The reek of disinfectant permeated every corner of the hospital, making him sick to his stomach.

He quickened his pace.

As he rounded a corner, he collided with a nurse and nearly lost his balance, scattering the stack of folders and papers she was carrying. Very important documentation, to judge by how frantically she scrambled to retrieve it all from the floor.

'What a mess,' Hugo apologized, reaching for a file.

'No, please don't bother! Just don't touch a thing!'

Hugo only managed to pick up a solitary sheet of paper. He handed it to her. They locked eyes in surprise. The nurse, still down on all fours gathering papers from the floor, broke into a smile that almost made him feel like a fool.

'Hugo Fischer!'

'Fräulein Adele . . .'

Chapter 11

Hidden down there, Duda had had time to reflect and realize when it all began.

The longer she thought about it, the more convinced she became that the root of it lay with that lady who used to come to the camp. A tall lady, blond hair tied back tightly and an impeccably pressed blouse. Grandma Rose shook her head every time she saw her coming, sheathed in white linen as she was. Grandma Rose who in contrast concealed the softness of her own body under layer upon layer of colourful fabric and shawls upon which she embroidered red roses. A rose for every different region they'd passed through since Duda's birth, until they finally halted their caravans in Berlin.

It was the blonde lady who had taught Duda how to read and write. She brought books with brightly coloured covers and sat among the children. The man who came with her, long-faced, almost bald, would watch from a distance, taking notes. Duda had always been annoyed by the way he looked at her.

Grandma Rose didn't like it any more than she did. That was pretty understandable though. They never taught Grandma Rose to read and write. They just took blood samples and measured her face. The first time the pair of them had shown up at the camp was the year of the Olympics. That was when they had been rounded up and taken to Marzahn. It was just to ensure they made the best possible impression on foreign visitors, Grandma Rose had explained. For some mysterious reason, Hitler didn't find their horse-drawn wagons scattered around the city to be properly decorous.

Duda got up and went to find a book. She picked one out of the stack, doing her best not to awaken the others, all still sleeping. All she needed now was to set Dieter to whimpering again. She pressed her nose close to the volume's leather binding and inhaled. She thought she could smell soot. Ash from the bonfires at the camp.

'That's one I rescued myself.' Frya's warm voice came from behind her.

'How did you save it?' Duda hugged the book to her chest and sat down, cross-legged, to leaf through it.

'By midnight we were all in Opernplatz.' Frya sat down beside her, bemoaning again the pain in her knees and hips and back. She had white hair and a fine scattering of wrinkles, but Duda never ceased to marvel at the timeless beauty of her face. 'There was the SS, young people from the university, and Party sympathizers,' Frya went on. 'And curious onlookers like me. They built a bonfire to burn all the *dangerous* books. I had already collected quite a few and was holding them under my skirt, but I'd missed this one. It had tumbled out to the very edge of the pyre. Only a small section of the cover had caught fire; the rest was intact. A minor miracle. I couldn't resist.'

'*The Magic Mountain*.' Duda read the title.

She opened the book to the very first page. At the bottom, in precise and elegant handwriting, was the name of the owner, Hugo Fischer.

The book's title had a magical tang, just like the tales Grandma Rose would tell them at night when she was a little girl and the fires lit up the field with a myriad of lights. They'd stay up late playing fiddles and tambourines, while she told tales of sorceresses, magic spells, and faraway lands.

'It must have been dangerous to rescue it. Why did you run the risk?'

Frya shrugged her shoulders. 'I take risks every day. It's the only thing that keeps me going.'

'You take risks to hide *us* . . .'

'Most of all.' Frya smiled and stroked the back of Duda's hand. 'But, you see, there are so many different ways to die, and often the death of a soul is a much worse thing than the death of a body. I keep the most important part of me alive by helping you.'

'You are a good person. But so many of those other men are bad . . .'

'I know, I know. Not all of them, though. And just a few might be enough.'

Grandma Rose died one winter morning.

The blonde lady was making a wax cast of Herr Paki's face. He sat quietly, letting her work. Duda understood that letting them do what they wanted was the only way to make the visits quick and painless. The blonde lady was tireless. She would measure, take notes, ask questions, and once she was done with the grown-ups, she'd move on to the youngsters, interrogating them about what they'd read in their books. And if they got a wrong answer, she would turn triumphantly to her collaborators. 'See?' she would say. 'A corrupted race. Beyond saving, even if we wanted to educate them all.'

Having finished the cast of Herr Paki's face, the blonde lady had asked Grandma Rose to undress. Grandma Rose, who covered every inch of her body with fabric even in summer, had refused. Because, as her mother later explained to her, while letting them do whatever they wanted might be a way to keep the peace, there was also a limit beyond which a person had to defend their dignity.

The blonde lady's face tightened at Grandma Rose's firm refusal, and her chest heaved under her coat. She made a flustered gesture to summon the SS, and they grabbed Grandma Rose, dragging her to her feet.

'Strip her naked, but first cut off her hair,' the blonde lady had said. 'Let her learn some respect.'

And so Grandma Rose's long grey hair fell to the ground. The braid that had been with her since she was a little girl fell, along with her whole childhood, her youth, and her old age. The SS shaved her head, without soap or water, until her head started to bleed.

They left her naked for hours.

Duda remembered the frozen grass crunching underfoot. The bitter wind that day swept through Marzahn with an unprecedented ferocity, turning Grandma Rose's withered arms and legs purple. She was forced to stand naked in front of everyone, unable even to cover her crotch or her breasts. Tears streamed down her cheeks, but she kept her lips tight and mute. Only once did she open them, to whisper something unknown. Some ancient curse of their people, and Duda hoped with all her heart that the curse would work. For the first time in her life, she wished for someone's death.

But it was Grandma Rose who died, three days later. Her soul had entered the wind that brushed through Marzahn's grass, the fires, and the music of the violins. It had entered everything in the world. It was probably there with Duda even now. Under Berlin and inside those books.

Chapter 12

'What are you doing here?' Hugo wasn't sure he'd be able to hold back his astonishment.

So he hadn't been mistaken; it was indeed Adele he'd glimpsed vanishing into the crowd when the sirens had started blaring.

Adele smiled, clutching the medical files to her chest once she'd retrieved all her documents.

They left the imposing hospital building behind and walked down the tree-lined avenue. The neighbourhood was still intact, but Hugo knew that war left its mark in more ways than just rubble and homelessness. You could see it in the ambulances, sirens wailing, racing across the city even on supposed days of respite. Just then, an ambulance parked nearby, and two men emerged with a stretcher. The boy they carried must have been sedated or unconscious because anyone with legs in such a state – nothing but stumps from the knee down – would have been screaming in agony.

'Unexploded bombs,' Hugo remarked. 'Those are the worst.'

Adele shook her head, watching the medics and the stretcher disappear into the front hall of the Charité hospital.

'Well?' he prompted. 'You still haven't answered me. What are you doing here?'

'I was transferred,' the nurse replied. 'Can we drop the formalities? We're on first-name terms, don't you think?'

Hugo thought back to the fleeting kiss they'd shared when he'd finished his investigation at Auschwitz's Stamm-lager. But that kiss had meant nothing; it was just a way to remind themselves they were still alive in that cursed anus of the world, *anus mundi*, as SS Tristan Voigt had called it. The kiss had been something to cling to, a lifeline in the snow-covered ash. It probably hadn't meant anything else. But dropping the formalities? That made him feel better.

'Let's sit over there,' Hugo said, pointing with his cane to a bench. 'I imagine *you* have quite a bit to tell me.'

Adele set the files down first, then sat. 'I was transferred thanks to Tristan Voigt. Things at the camp weren't going well at all . . .'

'What happened?'

'A man from Berlin came all the way to Auschwitz, de-manding the return of one of his employees, a Jewish wom-an. You should have seen him. A tiny little man, so thin . . . but so full of energy. He demanded to speak to the *Kom-mandant* personally. Of course, he didn't get anywhere.'

'And what did he expect? That they'd hand the Jewess over to him on a silver platter?' Hugo let out a bitter laugh.

Adele shot him a frosty glance before continuing. 'The man didn't find Liebehenschel in charge of the camp. Now it was Hess.'

'Liebehenschel was transferred?'

'Yes, to Majdanek. Hess is brutal, he's . . .' Adele couldn't finish the sentence. 'But this man, Otto Weidt, stood his ground. He owns a factory here in Berlin where only Jews work. No one knows how he managed to keep it running. They say he bribed the Gestapo.'

'Weidt, did you say?'

'Do you know him?'

'No.' Hugo leaned back against the bench. His breathing was becoming laboured again, that unpleasant sensation of not being able to fully fill his lungs. 'I'm working on a case involving a Herr Weidt. He killed his wife and then himself. A coincidence. But how did this Weidt get you into trouble?'

'I tried to help him. Together, we planned the girl's escape, but it failed. To avoid any unpleasant repercussions, Voigt arranged for my transfer as quickly as possible. For a few months, I worked with Dr *Fischer* at Ravensbrück.'

Adele emphasized the last name. Hugo sat up a little straighter.

'Assistant to Karl Gebhardt, does that ring a bell?' she pressed.

'Fritz Ernst Fischer,' Hugo exhaled. 'Yes, we're related.'

'Tristan Voigt managed to get the transfer expedited, claiming to be a close childhood friend of yours, and Fischer gladly agreed.' Adele placed a hand on the medical records, her expression darkening. 'These documents contain details of the experiments your cousin is conducting at the camp.'

'I'm not going to ask you what it's like in there . . .'

Adele said nothing. There was no need. Her green eyes reflected the Berlin sky, glistening visibly enough to tell him all about the experiments his cousin was performing just outside the city. He'd got a taste of it at Auschwitz – human guinea pigs sacrificed in the name of science, prisoners subjected to anything and everything imaginable.

For the first time, he realized just how deeply his family was entangled in the filth of Nazism. First his uncle, now his cousin – both the worst kind of perpetrators. There was no redemption for his bloodline.

'Is this employee of Weidt's still alive, or . . .' He trailed off, hoping for a more comforting answer.

'She's alive.' Adele's eyes cleared. 'She's an excellent factory worker, though she has problems with her vision. And as long as she's useful and able to work . . . well, you know.'

Hugo sighed, patting his coat pocket. He'd have given anything for a cigarette. He wasn't asking for morphine or Pervitin – just tobacco. But he remembered Meyer's advice from only a few minutes ago.

'And the others, how are they?'

'Still surviving.' Adele looked him straight in the eye. 'And *himself*?'

'He's doing well. He'd be so happy to see you again. You should come and visit . . .'

'Of course.'

Adele, who must have been holding back until that moment, broke into a storm of tears. She smiled through them, apologizing, but the more she tried to wipe them away, the harder they fell. Anyone passing by would have glared at him with disapproval, supposing he must be the cause of such a beautiful young woman's distress.

'I'm happy for Gioele,' she sobbed. 'I just can't bear to see the horrible things we've done . . .'

'You should request another transfer . . .'

'I did. As of yesterday, I no longer work at the camp.' Adele sniffled. 'I've secured a job at the Charité. A *normal* job, in a department full of life. I'm working in obstetrics. But at the camp, I at least felt useful somehow. I could help the prisoners, organize some resistance . . . Here, I feel utterly useless.'

'No one is useless if they're helping someone to be born.' Hugo tried to console her, but his eyes inevitably fell on the files. 'If you're no longer working at the camp, why do you still have those documents?'

'They're copies.' Adele tucked a strand of hair behind her ear, trying to compose herself after the tears. 'I copied all the reports. I just need to hide them somewhere safe. One day, they can be used to expose those doctors' crimes. Don't think these people will get away with it after the war, once Hitler is gone. The rest of the world needs to know exactly how far it went.'

The ease and innocence with which Adele undertook such dangerous acts left him speechless. Yet Hugo wasn't convinced that those torturers would ever truly pay for their horrors. Not even their consciences would punish them – they probably had none. He wasn't sure the war would end so soon, or that Nazism would fall with it. And even if it did, if they were all cogs in this machine of horror, all complicit in some way, who then would judge whom?

Hugo checked his watch, unable to bear the weight of it all any longer – a burden that already haunted him nightly.

'Forgive me, but I have an appointment with a colleague . . .'

'Not to worry. It was nice to see you again, Herr Fischer.' Adele smiled, the wind tousling her auburn hair.

Hugo thought back wistfully to that kiss, shared in the worst place on earth.

'Bombs permitting,' he said, 'we still have a working phone line at home. We're in Nikolaiviertel. Call me whenever you'd like to come and see Gioele. It would do him good.'

Chapter 13

Hugo crossed the Werderscher Markt and stopped to look at the Gothic church whose red bricks attracted all the attention in the square. Before the Olympics, Speer had tried to change the shape and appearance of that plaza. He aspired to achieve more uniform cornices, the removal of the newly planted saplings next to the Bear Fountain, and even the elimination of the advertising pillar, the streetcar pillar, the telephone booth, and the public fire alarm. The most radical solution, however, would have been the elimination of the road entirely to make way for a broad paved plaza. It seemed that the Nazi solution to *everything* was just to *eliminate it*.

No changes were ever implemented, though, except for the one involving Hermann Gerson's enormous shopping centre, which was fully Aryanized, transformed from a gleaming, glossy fashion house into the headquarters of the Kriminalpolizei, with its antiseptic and unadorned offices and laboratories.

Lukas Eder was waiting for Hugo just outside the big front portal of criminal police HQ.

He stood smoking right in front of one of the many strategic frontline maps posted on the city's many bulletin boards. Those had been good times, back when Berliners crowded in front of strategic maps, celebrating the Wehrmacht's stunning achievements, all marked out with little flags: these days no one was updating military progress, so everyone avoided looking at the maps, except fleetingly, in passing.

They had plenty of other things to look at, after all. For example, messages left for relatives and friends, written in white paint on what still survived of collapsed buildings, in the hope that they might be read by those who were missing.

Everything was shit lately, Hugo told himself, as he quickened his pace in Lukas's direction.

The boy saw this and immediately flicked away the cigarette butt.

'Heil Hitler!' This time he stretched upward in a perfect straight-armed salute. 'Thank you for the opportunity you are offering me, Herr Fischer!'

'Relax, Eder.' Hugo dampened all that enthusiasm with a wave of his hand. 'Have you had coffee yet? I mean, that ersatz gruel they're trying to pass off as coffee . . .'

'Not yet.'

A moment later they were inside Kriminalpolizei headquarters, focused on the uniformed girl busy handing out smiles and cups of hot ersatz *kaffee*. Hugo decided that even if he was drinking nothing but a roasted bean infusion, it might still somehow awaken him from the stupor Adele had instilled in him.

'Lately, even this slop seems like a luxury to me,' Lukas exclaimed.

'You don't have to tell me.'

Hugo lost himself in watching people as they passed up and down the stairs. The Reich Security Office had plenty of work to do. Strange to say – since most of the enemies had been neutralized. That turmoil must have been a reflection of the hot breath on German necks of the oncoming British, Americans, and Russians.

'Yesterday, I worked on studying the Weidt case.' Lukas's voice shook him out of his thoughts.

Hugo took another sip of ersatz. 'Discover anything interesting?'

'No. But I did think that if *I* had a mistress, the last thing I would do is keep evidence of her in the house; rather, I'd store it somewhere my wife couldn't find any of it. Maybe in the office where I work. That's what I would do . . .'

'Me, too, probably, although I have neither wife nor mistress, specifically to avoid such concerns.' Hugo placed his empty cup on the cart of dirty dishes and then pointed at the exit with his cane. 'Let's go. We can start at Frau Marlene's office.'

The Reich Health Office loomed against the bright sky of the Hansaviertel. The windows extended in close succession, one after another, and each one marked an office in which people were working busily for the Führer. Yet that imposing structure had also housed such visionaries as Koch, who had saved the nation from tuberculosis – not just demented slaves of the regime.

'Please, please.' Welcoming them to Marlene's office was her secretary, a petite woman, weathered by years of service. 'Dr Ritter said that you have complete carte blanche in Dr Weidt's office, if that can help to figure out what happened. We all loved her so. An unassuming woman, always very kind.'

Frau Plontz dabbed at her tears with a handkerchief. Her chest heaved with sobs beneath her charcoal-grey suit.

Hugo scanned the office with a quick glance. Like all Reich offices, it was clean, uncluttered, and simple. No distracting elements, few colours apart from a green lamp that broke the two-tone colour scheme of white and grey. On the walls were the products of Marlene's hard work: maps upon which she had highlighted Berlin's districts, with numbers pinned to them, and Gypsy family trees, complete with the transcribed names of every ancestor and descendant.

Frau Plontz sighed, hand on her chest. 'The doctor lived for her work. I believe every German should feel grateful to her. Do you know who deserves the credit for the way Berlin is now?'

Hugo tried to keep his own sarcasm at bay and studiously maintained as neutral an expression as possible. Not so Lukas, who instead stepped to one side to gaze out of the window: the buildings across the street were gutted and the zoo over the river had been destroyed in a mere fifteen minutes of incendiary hell. So was the secretary actually blaming Marlene for the city's current desolation?

'No Jews and no gypsies,' the woman continued. 'Before, a citizen rightly feared walking the city's streets. Look, these right here are the doctor's research studies, you see?' Frau Plontz pulled out folders and proudly spread documents and photos on the table. 'These are dangerous individuals, antisocial people, people who have crime in their blood. I wonder how many of them you see, with the work that you do . . .'

'Of course,' nodded Hugo.

He grabbed the magnifying glass that lay on the table and glanced at the photos. Marlene was depicted in the act of measuring the faces of men and women. It was an artful-ly constructed pose, in the context of propaganda for the regime, with the doctor showing off all her grace and *Ary-anity* while surrounded by the caravans of a Roma camp. He had a feeling that he'd already seen that photograph.

He flipped through a couple of folders. Dozens and dozens of documents. Years and years of work. Thousands of names sorted into tables of 'pure', 'mixed blood', and 'non-Gypsy'. The conclusion of that immense research, which bore the official stamps of the city of Berlin and the Reich, as well as the signatures of no fewer than four researchers, was, 'The Gypsy question can be considered resolved only once the bulk of these antisocial, layabout mongrels are rounded up and confined in concentration camps, where they can be set to forced labour, so that any further increase of these populations is finally put to a halt.'

Practical proposals for a solution to the Gypsy plague followed, and Hugo had seen with his own eyes, in Aus-chwitz, which one had been adopted. The most *effective* one.

'Frau Plontz . . .' Hugo put the papers back in their fold-er and handed it to the woman. 'You must know that Dr Weidt committed murder because driven, in all likelihood, by motives of passion. Are you aware of any rift between the couple?'

'Ach, *any* rift, you ask?!' The secretary's voice cracked with emotion. 'Dr Weidt despised his wife's work. A week ago I caught the doctor in tears, and she confessed to me that she was weeping for her husband; she actually feared that he might get into serious trouble with the Gestapo. A man who had no respect for morality . . .'

Lukas furrowed his brow. He adjusted his eye patch as if that might be sufficient to conceal his astonishment at the statement.

'How could two such different people still be married?' asked Hugo.

'I can't say.' The woman shrugged. 'But I'm hardly surprised that a degenerate like Dr Weidt should have murdered his wife. She certainly deserved nothing of the sort.'

'Might she have had a lover? Dr Marlene, I mean.'

'What?' Frau Plontz turned beetroot and came dangerously close to dropping the folders on the floor, which would have ruined all of Dr Marlene's painstaking efforts. 'And what if she did? Would that justify what that monster did to her?'

'No. My duty is to investigate, nothing more. Try to understand.'

Hugo received no answer. As the secretary walked away, clicking her heels disappointedly across the floor, he felt certain that the Weidts' marriage was anything but a vale of contentment. Perhaps Nebe had seen right through it. Perhaps there was a lover, some deep-seated passionate motive, and, above all, an Aryan couple squabbling over the regime's racial views. That would have explained the absolute secrecy that Nebe demanded: nothing could be seen to be imperfect in the perfect Nazi society.

'Let's see now . . .'

He took a seat at Marlene's desk. Next to the research volumes was a pretty photo of the two children, hand-coloured. Hugo opened a drawer and rummaged through the deceased doctor's personal possessions. A small mirror and a comb, an empty notebook, a half-eaten chocolate bar, and a metal case containing only two cigarettes.

'What are we looking for?' Lukas craned his neck to peek.

'Whatever may serve as a clue, as evidence. At work she was well-liked and admired, no one is ever going to undermine her cherished memory. All that's left for us to do is to sleuth . . .'

'With a candy bar?'

'No.' Hugo triumphantly displayed a box of Kaiser Café matches. 'With this.'

Chapter 14

Five Days Before the Massacre

Anything becomes tolerable when you're hungry and tired. That's the only way I can explain the zest with which my comrades and I are devouring this soup – a bowl of slop that, just a few months ago, we'd only have considered fit for dogs or to be used as fertilizer. But now, I'm freezing, every part of my body aches, I can no longer feel my toes, and we've run out of the last few doses of Pervitin. They've promised to resupply us soon. Right now, the sound of soup being noisily slurped is the only thing bringing me a semblance of peace.

'I need the bathroom.'

Ermanno leaps to his feet, nearly knocking over his bowl. His voice booms throughout headquarters, echoing off the windows that frame the grey view of Kiev.

For days, we've been ravaged by some illness that

forces us to drop our trousers at the worst possible moments – or otherwise soil ourselves as we trudge through the lands between the rivers Desna and Dnipro and the marshes of Prypiat, in the wake of the Panzer divisions. Maybe it's the Ukrainian chill, or else fear. Or perhaps both.

I try not to let it affect me. I force down another spoonful, hoping my stomach won't betray me. I'm safe for now. We've lost a great many men, but the grand encirclement manoeuvre worked. The Wehrmacht has trapped Soviet forces in a pocket and pushed them out of the city. It doesn't matter that, in their retreat, the Russians blew up water and power stations and destroyed food supplies – the worst is over.

I repeat this to myself, but I'm not all that good at self-deception. My thoughts keep drifting home – to my mother, my bed, my dog. I know I could lose everything in an instant. And for what? For whom?

'They've captured some nationalists,' I say, wiping my mouth. My bowl is empty, but I'm still hungry. 'They were distributing leaflets . . .'

'Leaflets don't kill,' Hans reassures me with a laugh. 'The city's under control.'

I first met Hans when I enlisted. He's the one who keeps me tethered to my duties, because he truly believes in this war. Without him, I'd probably have deserted by now. Without him, and without Ermanno and Walther.

'They don't kill,' I counter, 'but I don't feel safe knowing there are still communists around. Those leaflets are meant to stir up trouble – you know that . . .'

Hans and Walther don't get the chance to call me a coward, as they usually would, teasingly. Their mocking expressions freeze as a series of explosions rock the city, shaking the walls. The chandeliers flicker.

One after another, the explosions grow closer. Glass shatters. A cascade of sharp fragments assails us, and the detonation of the last shell pulls us into the maelstrom of collapsing walls, in the piercing shriek of rubble crashing down around us.

I try to breathe, but the only thing filling my lungs is the suffocating stench of death.

Chapter 15

Berlin, Ein Volk Editorial Offices

'Are you going to tell me why we're here?'

Lukas eyed the offices of the magazine that had, in recent years, aimed to entertain the population of Berlin with its grandiose mission of shaping a new people. A perfect people. *The* people.

It was a modest building, despite its ambitions: little more than a black sign on a glass door. On the bulletin board next to the entrance, the cover of the latest issue featured the proud Aryan features of a man and woman, both blond. The man stood behind the woman, while she cradled a baby – the future hope of a nation sadly diminished by war. An entirely false portrait, given that half the men were dying in Russia and half the women were working in factories instead of staying at home.

'That's the Kaiser Café,' Hugo said, pointing to the

wrought-iron tables arrayed outside, surrounded by plants and small trees – a tiny oasis beside two bombed-out buildings. 'We know Marlene came here because she had matches from the place.'

'But what does *Ein Volk* magazine have to do with it?'

'I'd seen Marlene's photos somewhere before,' Hugo explained. 'In an article from *Ein Volk*, actually. A very thorough interview.'

'You have quite the memory . . .'

Hugo accepted the compliment, though it wasn't memory that had etched that article into his mind. *Ein Volk* had been promoting the sterilization of genetically defective people. The year was 1938. Hugo's father had placed the magazine on the table, leafed through the pages, and pointed to the article, his expression betraying deep concern.

The article explained that people with mental or physical issues were a major economic burden on society and posed a threat to the creation of a new people.

'We need to make sure that Dr Meyer keeps his word.' Hugo's father's voice that day had been a whisper.

Among the illnesses listed in *Ein Volk* was multiple sclerosis. Just a few pages later, there was an article advocating for the sterilization of all Romani and Sinti girls aged twelve and up. Marlene Weidt smiled in the accompanying photos, diligently working in her tireless role.

'Maybe she got the matches during that interview,' Lukas objected.

'The article is from 1938. The Kaiser Café is much more recent – no more than a couple of years old. More importantly, the case only had two cigarettes left, while the pack of matches was full. She got the matches recently, no doubt about it.'

'So Marlene was here not long ago . . .'

'I think so. Maybe just for another interview we don't know about . . . That's why we'll go inside now and ask a few questions. Remember, the most important part of this job is knowing how to listen.'

The interior of the newsroom was far less austere than its exterior, and Hugo thought it could have been a perfect set for a Murnau film. Light struggled to filter through the ground-floor windows, and the lighting relied entirely on desk lamps at each workstation, casting dramatic shadows over typewriters, telephones, and boxes stacked in corners. Everything seemed designed to make *Ein Volk*'s newsroom feel like a place where the history of a people was being written.

Hugo approached a woman who appeared to be the secretary.

She adjusted her hair as he approached, smiling coquettishly.

'Can I help you?' she asked.

Hugo said nothing, merely sliding a brass Kriminalpolizei badge across the counter in response. That alone made the secretary tense up like a wooden rod – not out of excitement, but fear. Once she noticed Lukas in uniform, the effect was overwhelming.

'Is there something wrong?' The woman forced a smile. Without her make-up, she would have been as pale as freshly laundered linen.

To Hugo, her reaction seemed exaggerated.

'We need to speak with one of your journalists,' he reassured her. 'The author of a 1938 article on Romani racial studies . . . Maybe you can check the archives.'

'Marlene Weidt . . .'

The secretary whispered the name so softly that Hugo had to strain to hear it above the relentless clacking of type-writers. Realizing her mistake, she instinctively closed her eyes and took a deep breath.

Lukas sought eye contact with Hugo, who returned the glance. The woman had brought up the deceased without pausing for thought. There must have been dozens of articles and interviews on the Romani issue, yet the name that slipped from her lips like an involuntary reflex was Marlene's.

'Who wrote that article?' Hugo asked, seizing the moment of weakness.

'The director . . .'

This time, not even her make-up could help her. She began tapping her nails on the counter in rhythm with the stenographers' typing. Her lips trembled just enough to confirm Hugo's suspicions. The director and Marlene had known each other well. Not only that – the secretary knew how well they had known each other. Their visit, so soon after the tragedy now on everyone's lips, could only mean that the criminal police were well aware of everything.

Hugo decided to play a sneaky card. He leaned towards the woman, resting his elbow on the counter, his gaze indicating the oblivious journalists at their desks.

'We'd like to handle this discreetly, you understand. If word gets out . . .'

'What?'

'The director . . . Herr . . .?'

'Basilius. Basilius Brecht . . .'

'Basilius Brecht has a wife and children.'

'Yes, discretion . . .'

'And Frau Weidt has a reputation to protect.'

'Of course, of course . . .'

'When did the director and Marlene last meet?'

'A few days ago . . .' The woman shook her head, scanning the room to ensure no one was paying attention. 'What happened is . . . awful.'

'Brecht must be heartbroken.'

'Yes . . . They cared for each other deeply . . .'

'We'd like to have a word with him,' Hugo concluded. 'In the most . . . discreet way possible.'

He cast a knowing glance at Lukas, who struggled to suppress a laugh. The woman nodded, picked up the internal phone, and announced their visit. Then she pointed to a wrought-iron staircase, decorated with a Black Sun emblem, leading directly to the director's office.

Chapter 16

The black market at Alexanderplatz was not exactly as he had imagined it. No indoor stalls or hidden tunnels away from the police's watchful eyes. Everything was right there, out in the open, under Berlin's blue sky.

'Remember, speak as little as possible.' Edmund squeezed his shoulder firmly.

He hadn't stopped repeating this since they left the house. He had gestured dramatically in front of the bathroom mirror before leaving, denouncing himself as good-for-nothing and dangerously reckless.

'Say nothing to Hugo,' he had said. Then: 'To hell with it. I'm his father. What's the worst that could happen? You've got almost blue eyes, you speak German, and we have an identity document . . . Didn't things go fine the other day?'

Gioele held Edmund's calloused, rough hand as they weaved through the crowd thronging Alexanderplatz. Being outside filled him with joy, but he was no fool: he knew Edmund was taking a risk, and that most other adults were much more cautious and rational than he was. That was exactly why Gioele liked him so much.

'What are we getting?' Gioele spotted the stall where bread was being handed out.

The line was long and orderly, despite the gaunt faces of people who would have happily lunged forward to devour the loaves on the spot. He had always pictured Berlin as a gleaming city, and Germans as superior beings. But they were just like everyone else – hungry, thin, dirty, and homeless.

'Just watch.' Edmund took him by the shoulder. 'And don't speak,' he repeated.

He handed Gioele a ration card. Gioele ran his fingertip over the eagle with spread wings clutching the swastika. He slid his fingertip over the Bear of Berlin emblem below, and then to the handwritten name, which belonged to neither Edmund nor Hugo.

Edmund put a finger to his lips, and Gioele obeyed. No questions.

When it was their turn, Edmund pulled out other pads of ration cards from his pocket. The man at the stall took them without batting an eye, continuing to chew the tooth-pick in his mouth. He tore off a coupon from each pad and handed them three loaves – two more than their allocation.

'Anything else?' the man asked.

'If you had some chocolate for my nephew and some-thing . . . heartier . . .'

'A piece of smoked bacon.'

In response, Edmund slid a wristwatch with a brown leather strap into the man's hand. The tradename 'Jung-hans' gleamed on the dial for just a moment before disap-pearing into the vendor's pocket.

Edmund took the goods, packing them into a bag. While

he fiddled with the bag, he raised his glasses and scanned the square to ensure they weren't being watched. Straightening up with a hand on his lower back, he let out a faint groan.

'My back,' he grumbled. 'Sixty years, every year as heavy as stones!'

'Want me to carry the bag?' Gioele offered.

'Why not.' Edmund slipped a hand behind Gioele's ears and pulled out a coin. 'Look at that, coins keep growing out of your ears . . . you should clean them better.'

Gioele laughed, taking the coin, then slung the bag over his shoulder and followed Edmund through the crowd.

But they hadn't gone more than a few metres when Edmund grabbed him by the scruff of his neck.

At that gesture, a few people quickened their pace, and no one in the crowd failed to notice it.

'The Gendarmerie,' Edmund hissed. 'Boy, not a word . . . Let me handle this, okay?'

Gioele felt his lips tingle. It was as though all the blood in his body had drained away. He spotted the two men in green uniform pushing through the crowd. They grabbed one boy roughly, searched him from head to toe, and then shoved him to the ground, pinning his face to the pavement and his wrists behind his back.

Gioele tried to swallow. Suddenly, the bag on his back felt unbearably heavy. Edmund signalled to him to veer eastward, away from the square, while the policemen were busy with the boy.

'Sir, wait.' The sharp, low voice of one of the two officers halted their attempt to slip away. 'Just a quick check.'

Gioele tried to take a step, but his feet felt like lead. The Auschwitz tattoo beneath his bandage burned so intensely it made his stomach churn and his bladder clench. What if he wet himself right now, in the middle of a police round-up? He tried to calm himself, but it was no use – his ears were probably red and burning. They'd know something was wrong.

'Can I help you?' Edmund's voice, however, was calm.

'Open the bag,' the other man ordered.

Gioele tightened his grip on the bag's drawstrings. Edmund smiled gently at him.

'You heard the officer,' he urged. 'Go on, open it.'

Gioele set the bag down. The police would find three loaves instead of one, along with black-market food. Both of them would hang for it. He vividly remembered the prisoners dangling from the gallows at Auschwitz, their tongues blue and their eyes wide open. They swayed for hours in the snow and howling wind.

'Here you go.' Edmund swiftly untied the strings. 'You have a familiar face, you know that?'

'I doubt it,' the officer replied curtly.

'Actually, yes, I think so. Perhaps you've worked with my son, Hugo Fischer, the criminologist . . .'

'Fischer . . .' The officer nodded. 'I've heard the name. I'll just have a quick look, then?'

'Of course.' Edmund widened the bag's opening.

The officer reached in, pulling out the bread, scrutinized the contents, and then put everything back.

'Is that your grandson?' he asked.

'Yes.'

'Such . . . unusual eyes.'

'Oh, heterochromia. Ever heard of it? Just think, he was even studied by Dr Mengele as an example of Aryan traits! You know Mengele, don't you?'

'Can't say I recall at the moment . . .'

'Don't worry, no need to know everything, though it often helps. Anything else you need to check?'

'No, everything's in order . . . you're free to go. And give my regards to your son.'

'Will do!'

Gioele bit his tongue to make it salivate, but his mouth was so dry he couldn't even muster a thank you. Edmund slung the bag over his shoulder and signalled for him to hurry.

His legs moved on their own, still numb.

Once they were far from Alexanderplatz, Gioele finally took a deep breath, which only filled his throat with the irritating dust hanging in the air.

'How did you do that? What happened?' he whispered.

Edmund smiled, winking mischievously. 'A false bottom in the bag. An old trick from when I was a magician.'

'You were a magician?'

'An illusionist. And a mind manipulator. Something I'm clearly still good at.'

'Why didn't you tell me before?'

'Because telling things only at the right moment is also a form of magic. When we get home, I'll show you my study . . . But for now, we've got other errands to do. Can you manage to stay out a bit longer?'

Gioele nodded. With Edmund, even the ruins of Berlin seemed brighter and danger less terrifying.

Chapter 17

'A cigar?'

Basilius Brecht opened a wooden box, releasing the rich aroma of tobacco leaves into the office. It was such a rare luxury that Hugo immediately recognized it as a tactic to soften them up.

'To what do we owe the honour of your visit?' Brecht's eyes were uneasy, slightly narrowed in an effort to mask his discomfort. He knew why they were there. He was a sharp and cunning man.

Hugo played along.

'We're here about the murder of Frau Marlene Weidt. Have you read the papers?'

Basilius Brecht extended the box of cigars. Hugo declined with a curt wave, more to underline his incorruptibility than from any concern for his lungs. Lukas, however, accepted, despite the fact that his uniform actually demanded greater decorum.

'I never know what to make of a man who won't smoke in company,' Basilius chuckled.

'I never know what to make of a man who stalls before answering,' Hugo shot back.

The director absorbed the jab, lighting his cigar and taking a long draw. The crackling of tobacco was the only sound in the room.

'I interviewed her a few years ago,' Brecht said finally. 'A charming woman . . .'

'Certainly.' Basilius clamped the cigar between his teeth and leaned back, clasping his hands behind his head. The overly casual posture only underscored his tension.

'When did you last see her?'

'I couldn't say . . . It's been quite some time.'

'Your secretary tells me that she saw Frau Weidt right here just a few days ago.'

Basilius laughed. 'Fräulein Margot confuses faces all the time. She probably saw my wife . . .'

Hugo caught the deliberate emphasis on that word. Basilius Brecht, happily married with as many children as the regime encouraged, was pleading for absolute discretion.

'Nothing you say in this office will leave this room, you have my word,' Hugo reassured him.

'But I have nothing to say.'

Hugo surveyed the room. The dim light softened the black leather sofa, the gramophone in the corner, and the glass cabinet stocked with liquor. It dulled every sharp edge. This was where their rendezvous had taken place, neither at her house nor at his. Here, in this office, with the complicity of his secretary and under the enormous colour print of the magazine's first issue – a swastika looming over a model Aryan family. Certainly, Marlene shared more ideas and ideology with Basilius Brecht than with her husband.

'Was Frau Weidt acting nervous recently?' Lukas interjected.

'I told you, I haven't seen her in a long time.'

'Did she mention anything that might have concerned the police? About her husband, for instance . . .'

For the first time since they entered, Basilius Brecht abandoned his confident posture. His chest, encased in a tailored Italian suit, deflated, and behind the fresh scent of cologne – applied generously – Hugo detected the acrid undertone of fear.

'No,' Brecht repeated, less defiantly this time. His gaze dropped down and to the right. Hugo knew he was lying. 'I haven't seen Marlene since the day of the interview, as I said. I'm sorry for her passing, but I fail to see how I have any involvement in this matter.'

Hugo motioned to Lukas, cutting off the next question. Pushing harder wouldn't get them anywhere. Brecht needed to feel safer talking to them than keeping quiet and, at the same time, under no pressure to speak.

'Thank you for your time, Mr Brecht. Please call me if anything comes to mind. As long as the investigation remains with the Kripo, I can assure you the necessary discretion. But if the Gestapo becomes involved . . . you understand.'

'Of course . . .'

Brecht's voice cracked. He was weighing whether to trust them. They needed to give him time to deliberate, to foster the illusion that the only way to keep his affair secret was to confide in them.

'I look forward to your call,' Hugo concluded.

Chapter 18

Gioele had never been inside a print shop, but he immediately understood it was a place he could grow to like.

As soon as they stepped inside, they were engulfed by the smell of paper and the relentless sound of machines, echoing off high ceilings decorated with frescoes. He stood for a moment with his head tilted back to admire the art. Amidst the lush vegetation painted in every imaginable shade of green, a majestic stag with spreading antlers was being pursued by a pack of hounds. The night sky above was deep and starry. Gioele thought that, when he grew up, he'd like to paint ceilings as beautiful as this one.

'Do you like it?'

A woman with white hair, dressed like a man, approached to greet them. She watched him with her hands in her trouser pockets, a faint smile lining her weathered face.

'It's beautiful,' Gioele replied.

Edmund rested a hand on his shoulder. 'This is Bastian,' he said, introducing him with the alias Voigt had provided, along with the false identity papers of his deceased son. 'He's very good at drawing. You'd find his work impressive.'

'Is that so? I'm Frau Volker, but you can call me Frya. Want to see how the machines work?'

Gioele nodded, catching the fetching look Edmund gave the woman. She didn't seem offended; in fact, her sunny smile made him feel he could trust her, despite the walls of the print shop being covered in posters he didn't like at all.

He followed Frya towards the room with the machines, studying the illustrations bearing swastikas as they passed. One poster was so dark and menacing he had to stop. A skeletal figure with a sinister face was wielding a bomb and riding an airplane, ready to drop it onto the sole illuminated window of a darkened city.

'Creepy, right? But it works. People pay attention, and as soon as it gets dark, they close their windows and turn off the lights.' Frya led him into a noisy room and pointed at a contraption resembling a massive typewriter with a great many more keys. 'Nearly three hundred of them,' she said, brushing her fingers over the keys. 'Upper case, lower case, italics, small caps, bold . . . Then there are the numbers, punctuation marks, and symbols. These keys control the perforator apparatus. The perforated sheet is then placed there, in the pneumatic reader of the casting machine, and the printing begins.'

Frya gestured towards the machine currently in operation. The rhythmic noise of the casting machine was steady, almost like a dance – a constant, tireless hum.

Gioele circled the enormous dark iron machine, bristling with levers, cylinders, and tubes. If he could, he would attach canvas wings to it, with a sturdy frame, and turn it into a flying machine to soar over Berlin and then Bologna, scattering cheerful and colourful prints over the world. No bombs.

'I've got something for you,' Edmund's voice, directed at Frya, pulled him back to reality. 'It's not much . . . It's getting harder and harder to find things.'

Frya rolled up the sleeves of her shirt. She picked up a cardboard box and emptied out the sheets it contained. Edmund pulled out the loaves of bread and the piece of bacon and placed them inside.

'That's all there is . . . I'm sorry,' he murmured.

'It's enough,' she reassured him.

Gioele pressed a finger to his lips, pre-empting his grand-father. No questions.

He didn't ask any when they left the shop and made their way home, leaving behind the print shop and its little secrets.

When they got home, Edmund kept his promise and let him enter his personal study for the first time. The room smelled of cigars and resembled a sanctuary: the walls were covered with photos and there were strange instruments that he must have used in his days as a magician. In the photos, Edmund was just as young and handsome as Hugo, performing onstage dressed in tails and a top hat. Behind him, an orchestra could be seen. In some images, he was pictured with a jovial-looking man with a handlebar moustache. They seemed very close.

'Were you famous?' Gioele asked.

'Even better than that. I was beloved.' Edmund's eyes sparkled behind his round glasses.

In one photo, Gioele recognized Hugo's mother. Her long, glittering gown made her look like a movie star.

'She was your wife . . . Was she an actress?'

'She was as beautiful as an actress, but no.' Edmund sighed. 'Vera was a professional skier. A slalom champion.'

'How did she die?'

'Doing what she loved most. Skiing.'

'And how did you meet?'

Gioele felt a deep hunger for knowledge. They'd shared the same house for six months, Edmund was risking the gallows to hide him, and yet he knew so little about him.

'I met her during one of my shows.' He laughed. 'I practically enchanted her.'

'How did you . . . I mean, there's always a trick, right?'

'What trick? I have real magical powers, that's the truth.'

Edmund closed the doors to that small temple to magic and led him to the kitchen. He took out a cutting board and began slicing onions and bread for a snack. The sound of the knife on the wood was the same as when his mother used to make him a snack. Gioele couldn't tell if the sting in his eyes was from the memory or the onion juice spraying into the air.

He sat at the table and bit into the food Edmund placed on his plate.

'How does a magician really perform his tricks?' he pressed.

'You won't let this get around, will you? Well, first, you learn to read people from the smallest details and in the very first instant. People tell you everything about themselves, even without meaning to. For example, that policeman earlier – did you notice how cocky he was? Perfectly groomed hair, neatly trimmed nails . . . Someone like that is terrified of looking foolish or being caught discussing something he doesn't know about. Once his guard was up, he just wanted to be done with the search as quickly as possible.'

Gioele chewed voraciously. 'And then?'

'Then, the magician studies human psychology to find those cracks to slip through. Where do you think Hugo learned it? I taught him more than his criminology professor ever did. One of the mind's flaws, for instance, is logical completion.'

Edmund opened a drawer and pulled out a ball. He passed it from one hand to the other, but when he opened his hand, it had already disappeared. He closed his hand again, and the ball reappeared out of nowhere. Gioele's jaw dropped, losing a piece of onion in the process.

'The flaw is in your mind,' Edmund chuckled. 'It's your brain that assumes the ball went from my right hand to my left. But I never passed it at all.'

'Could I learn?'

'With some practice.'

Gioele bit the last piece of bread. 'These past two days have truly been magical,' he exclaimed.

'I'm glad.' Edmund, hunched over the worn kitchen table, suddenly grew serious. 'But we need to stop these outings. Today, I exposed you to a great risk. I've thought about it, and I've been a real fool. Don't tell Hugo.'

Gioele lowered his gaze. *Stupid rat*, they used to call him in Auschwitz. He didn't want to be a rat hiding forever.

'The flaw is in their minds,' he blurted out. Edmund raised his eyebrows. Gioele elaborated: 'Logical completion means the Nazis see me walking calmly on the street and deduce that I must be German . . . Logic tells them that Jews hide. I'm more suspicious staying indoors all the time . . .'

'It doesn't work like that. Not here. Not with the Nazis.

Keeping you safe isn't a magic trick. Do you know what happened to the man in the photo, the one next to me?'

Gioele shook his head.

'He died four years ago in Plötzensee prison for telling a joke about Hitler during one of his last performances. For a joke, you understand? They sentenced him to death for undermining the war effort. They erased his name from every film he'd appeared in . . .'

'But I . . .'

Edmund didn't let him finish. He pulled off the bandages, exposing the small tattoo.

'If someone decided to check the data on your documents, only God knows what would happen. And if they saw this . . .'

Gioele stared at the tattoo. He was condemned to remain a rat forever, and that verdict was engraved in that brief string of numbers.

Chapter 19

Marzahn Camp

Snow fell gently, piling up around the wheels of the wagons.
Duda sat huddled on the step of the caravan, wrapped
tightly in the shawl that had belonged to her grandmother.
Before her stretched the bleak landscape of Marzahn, a
barren field where grass had withered beneath the ice. The
relentless stomping of SS boots had trampled the ground so
thoroughly that Duda was certain no flowers would bloom
there, not even in spring.

'Are you all right?' Her mother approached.

Duda avoided looking at her face. She barely recognized
it any more. Her mother's cheeks were hollow, as if being drained from within, her skin dull and growing thinner
with every cough. Her teeth were rotting.

'They're coming for you tonight,' her mother whispered.

'I don't want to leave.' Duda clenched her fists, hiding

them beneath the shawl. The cold was biting, tearing at her skin. 'I don't want to leave you.'

'You're so beautiful.' Her mother brushed a rough hand against Duda's cheek. Despite the freezing air, her touch was warm. 'Your eyes, your hair . . . You're a flower that mustn't be trampled.'

'I said I don't want to leave.'

'They want to sterilize even the little girls . . . and you're twelve. I won't let that happen.'

'So what?' Duda turned to meet her mother's gaze, though it pained her. 'They only want to sterilize us, not kill us! I want to stay here with you!'

'You're still a child; you don't understand what you're saying.' Her mother shook her head, her lips compressed. 'You'll understand when you're older. In here, you're losing the ability to feel wonder, to dream . . . and believe me, that's not who we are.'

Duda jumped down from the caravan step. Snow seeped into her wooden clogs. She ran to fetch her violin and placed it on her shoulder. She didn't want to hear any more nonsense.

The uncertain melody mingled with the falling snow and the wind that crept through the cracks in the wagons, making them groan softly. Her father had been taken away six months ago, along with most of the men. No one knew where. The women had been sterilized, whatever that meant, and most had died – some from fever, others from agonizing pain that made them scream through the night, while others still, like her mother, simply withered away. What was left to marvel at or dream about?

Her mother's hand landed gently on her shoulder, stopping her violin playing.

'Now you must listen to me.' Her voice was no longer tender or open to discussion. It was as cold and hard as the ice around them. 'At dawn, they'll come to finish the well. A man will put you in a sack and load you onto his truck with the sandbags. He'll take you somewhere safe. Your only job is to stay quiet.'

'Can I at least take the violin?' Duda could think of nothing else to say.

Her mother laughed, though tears fell from her eyes like those of a child, and she clutched Duda tightly against her trembling chest.

'Of course you can. We'll see each other again, as soon as things get better,' she whispered into Duda's hair. 'Flowers always bloom in spring. And they're beautiful.'

Dawn crept in slowly, shaking off the lethargy of night.

Duda followed her mother's instructions to the letter. She hid behind the hut across from the well, trembling in the cold, clutching her violin. While waiting, she picked up a sharp stone and carved her name into the wooden instrument. She didn't want to lose it.

A worker paused, taking advantage of the distraction of the SS officers as they drank their hot coffee. He scanned the area, searching for something. This had to be her man. Duda tossed a stone that clicked three times against the frozen ground. The man approached her with a thick burlap sack.

They didn't need to speak. He gestured for silence, then carefully helped her into the sack and tied it tightly. Now, curled up inside the rough fabric, hugging her violin to her chest, she was alone. Her heart pounded against the instrument's soundboard, resonating through the strings.

Her ears rang as the man hoisted her up and loaded her onto the truck. She felt the hardness of the metal beneath her. More sacks were thrown in, landing with dull thuds nearby.

She closed her eyes. The cold made her shiver, but she knew she had to remain still.

The engine roared to life. Exhaust fumes filled her nostrils. The vehicle jerked into motion. Sunlight began to filter faintly through the burlap, revealing slivers of the waking camp. Her head ached. Marzahn was her world, horrible and grim as it was. She had no idea where they were taking her, only that it would be far from home.

'Halt!' A guard's voice sliced through the air. Dogs barked.

'We're done with the well,' the driver said.

'We'll do a check,' the guard barked. 'The dogs are suspicious.'

The engine stopped. The Alsatian whined. Duda loved animals, but she swore she could strangle this one. She prayed it would stop.

'What's in the sacks?'

'Sand for cement.'

'There's plenty left . . .'

'Yes.'

Duda heard a sharp whistle cut the air. A series of blows struck the sacks.

'You're spilling all the sand!' the driver complained.

'Then you'll clean it up,' the guard retorted, delivering another couple of what Duda realized were knife thrusts. The last one hit the sack next to hers, and sand cascaded down with a loud hiss. The dog barked furiously. Her ears throbbed painfully.

'Ah, that's why you were so worked up.' The SS man laughed. Duda felt as though she were swallowing stones. 'This piece of bacon is for the dog.'

'Of course, sir . . .'

'You wouldn't be trying to feed these subhumans, would you?'

'No, sir. It's for me, for my wife's stew tonight. I hid it among the sacks to keep the thieves from finding it.'

'Then thank your wife on behalf of my dog.'

The SS officer whistled sharply. Duda heard his boots retreat and the engine restart.

As the truck jolted along the road, she placed her hand against the burlap. Tiny beams of light streamed through the weave, like a cascade of shooting stars piercing the camp's night sky.

'See you soon, Mama,' she whispered.

'We've arrived.'

When the man freed her from the sack, the sun was high in the sky, making the snow sparkle.

The banners of the Hoff Circus fluttered in the icy December wind. A man emerged from the circus building, paid the truck driver, and offered Duda his hand to help her down.

'Welcome, Duda. Are you ready to be amazed?'

Chapter 20

'Brecht fears for his reputation,' Hugo said, stepping briskly into the Werderscher Markt building and heading straight for the lift.

'Those two were lovers.' Lukas followed at a sharp pace. 'It's so obvious . . . Dr Weidt finds out about the affair, fights with his wife, kills her, and then, overcome with guilt, takes his own life.'

'Not so fast, Eder,' Hugo said, stepping into the paternoster lift, cursing the outdated contraption that required him to leap into the moving compartment – a task that always reminded him of his limp.

Lukas hopped in after him, and the cabin continued its rhythmic descent.

'I prefer to draw conclusions after the autopsy,' Hugo added. 'We've heard from the living; now let's hear from the dead.'

The lift reached their floor, ready to reverse its journey. Hugo had to move quickly to avoid missing his stop. His bad leg threatened to betray him at any moment.

'Are you all right?' Lukas asked with genuine concern.

Nothing grated on Hugo's nerves more than pity. Though no one but Meyer and Sauerbruch knew about his multiple sclerosis, he loathed any sign of sympathy.

'I'm fine,' he replied curtly, trying to mask his irritation.

After all, it wasn't Lukas's fault. It wasn't anyone's fault – not other people's, not even God's, if there was such a thing as God. His condition was the result of his erratic nervous system, nothing more.

As they headed towards the morgue, Hugo focused his mind on the case. His illness was unpredictable; humans were not. They all acted according to the same motives, ambitions, and patterns. Logic, reason, and evidence always brought order to the chaos.

In the morgue, they would uncover the first tangible piece of that order. The Weidts' bodies, soon to be dissected under the cold, sterile light of the Charité's autopsy room, would finally *tell* their side of the story.

The air in the morgue greeted them, heavy with the scent of disinfectant, an ineffective attempt to counter the stench of death. There were two corpses, already prepared for transport, their feet protruding from under white sheets – swollen, discoloured, unnatural. Yet there was nothing more natural than death itself.

Hugo checked the tags tied to the corpses' toes. He flinched. Neither body belonged to the Weidts.

'Herr Fischer!' Dr Schmidt approached, flustered, his white lab coat hanging open. He waved his hands in nervous, exaggerated gestures, a dissonance that immediately annoyed Hugo.

'I was expecting you at eight this morning . . .'

'I'm fairly certain the appointment was set for three this afternoon.' Hugo glanced at his wristwatch, a familiar prickle of unease creeping along his neck. Something wasn't right. 'Where's Dr Keller?'

'Intestinal infection,' Schmidt replied. 'He went home immediately after the dissection.'

'You've *already* performed the autopsy?' Hugo worked hard to suppress his growing anger. He had studied medicine precisely to ensure that he could assess autopsies himself, free from reliance on others' potential errors.

This time, the pathologist had circumvented him completely.

'Did you or did you not dissect the bodies without my presence?' Hugo's voice was tight with restrained frustration.

'I . . . I'm sorry . . .' Schmidt stammered. 'You weren't here, so—'

'Do you have the reports?'

'Yes, of course.' Schmidt opened a metal clipboard case and handed over a file. 'Everything's in here. I tried to be as thorough as possible.'

'*You* tried? Alone? What about Dr Keller?'

'We tried . . .'

There was something off about that phrasing. A forensic pathologist should *always* be precise. Why emphasize *effort* on that one occasion, as if precision was optional?

Hugo snatched the file folder and gestured to Lukas. There was nothing more to be gained in this room.

'Thank you for your cooperation,' he said, locking eyes with Schmidt.

The doctor visibly shrank under his gaze, his pale blue eyes retreating behind his gold-rimmed glasses.

Once outside, Hugo exploded. 'Goddammit!' he yelled, indifferent to decorum or Lukas's startled reaction. He lit a cigarette, but instead of easing his tension, the smoke stoked the stabbing pain in his head. All he wanted now was a dark room, a bed, and enough morphine to blot out the day.

'That man deliberately excluded me from the autopsy!'

'Maybe we really were late . . .' Lukas offered weakly, hands spread in a conciliatory gesture.

'The appointment was at three!' Hugo snapped.

He took a deep drag from the cigarette, but doubt gnawed at him. What if this was another cruel trick of his illness, or a side effect of the Pervitin?

'I need to speak to someone,' he muttered.

His gaze travelled upward, towards the row of windows overlooking the square. The person he needed was up there – the only one with the answers.

Chapter 21

'Fischer, any updates on the Weidt case?'

Arthur Nebe didn't stir from his seat. Not a salute with a raised arm, as protocol demanded, nor any show of surprise at the unannounced visit. He remained reclined against the leather chair's back rest, hands clasped on the desk strewn with documents. The great Thousand-Year Reich never stopped working.

Hugo stepped closer, making a concerted effort to maintain his composure.

'I just spoke to the medical examiner,' he declared. 'The autopsy on the Weidts was conducted in my absence.'

Nebe straightened, as if jolted by an electric shock. Hugo couldn't tell if his reaction was genuine or that of a skilled actor.

'How did that happen? I personally stressed the importance of your presence . . .'

'The autopsy was scheduled for three in the afternoon.'

'There must have been a mistake.' Nebe shuffled through the papers on his desk, searching for a specific document.

Once found, he slid on his glasses and read it carefully. His finger stopped at the typewritten time. 'It seems the medical examiner was correct. It was scheduled for eight in the morning.'

Hugo blinked repeatedly, trying to regain clarity. His vision was starting to blur.

'What's the matter, Fischer? You're pale . . .'

Nebe's voice became a lifeline to cling to for lucidity. Hugo sat down heavily in the chair. He was sure of the time. He couldn't afford to lose his memory too. What would he have left, then?

'The crime scene photos?' he asked. 'Are they ready?'

Nebe raised his thick eyebrows high. The smile that crossed his face was a blend of gentleness and regret. He clasped his hands before him and pursed his lips.

'We don't have any photos . . .'

'What?'

'The film was destroyed in an accident. I know how absurd this sounds, but . . .'

'What game are you playing, Herr Gruppenführer?' Hugo rose from his chair. Nebe stared at him, unperturbed, as though anticipating this outburst. 'You cleared the crime scene before I could examine it, excluded me from the autopsy, and now tell me the photos don't exist? One mishap is an error . . . three mishaps amount to deliberate obstruction! What's the point of assigning me a case only to hinder my investigation?'

'Sit down, Fischer.' Nebe locked eyes with him. 'These are three mistakes; I give you my word. There's no malicious intent. Why would I assign you a case just to sabotage it? What are you suggesting? That I want to ruin your career? Think it through – what sense would that make?

Why would I do it? To what end? I'm genuinely concerned about you. You look terribly fatigued – perhaps you need a break . . .'

Hugo gripped his cane's handle tightly to stay grounded. Sweat trickled down his neck. He was overheating and couldn't catch his breath. Was this a paranoid delusion brought on by his condition?

'My apologies,' he said, trying to compose himself. He had seen enough delusional people, convinced they were being persecuted, consumed by fear and distrust, paralysed by their hallucinations. Most of the serial killers he'd profiled were paranoids. He didn't want to end up like that.

'The bombings we're enduring wear on the nerves,' Nebe said reassuringly. 'I think you're just overtired. You mentioned you're not sleeping well at night . . .'

Hugo nodded.

'Maybe you've overcomplicated this case,' Nebe continued, pouring whisky into two glasses from the decanter on his desk. He handed one to Hugo. 'Perhaps the last case took a greater toll than you realized . . . Auschwitz would test anyone's mettle.'

Hugo downed the whisky in a single gulp, feeling it scorch his throat and stomach.

'Let's focus on the Weidt case. Have you identified Frau Weidt's lover?'

'Yes,' Hugo replied. 'There's a lover. Basilius Brecht, the director of *Ein Volk* magazine.'

'Good. See? Despite the setbacks, you're making progress.'

'Yes.' Hugo weighed the autopsy file in his hand. 'I'll have a definitive answer after reviewing this, but you're right – the case might be simpler than I initially thought.'

'It is. Let's close it quickly. The journalists are hounding me, and I want to give them answers as soon as possible.'

'One more question,' Hugo added. On this point, he needed clarity to rule out any flights of fancy. 'The Weidts argued over a . . . political matter. You want to keep it quiet that a regime-endorsed couple had conflicting views on race, correct?'

'I *truly* believe Dr Weidt killed his wife out of passion,' Nebe sighed. 'But . . . yes, I'd prefer it not be known that there are individuals in the Party who don't share the Party's ideology. That's why I want this resolved swiftly. We're already weak enough these days.'

'Very weak . . .'

'Ah, Fischer, one more thing.' Nebe handed him a flyer.

Hugo examined it. Simple paper, typewritten. The 'v' key was clearly worn, leaving part of the letter missing. It was nothing too concerning – except for the message: '*We are losing the war. Germans, time to wake up!*'

'They've popped up all over Mitte,' Nebe said. 'It narrows the search area considerably. The Gestapo is already on it, but Himmler asked the Kripo to take a look as well. They want the culprits on the gallows before Berliners start getting ideas. See if you can find anything.'

Chapter 22

The drip of water in the sink was the only sound in the empty kitchen, apart from the soft crackling of burning wicks.

Hugo leafed through the autopsy report by candlelight. A precise report, as Schmidt had promised, with nothing to suggest anything other than a murder-suicide. Neither of the bodies showed any defensive wounds. Frau Weidt had a lacerated wound on the back of her head but had died from the gunshot wound inflicted by her husband with the pistol officially registered in the household. The blow to her head had merely stunned her, taking her by surprise. Mr Weidt had died from a gunshot to the temple, fired at close range. Very close range, as evidenced by the state of his shattered head.

Nebe had been right. For once, there was no need to dig deeper, no puzzle pieces to find. He didn't need to do anything; it was all there, laid out in front of him.

And yet, something felt *wrong*. Hugo considered closing the file. He was giving in to his paranoid delusions again. Instead of stopping, however, he flipped back through the report. The bodies had not been moved. The time of death matched the emergency call. Everything was in order. So what was this nagging feeling? What had his eyes noticed that his mind hadn't yet processed?

Exhausted, Hugo got up and walked into the living room. He poured himself a glass of cognac and set Bach on the gramophone. He adjusted the needle. After the first scratch, the notes of the Crab Canon filled the room.

This had been his mother's favourite piece of music – a melody that could be played synchronously, from the first note to the last, and in reverse. A perfect allegory of life and death, of their continuous cycle on earth.

He took a deep breath.

'From the first note to the last,' he murmured. 'From the first page to the last . . .'

That's when it hit him – what his eyes had seen. He hurried to grab the report and flipped quickly to the last page. The document was signed only by Dr Schmidt, not by Dr Keller. But Keller was the one who always authored the reports.

Hugo grabbed the phone receiver and dialled the operator.

'Get me Dr Peter Keller immediately,' he told the woman on the other end, his urgency unmistakable.

The operator must have sensed it because only a moment passed before the call went through. Hugo's hands were tingling. He was sure the call was being monitored because of his hasty intensity.

'Professor Keller speaking.' The pathologist's voice was thick with sleep.

'This is Fischer. I apologize for disturbing you at this hour . . .'

'Fischer . . . go ahead.'

'I have a question, Professor. I just noticed that my anatomy exam was signed by only one of the instructors. Is it still valid?'

Keller's pause was too long for him not to have understood what Hugo was really asking.

'Perhaps the other professor didn't feel the exam was passed with distinction,' he replied.

'I see. Should I retake it?'

'It should indeed be retaken, but it's too late for that now. Goodbye, Fischer.'

'Thank you, Professor . . .'

Hugo replaced the receiver. As he had suspected, Keller had refused to sign off on the autopsy. What had been left out of the reports?

He collapsed onto the couch, exhausted, as if carrying the weight of the world on his shoulders. He massaged his legs, but it was no use. His muscles were fatigued, and yet there had been a time, before the illness, when he had scaled mountain peaks alongside his mother.

He reached for his case and took out the morphine.

He rolled up his sleeves. Tightened the strap.

'Why didn't you sign, *Herr Doktor*?'

He shook his head. He shouldn't ask questions. Some questions only led to trouble.

He clenched his fist, the vein pulsing as it surfaced. All he had to do was close his eyes, as he always had. Like when Hitler had come to power and the communists and dissidents were purged. Like when the Jews were confined to ghettos and then camps. He just had to close his eyes. He was very good at that.

He pushed the plunger. The warmth of the morphine engulfed him like a hot wave, erasing every pain, leaving him dazed, his head tilted back against the sofa. No more questions.

Chapter 23

Two Days Before the Massacre

The city's buildings are charred shells. In the presence of the smouldering ruins, the cold becomes irrelevant.

I sit across from a gutted church. The walls have collapsed, leaving only the bell tower and part of the frescoed dome beneath it. The painted saints look down, full of sorrow. Perhaps they're lamenting my torn and dust-covered uniform – or the bodies of my comrades, now wrapped in sheets. Ermanno died in the bathroom, trousers around his ankles, and for some reason, that fact makes me weep like a child. We set off for this war thinking we wouldn't die – or if we did, it would at least be heroic.

But Ermanno died like this. In the middle of a bowel movement.

I don't even remember how long I was trapped under the rubble before someone pulled me out. I recall the screams and groans, Hans's curses of 'damned Bolsheviks' cutting through the chaos. That rant of his reassured me some-what – if he had that much breath, he had to be alive and well.

The city, now that the worst has passed, is plastered with proclamations. The edges of the paper flutter in the Ukrainian wind, which grows colder by the day.

I get up from the pavement where I've been resting and approach one of the notices:

'All Jews living in Kiev and its surroundings are to gather at 8 a.m. on Monday, 29 September 1941, at the corner of Melnykovska and Dokhturov Streets. They must bring their identification papers, money, valuables, warm clothing, and linen. Any Jews who fail to comply with these instructions or who are found elsewhere will be shot. Any civilians en-tering vacated apartments to loot will also be shot.'

The Soviets have been driven out; now it's *their* turn.

'Do you think they'll actually believe it?' Hans stands beside me, shifting his weight from one foot to the other, exhausted from hours of digging through rubble to recover bodies.

'Believe what?'

'Sometimes I wonder if you even have a brain.' Hans smacks me lightly on the forehead. 'They're not being evacuated for real.'

'What do you mean?'

Hans lights a cigarette and offers me one. It tastes more bitter than usual – maybe because of all the dust I've inhaled.

'Haven't you heard what the Wehrmacht did in Poland?'

'Something, vaguely . . .' I shrug.

'Walther says they made them all lie face down, or kneel,

and shot them one by one, straight into the pits. I bet that's what they'll do here too.'

I take such a deep drag that my lungs burn.

'This afternoon, the Obergruppenführer wants to speak with us,' Hans continues. 'Walther overheard him arguing with the Wehrmacht because he wants our battalion to handle the operation. After all the shit we've dealt with these past days, someone has to pay . . .'

'And you'd do it?'

'Shoot Jews? If those are the orders, I'll obey. What about you, coward?'

'I don't know . . .'

Hans shrugs. 'If it's come to this, they must have done something to deserve it.'

'And what would that be? Look, it was the Soviets who planted the mines . . .'

'They dragged us into this war, isn't that enough? If we almost died, it's partly their fault!'

'How so?' I prod him further, bile rising inside me. I just want to go home – I don't want to kill anyone. 'How did the Jews drag us into war?'

'That's enough!' Hans grabs me by the collar, slamming me against the proclamation. Plaster flakes off the wall and falls to the ground. 'Shut that hole in your face and stop acting like a woman. I don't want any trouble, got it?'

I nod, dazed.

Hans lets go of me and pats my shoulders, brushing off the dust from the wall.

'You'd better obey every order they give us. I don't want to lose another friend, understand? It's us or them.'

'I didn't go to war for this . . .'

'You're so naive.' Hans rubs his palms together and

blows on them to ease the sting of his injuries. 'What did you think war was about? Braiding dolls' hair? In war, this is what you do – you kill.'

'You know what I mean . . .'

'Don't screw this up. Just follow orders and shut up. There's no room for the weak here.'

I can't find anything else to say. I take one last look at the proclamation before returning to shovel the rubble.

Chapter 24

Berlin, Hansaviertel

The Spree flowed quickly through this part of Hansaviertel, creating a whitish foam along the riverbank that resembled frost. The sound of the current was interrupted only by the murmurs of police officers gathered on the shore, where the river bent into a curve amidst the bomb-ravaged neighbourhood. There, among the debris carried by the current, lay a dark mass, a shapeless figure that Hugo only recognized as a corpse once he got closer.

The corpse of Basilius Brecht.

Hugo pushed his way through the officers. Among a group of onlookers standing further back, he spotted the secretary from *Ein Volk*. She was crying, her make-up streaked down her cheeks in uneven lines.

The body of Basilius Brecht was not a pleasant sight. He lay face down in the mud, his face battered and his clothes shredded by the force of the current, which must have tossed him around for some time before leaving him on the shore, only a short distance from Marlene's office. Whether this was a twist of fate, Hugo couldn't say.

He approached Dr Schmidt, who was crouched near the body. Nebe stood silently nearby, holding a rolled-up newspaper under his arm.

'Drowned,' Schmidt announced, pre-empting any questions. He stood to give Hugo room to examine the body.

Hugo knelt beside the corpse, setting down his cane. Brecht's blue eyes, frozen in the last moment of his life, still gleamed faintly. His tie was loosened, and his trousers and shirt were torn, revealing multiple abrasions beneath.

'Bright red livor mortis,' Hugo commented, touching the face.

He prised open Brecht's mouth with two fingers. The jaw resisted at first but finally opened with a loud crack, silencing everyone around. Hugo observed the foam clogging the trachea and rising to the palate. Even the goosebumps on the skin hinted at death by drowning. The real question was whether he had simply drowned or *been* drowned.

Leaning heavily on his cane, Hugo rose. In response, Nebe waved the *Ein Volk* issue he'd been carrying.

'Read the front page,' he said.

Hugo took the newspaper. The publisher's letter was a brief note of farewell. Basilius Brecht announced his suicide, confessing his tragic love affair with the late Marlene Weidt. He begged forgiveness from his wife, children, and the nation.

'The printer raised the alarm when he noticed it,' Nebe explained as he lit a cigarette, scanning the river and the ruined buildings visible beyond the treetops. 'He couldn't bear to live without Marlene. He must have loved her deeply.'

Hugo struggled to find the right words to reply to the Gruppenführer. There were countless ways to commit suicide, and drowning oneself was among the least convenient.

'This was found in his jacket pocket,' Nebe said, handing Hugo a transparent envelope containing a letter with ink blurred by the river water. 'It's the handwritten draft of the letter printed in the paper. The secretary confirms the handwriting; she says there's no doubt it's his.'

'Then the case is closed,' Hugo declared, exhaling deeply.

He knew this was what Nebe wanted to hear, and as he uttered the verdict, he felt the tension leave his body. He was free now. Whether or not there was more to uncover, it was no longer his concern. There was a jealous and obsessive husband, a dead wife, a suicidal lover, and a story that would now be on everyone's lips. People would talk about a crime of passion, ignoring Marlene and Benedict's disputes over racial issues. The German people needed unity now, in a time of falling bombs and waning faith in the Führer.

'I have nothing more to do here,' Hugo said, handing back the magazine. He studied Nebe's face, but his eyes were an impenetrable wall. 'I'll draft the report and archive the case.'

'Well done. See you soon, Fischer,' the Gruppenführer said, extending his hand.

Hugo shook it, holding the grip longer than necessary. A part of him – the part that had fallen in love with criminology and the pursuit of truth – knew he was leaving the job unfinished, with an ending that fit poorly, designed only to serve everyone's convenience.

'By the way,' Nebe added, 'have you made any progress on those flyers I mentioned?'

Hugo shook his head. 'I haven't had time, but I'll update you if I find anything.'

He left the riverbank, the weeping secretary, the corpse, and the cluster of officers preparing to remove the body.

Standing on the street, he searched for a sliver of sunlight amidst the desolation of the crumbling neighbourhood. He promised himself he would return home, to care for his father and Gioele. For once, he could focus on the living instead of the dead.

Chapter 25

The sight of the Nikolaikirche filled him with immense sorrow. The spires were gone, the roof had caved in, and part of the choir had been destroyed by the bombings. For the first time, Hugo fully realized how deeply the city had been wounded. He had continued to see Berlin through the proud eyes of a German, refusing to accept the idea of total defeat. But now, everything was painfully clear: they were truly on the brink of ruin.

Walking through the rubble, he couldn't help but feel even more exhausted and lost. He couldn't tell if it was due to the drugs, the Weidt case, or the war itself that had reached them where they once felt safest. He sat down on what remained of the fountain, staring at his dust-covered shoes.

He pulled a cigarette from its case. A woman's hand appeared in front of him, flicking an open lighter. Hugo looked up.

'Why the long face, Herr Fischer? You should smile now and then. It would do you good.'

The dimple in Adele's right cheek made her look like a child. When had a woman last captivated him like this? He almost failed to notice the slender, quiet man standing beside her. Yet he was hard to miss, Hugo realized a moment later: he stood out against the rubble of Nikolaiviertel like a figure misplaced in time. His gentle, composed face contrasted sharply with all the desolation.

'I'd like you to meet Otto Weidt,' the nurse said. 'You remember? I've mentioned him to you.'

'Pleased to meet you . . .' Hugo stood, caught off guard by this encounter, which felt far from coincidental.

'The pleasure is mine, Herr Fischer. We were looking for you.'

'And why is that?' Hugo turned his questioning gaze to Adele.

'I heard you're handling the case of Benedict Weidt,' the man continued. 'My cousin.'

'My condolences. It would be more accurate to say that I *was* handling it. The case was officially closed just this morning.'

'That's precisely why I'm here. Fräulein Adele, whom I discovered we both know, kindly offered to bring me to you.'

Hugo felt a faint ringing in his ear, a familiar herald of trouble. He couldn't resist casting a disapproving glance at the nurse, though he couldn't maintain his stern expression for more than a few seconds.

'I'll be brief.' Otto Weidt tapped his cane against the ground, moving closer. 'My cousin never harmed anyone. He had immense respect for life. He would never have killed his wife, nor would he have abandoned his children by taking his own life.'

'Herr Weidt, you have my deepest sympathy, but every element of the case points to a murder-suicide. I understand it's hard to accept, but that's the reality.'

'Let me show you something that might change your mind. Then you can decide whether to take this on or not.'

'I don't do private investigations.'

'Money isn't an issue.'

'This isn't about money, Herr Weidt. My family situation right now doesn't allow me to take on any personal work.'

'Hugo, at least give him the chance to show you what he's talking about,' Adele interjected.

The air raid sirens saved him from the combined on-slaught. They pierced the sky, suddenly making the clear blue heavens menacing.

'Not now,' Hugo said. 'Let's find shelter.'

The line into the shelter moved silently. Every motion had become mechanical by now, repeated so many dozens of times before. They funnelled through, pressed close together, following the painted directions on the walls leading to the various rooms in the bunker. Should the bombing hit the neighbourhood and electricity fail, the phosphorescent paint on the ceiling and signs would illuminate the room. But it made no difference to Otto Weidt: he already moved through darkness, unbothered by it.

They found seats on one of the wooden benches, tucked into a corner. Otto Weidt sat upright. His nerves seemed to be made of steel, Hugo thought, marvelling at the man who had dared to challenge the Kommandant of Auschwitz – not the jovial Liebehenschel, but the sadistic Rudolf Hess.

'Here.' Once seated, Otto handed Hugo a white envelope. 'Open it.'

Hugo sighed. He was facing a mastiff – a mastiff who swam among sharks. If this man had managed to bribe even the Gestapo to protect the Jews in his factory, how could Hugo possibly resist him?

'What is it?' Hugo whispered.

'You can see for yourself,' the man replied wryly. *'I had to borrow my secretary's eyes.'*

Hugo opened the envelope. He pulled out a sheet of paper, flipped it from one side to the other, and felt like he was being taken for a fool. He didn't have time for this.

'What's the meaning of this?' he hissed. 'It's blank. Your secretary must have been playing a joke.'

'A month ago, Benedict gave me this envelope with the paper inside,' Weidt explained, 'and told me to read it by candlelight only if something bad happened to him. So I did, after his death. Now it's your turn.'

Hugo glanced at the others in the shelter – a woman nursing a baby, an elderly couple, a young girl telling a story to children, those unlucky enough still to be in the city and not sent to relatives in the countryside. The guards stood on the stairs, waiting for the all-clear. At that moment, everyone's sole interest was surviving to see daylight again.

He flicked his lighter and passed the flame under the paper. Words appeared, one by one, then faded:

'If you're reading this, I am already dead. Remember me kindly, for I am guilty of nothing, though others will say otherwise. I love you, my children.'

Hugo folded the paper and returned it to the envelope, handing it back to Weidt. His fingers felt scorched.

'It reads like a confession,' Hugo murmured.

'A confession?' Adele's fiery red hair seemed to bristle. 'It's the opposite! Herr Weidt knew he was in danger, afraid for his life. Someone must have threatened him and his wife . . .'

Hugo breathed in and then exhaled sharply. Of course, it wasn't a confession. It was something far more dangerous. It was the sort of message that needed invisible ink to exist, and Hugo had no desire to dive into the depths of a mess that might drown him. Benedict, the kind man incapable of harming a fly, had clearly got himself into serious trouble.

'I'm sorry, Herr Weidt. I can't take this on.'

'I tried,' the man sighed. 'I wanted my nephews to know the truth about their father. But I also thought this case might make you feel *alive*.'

'Don't insult my intelligence with amateur psychology,' Hugo snapped.

'Young man, I may be blind, but doing what's right has always made me see clearer than anyone else. I'd wager you're dying to uncover the truth and that you know that the right thing to do is to restore Benedict's honour for his children's sake.'

'The dead don't care whether they're seen as guilty or innocent. In a few months, we'll all likely be in the same grave.'

'Ah . . . If you're such a nihilist, then you have nothing to fear. If you'll be dead in a month anyway.'

Hugo laughed. The man's tenacity was admirable.

'Herr Fischer,' Weidt pressed on, 'when someone dies, the pain belongs to the living. And when the living are children . . . it's our duty as adults to protect their memories of their parents. Not for Benedict and Marlene's sake, but for their children's.'

Hugo thought of Gioele, the way the boy clung to memories of his parents to keep them alive in his mind, and

Hugo also thought of his responsibility to help Gioele remember them, seeing that he had been unable to rescue them from the gas chambers.

'I'll consider your request,' Hugo finally said. 'I might ask around, speak to Weidt's secretary. But if I sense even a whiff of danger to me or my family, I'll stop. I also have a duty to protect my son. Agreed?'

'You're afraid,' Weidt murmured.

'Of course I am. I have reason to believe Benedict and Marlene's autopsies were falsified.' Hugo scanned the air raid shelter, lowering his voice to a whisper. 'The second medical examiner refused to sign the report. That suggests the Kripo wants to suppress something explosive, and I have no desire to get stung by that hornet's nest.'

'Courage defeats fear.'

'Nice words, but just *words*.'

Weidt fumbled in his jacket pocket, producing an envelope thick with cash. 'I have more, if this isn't enough. Does money trump fear?'

'You insult me again.' Hugo shook his head. 'Keep it for your factory workers when they return from the camps. If I decide to work for you, it won't be for money.'

'You're a good man, Herr Fischer,' Weidt said with a serene smile. 'Better than you think.'

Chapter 26

Berlin, Hoff Circus

Duda couldn't close her mouth for her amazement.

The Hoff Circus was nothing like their caravans. It was immense. The red fabric inside ignited everything, and even the flags with the swastika were a little less frightening in that magical place.

The seats stretched one after another in circular rows, silent now that the circus was empty. In the central ring, however, a woman was practising. She swung lightly on the trapeze, twisting in the air, moving her legs and arms like wings. Somewhere, the sound of a piano played. To that melody, the woman soared and glided. A graceful, remarkable bird. Duda envied her that freedom. She was high, distant, far from brutal men like those in the camp.

'How are you?'

The man who had welcomed her crouched to look her in the face. 'You must be starving.'

'Yes,' she whispered.

'I'm Mr Hoff. From today, you'll be staying with us. There are three rules here.' The man spread his fingers to enumerate them. He was tall and thin, his blond hair slicked back with pomade, and his moustache thin. 'First rule: help. Everyone here has a job to do – no idle hands. Second rule: hide well if there are inspections, or they'll kill both you and us.'

'The third?' whispered Duda.

'The third is to marvel.' Mr Hoff made a deep bow, then pulled a clown nose from his pocket and put it on.

Duda laughed. Looking around, she spotted the piano from which the melody came.

'Would you like to play with Dieter?' Hoff gestured to her violin.

'I'm not very good . . .' Duda clutched the instrument. Rising on her toes, she tried to see better. 'Who is Dieter?'

'A rascal. A scamp who spends his free time here, though at least it keeps him distracted. His father died in Kiev. Blown up by the Russians.'

Mr Hoff whistled. The melody stopped. A boy with blond hair, shaved on the sides, and wearing a Jungvolk uniform, leapt from the piano stool.

'Dieter, come here,' Hoff ordered. 'This is Duda. I knew her father well. We need to look after her for a while, understand?'

Duda shot a scornful glance at the boy. On his arm was an emblem similar to that of the SS, with a single menacing lightning bolt against a black background. One day, he would become one of them. She didn't feel safe around someone like that.

'You can trust him,' Hoff reassured her. 'You can trust all of us. I promise, no one here will hurt you.'

'Can I show her the elephants?' Dieter exclaimed.

'Of course!' Mr Hoff laughed. 'That's a great idea! Then take her to eat – she must be hungry enough to bite you!'

If the arena had amazed her, the elephants left her speechless.

She hadn't believed animals so large and yet so elegant could exist. They moved slowly in their enclosure, and she could swear that the ground vibrated with every step.

Dieter grabbed a handful of hay to coax them closer. Their trunks reached out delicately to take the food. Big and gentle, Duda thought.

'See this?' Dieter pointed to a pin on his shirt. 'I got this as a prize last year when I used an elephant to knock down the wall of an old, crumbling house. During an exercise, we had to find unorthodox methods to prove we could handle anything. Nothing more unorthodox than an elephant . . .'

'And Mr Hoff let you do it?'

'He lets me do whatever I want. I think he's having an affair with my mother . . . Besides, he likes me. Sometimes, I wonder if he's my real father.'

'And what else do you do in these stupid exercises?'

'They're not stupid,' Dieter snapped. 'You're stupid.'

'At least I'm not wearing that thing on my arm . . .'

Dieter glanced at the black armband and shrugged. 'The Jungvolk is fun. We go on trips without parents, cook outdoors, swim in lakes. I have loads of friends. Soon, I'll be in the Hitlerjugend.' He grabbed another handful of hay and pushed it into her hand. Then, with a nudge to her back, he urged her, 'Go on, feed them. They need to trust you.'

'Trust me?'

'Yes.'

Duda extended her hand, trying not to tremble. One of those beasts could easily tear off her arm or crush her with its trunk. Instead, it took the food gently. Duda felt its warm breath on her palm. She stroked it, and its skin was soft and warm – a kind of velvet.

'Can you play that?' Dieter pointed at her violin.

Duda lowered her gaze to the instrument. 'A little. My father was the talented one.'

'Play it. Go on.'

Duda obeyed. As the bow moved, she realized that the emblem on his uniform, even if from the Jungvolk, had made her follow an order. She thought of Marzahn and the cruel faces of the guards.

'Do you know what I am?' she asked, suddenly lowering the instrument.

'A Gypsy,' Dieter replied. 'So what?'

'You'll go out and tell everyone.'

'You're ridiculous.' The boy shrugged. 'If Hoff says to keep quiet, I keep quiet. I don't care what you are. Just don't steal anything . . .'

'I don't steal things!'

'You never know.' Dieter smirked, then opened the gate to the enclosure. 'Now, listen to me. If there's an inspection, you have to hide in here.'

'With the elephants?'

'The SS never check inside the enclosures,' Dieter chuckled. 'They're afraid of being crushed.'

Dieter grabbed her hand and pulled her into the pen. Caught off guard, Duda nearly stumbled, but he held her firmly by the waist. Her cheeks flushed at the unexpected contact.

'No sudden moves,' he whispered in her ear.

They moved among the animals. One reached out its trunk to touch her hair. Duda laughed at the ticklish sensation.

'You need to learn to be silent and anticipate their movements.'

Step by step, circling and weaving between the elephants, she and Dieter moved in a graceful dance, as light as the trapeze artist's performance. For a moment, Duda remembered what freedom felt like.

Chapter 27

26 June 1944

Berlin, Hotel Adlon

A gentle warm breeze swept across the Adlon terrace, making the swastika flags and the flags with the Berlin Bear wave in unison. It carried the scent of linden trees and blooming flowers.

Seated on the veranda, Hugo could see a glimpse of the Brandenburg Gate, its four-horse chariot, or quadriga, silhouetted against the sky. It was a mild summer. Only a year earlier, people would have flocked to the beaches of Wannsee to swim, indifferent to the initial bombings of the war. But over the course of the year, things had escalated, and now no one felt like having fun any more. Still, the newsreels portrayed a different Berlin: sunny, festive, its inhabitants working tirelessly to rebuild it, performing their duties as if nothing had happened. The power of propaganda.

'Good morning, Mr Fischer!'

Adele joined him at the table, her green dress swaying gently. Hugo couldn't help but notice that it matched the shade of her eyes perfectly. Eyes so large that some might say they were *too* big, but he liked their depth and the energy they radiated.

Adele sat down.

'Coffee?' Hugo asked as he lifted the porcelain pot. 'Real coffee . . .'

'If it's *real*, then yes. I imagine the Adlon is one of the few places you can find it.'

'Not for much longer.' Hugo filled her cup. The aroma fully woke him up. 'The restaurant's menu has been steadily declining,' he added. 'Soon, it'll just be boiled potatoes.'

'And we'll adapt.' Adele smiled and took a sip. Her satisfied expression revealed that, adaptable though she might be, she had sorely missed the taste of genuine coffee.

'Have you decided whether to help Weidt?'

Hugo pulled out a cigarette and placed it between his lips. He weighed the lighter in his hand.

'I'm torn,' he replied. 'I haven't been well lately, and I don't want to make any missteps that could put our little friend at risk.'

'Your illness . . .?'

'It's getting worse by the month.' Hugo lit the cigarette. The crackle of the tobacco reminded him that he was his own worst enemy. 'I shouldn't smoke, and I definitely should rest, sleep, and avoid anything stressful. As you can see, I'm doing the exact opposite.'

'I'm sorry. If I had known, I wouldn't have encouraged Weidt . . . Now I feel guilty for getting you involved.'

'Don't worry.' Hugo took a deep drag and closed his eyes. For the first time in days, he felt he could breathe almost normally. He savoured the nicotine. 'You were just trying to help that man . . . And he deserves it.'

'Do you think Benedict Weidt is innocent?'

A boisterous couple sat down at the next table. The man was an officer, and the woman was likely a prostitute recovering from a hangover. The woman collapsed into her chair with a loud, drunken laugh, but the waiter dared not say anything.

Hugo stood and gestured for Adele to follow him to the outer part of the veranda, away from prying ears. They walked past the fountain and stopped at the far end of the terrace. Below them loomed the Brandenburg Gate, and beyond that, the vast greenery of Tiergarten, swaying in the wind.

'I'm sure of two things: the autopsy report was altered, and I've been hindered in the investigation from the very beginning.'

'Why?'

'I think the Weidts represent a threat to the propaganda machine, but there has to be more . . . Without the original autopsy reports, I'm at a dead end, even though . . .'

'Even though what?'

Adele looked at him expectantly, as if she knew he could untangle the mess. That faith in him brought him an unexpected sense of pride, amplified by the Pervitin that was subtly inflating his self-image.

'Just suppositions. You know, what you do when you have facts and you try to line them up . . .'

'Then do it. You're great at this.'

Hugo leaned his elbows on the balustrade. He was so close to Adele that he could smell her. She wore no perfume. She was beautiful because she didn't care to hide or strive to please. He realized he was slowly slipping into a familiar trap, one where he could only get badly hurt if the feelings weren't mutual.

'Well?' she pressed.

Hugo took a deep breath. 'When I inspected the crime scene, I had a feeling something was missing, but I couldn't pinpoint it. Until this morning, when it hit me: there was no bullet near the Weidts' sofa.'

'Could it have been lodged in the skull?'

'Possibly. That can happen if someone is shot while lying on the ground. The bullet can't exit because it hits the resistance of the floor, causing devastating injuries – like those on Benedict's face . . .'

Adele gripped the railing with both hands. The swastika banners fluttered below, like a sea of blood ready to swallow them whole.

'Could they have made him lie down to shoot him?' she whispered. 'An execution.'

'Or else the bullet was there in the living room, and I missed it. Lately, I've been having trouble with memory and focus. Benedict's facial injuries, however, are also entirely consistent with suicide.'

'But you believe one of the medical examiners refused to sign the report . . .'

'I'm certain of it.'

'Do you think he'd be willing to talk?'

'Nobody wants to get into trouble.'

'True.'

'I'm hoping to get some information from Weidt's secretary at least. I really don't know which lead to follow.'

'Do you remember the fairy tale of Hansel and Gretel?' Adele turned towards him. The wind tousled her hair, erasing the crumbling backdrop of a dying Berlin.

'Of course . . .'

'We all leave traces. Many breadcrumbs get eaten by the birds, but some always remain . . .'

A Grimm fairy tale. A clever way to encourage him, considering the siblings narrowly escape being roasted alive by the witch.

'Let's hope there are enough breadcrumbs, then.'

'You'll find them, one step at a time.'

'What did you just say?' Hugo chuckled. 'That's what my mother always used to say . . . "One step at a time."'

'She must have been a wise woman.' Adele smiled.

They returned to the table to collect his hat and her bag. The officer and his companion were leaving, wrapped around each other. Even in wartime, people found ways to enjoy themselves.

'Come to dinner at my place tomorrow?' Hugo asked, realizing only afterward that he'd been a bit forward.

Adele blushed.

'I meant, you could come to see Gioele,' he clarified.

'Of course, why not? I'd like that very much.'

Chapter 28

'Please, come in.'

Dr Weidt's secretary led him into the office. The doctor's desk was covered with boxes and files as the woman cleared out the space in preparation for a new occupant. The equipment had been thoroughly cleaned, and the floor smelled of disinfectant.

'You're not the first one to come here,' the woman murmured.

Hugo approached the lenses used for eye examinations and fiddled with them, despite the stern look from Frau Braun, who made it clear how much she cherished the doctor's instruments. It was evident she had been very fond of him as well.

'What do you mean, I'm not the first?' Hugo asked.

'Others have been here to search through the doctor's belongings. They wanted to know if he kept diaries, correspondence, or anything like that.'

'The Gestapo?'

'No, two Wehrmacht officers. I can't recall their names.'

What did the Wehrmacht want with Weidt? Hugo kept the question to himself as he surveyed the desk and equipment again. Everything seemed in perfect order, no personal details visible. He turned his attention to the secretary. If anyone could offer him a clue, it would be her.

She was a middle-aged woman, short and plump, with a comforting softness that likely made others feel at ease. Hugo decided to take a gamble.

'Weidt was truly an exceptional man,' he said, peering into the boxes. A family photo, fountain pens, ink bottles. 'He spoke about you once, you know? "Frau Braun," he said, "that angel."'

The secretary's smile was both melancholic and flattered. 'I'll tell you this right now: Weidt wasn't a murderer, and I don't believe what the papers are saying.'

'Neither do I, or I wouldn't be here. What can you tell me about his wife? I didn't know her well . . .'

'She was a beautiful woman, no doubt about it, but heartless. She got him into trouble more than once.'

'Are you referring to the controversial issues with Gypsies?'

Frau Braun glanced around nervously before locking the door.

'Yes,' she whispered. 'The doctor was completely opposed to his wife's work. The Gestapo got involved, but thankfully it was resolved. Then there was the altercation with the *badogliano* . . .'

Hugo chuckled. The peculiar nickname for Italians arose from when they had switched sides with the armistice – led by General Badoglio. He tried not to fall into the trap of stereotypes, but when Italians were involved, there was often a scuffle or some kind of vendetta or reckoning.

'What kind of altercation?' he asked.

'Dr Weidt rented an apartment near Bahnhof Börse to a German woman and her Italo-German husband, who died at the front.' Frau Braun sighed and waved her hand dismissively. 'For Marlene, even the tiniest drop of Italian blood was too much. She wanted them and their son out of the house the same day as the armistice. Heartless, as I said.'

'And Weidt agreed . . .'

'Yes. And the couple's son, just a boy, attacked him because he didn't want to leave. The police had to intervene.'

'Do you remember his name?'

'Wait.'

Frau Braun grabbed a chair, dragged it to the medicine cabinet, and climbed up. She rummaged around, opened a false bottom, and retrieved a notebook.

'Here it is.'

'Why was it hidden there?' Hugo's eyes widened, as he sensed a small breadcrumb no bird had yet gobbled up.

'Because that's where the doctor hid it. I figured there must be a good reason, so I didn't touch it, even when those other men came to search. But you seem more trustworthy.'

She placed the notebook on the desk, moving aside some boxes. Her finger traced down the list of the doctor's patients. 'Here he is,' she exclaimed. 'Dieter Costa.'

'The appointment was a month ago . . .' Hugo leaned closer to read.

'Yes. Costa and the doctor had reconciled. The boy lost his father in the war and his mother to a heart attack on the day of their eviction. The doctor always felt responsible for that. He took a liking to the boy, who would often come to visit. Naturally, without Marlene knowing.'

A month ago. The same time Benedict had given Otto the letter.

'Do you think Dieter was looking for revenge?'

'No . . . He always seemed very attached to the doctor.'

'May I look at the other names?'

The secretary stepped aside without hesitation. Hugo scanned the appointments. None of the names rang a bell, and he couldn't investigate every single patient. He needed to find patterns or recurring names to narrow it down.

The secretary was the one to help.

'Look . . .' She flipped through the pages quickly. 'Dieter Costa came to see him three times in the past two months. And so did Walther Rumer, remember him?'

'The comedian?'

'Yes, that's him. He visited regularly. I don't know if it's helpful.'

'When all you have is nothing, then everything is helpful. Maybe he knew something and can give me a lead. Do you know where I can find him?'

'He's working at the Hoff Circus now.'

'The Führer's favourite circus. I used to go there with my mother.'

'I used to take my children there . . .'

Hugo noticed the shadow of pain in the woman's eyes. He didn't ask anything further. He had come to recognize that look, specific to mothers who had lost sons at the front: a living grief that made any further words unnecessary.

As Hugo went to return the notebook, a slip of paper tucked into the page of Costa's last appointment caught his attention. He placed the notebook back on the desk.

'What's this?' he asked.

'I have no idea . . .'

The strip had eight numbers written on it:

9,058, 7,058, 10,402, 7,258, 4,879, 9,171, 6,192, 9,081.

Hugo read them aloud softly as his mind tried to puzzle out their meaning. Money that Weidt owed someone? Money that was owed to him? And the fact that the slip was in the same page as Costa's appointment, the only appointment that day – did it mean the boy had given it to him? Or were they disguised radio frequencies? Perhaps the doctor had got into trouble much deeper than debts.

'Can I keep this note?' he asked the secretary.

'Of course, if it helps . . .'

'In the meantime, tell no one about it.'

Chapter 29

Hugo skirted the Reichstag building, illuminated by the noonday sun. The stone exuded heat, softened only by the nearby city park, where the strong scent of linden trees filled the air. Nature continued its cycle, even in a world on the brink of collapse.

If not for the extensive damage from the 1933 fire, the Reichstag would still have been the central seat of power in Berlin. Instead, it had been profoundly scarred, burned until it became a useless shell. The German populace had also been trampled that same night, though no one realized it at the time – not even Hugo.

He remembered every detail of that February. The sky was dark, pierced with stars. A biting cold froze the windows of the tavern where he and his university friends were enjoying their last beer of the evening. At a quarter past nine, the fire brigade's sirens began to wail, and central Berlin erupted in shouts and people rushing to witness the Reichstag engulfed in flames. When Hugo and his friends passed through the Brandenburg Gate, a massive explosion set the deputies' chamber ablaze. Tongues of fire rose high, wrapping around the dome and casting a shadow of blood all around, scattering sparks like falling stars. The police arrested a deranged man. Van der Lubbe claimed to have set the fire in protest against the growing power of the National Socialists. He confessed under torture and implicated the head of the Communist Party. With their leaders imprisoned and access to the press denied, the communists were crushed. In hindsight, after so many years, it didn't take a criminology degree to realize someone else had orchestrated the fire.

Hugo passed the charred building, crossed the street, and walked past the fountains of Hindenburgplatz. The eagles perched on the columns, still intact but weary, gazed silently at the sky. He crossed the colonnade of the Brandenburg Gate, where the monument's massive shadow provided a brief respite from the noonday sun.

Before him stretched Unter den Linden, strewn with rubble. The Reichstag stood behind him, mirroring the ruins of other buildings. The beginning of everything, and the beginning of the end, facing each other.

Hugo made his way to the Ordnungspolizei headquarters. If this Costa had been arrested for assault, he had to be on record, and Lukas Eder would be able to help him.

He entered the lobby and asked to speak with the officer.

Lukas appeared a few minutes later, flustered and surprised to see him.

'Heil Hitler!' Lukas said, extending his arm in salute before relaxing somewhat. 'Herr Fischer, to what do I owe this visit?'

'I need a favour,' Hugo replied, pulling out his cigarette case. 'If you join me for a smoke, I'll explain everything.'

Lukas followed without question, taking a cigarette and lighting it. Hugo thought that the missing eye was his blessing; otherwise, he'd likely have ended up dying like Frau Braun's sons. The Eastern Front was the worst: twenty-year-old boys rotting in the snow, slaughtered by enemy artillery. The luckiest returned without arms or legs, limbs claimed by the minus-forty-degree inferno of Bolshevik hell, rewarded with the Gefrierfleischorden, the 'Frozen Meat Medal'. Some consolation.

'What do you need?' Lukas asked, his good eye fixed on Hugo.

'An address.'

'I'm not sure how I can help . . .'

'It's someone who was arrested for assault. I need you to check the records and tell me where they're living now.'

Lukas finished his cigarette, dropped the butt to the ground, and stamped it out.

'Come with me,' he said, leading the way. 'It'll be a pleasure to help.'

The underground archive housed hundreds of files, catalogued by year and alphabetically. It smelled of paper and dust – the sweet, sacred scent of old libraries.

Their footsteps echoed among the shelves in the dim light, broken only by wall-mounted lamps. Lukas stopped at the section for the previous year.

'Costa, you said?' He pulled out the folder labelled 'C' and extracted the documents in question, handing them to Hugo.

Dieter Costa, just fifteen years old, had resisted eviction and punched Dr Weidt, breaking his nasal septum. He must have been a powerfully built fifteen-year-old, Hugo thought. The complaint, unsurprisingly, had been filed by Marlene. After a week in juvenile detention, Dieter was placed under the care of the Carmelite Sisters at St Teresa's Convent because his mother had died just hours after his arrest, and his father had been killed at the front. Fate had certainly not been kind to the boy.

Hugo closed the file and handed it back to Lukas.

'Did you get the address you needed?'

'Yes.'

'Herr Fischer . . .' Lukas hesitated but finally spoke. 'I couldn't help but notice. The complaint was filed by Marlene Weidt. Has the case been reopened?'

'The case is closed,' Hugo replied, adjusting his hat.

'Then why are you investigating this boy?'

'Out of . . . personal curiosity.'

'You think there's more to it?' Lukas lowered his voice. 'Everything adds up in that case . . . doesn't it?'

'No, Eder, nothing adds up.' Hugo fixed him with a steady gaze, his expression as sharp as his words. 'I don't know if I can trust you, so I won't say anything more.'

'I understand, and I don't expect you to.'

'Take care, Lukas,' Hugo concluded.

Chapter 30

St Teresa's Convent stood untouched amidst the ruins. A miracle, the nuns would have said, considering it emerged unscathed while all the surrounding buildings lay gutted. Even the nearby S-Bahn station had been severely damaged; the area had borne the brunt of relentless bombing.

Hugo walked past a construction site where prisoners from a labour camp worked to defuse an unexploded bomb. A single misstep could spell disaster. An SS guard overseeing the workers cast an indifferent glance as Hugo paused to observe. A scrap of white paper fluttered down, landing near the barricades. Its bold lettering caught both their attention: *'The Russians are coming! Hitler is lying to you!'*

Quickly pulling out his Kripo badge, Hugo displayed it to the SS officer before he could retrieve the leaflet. 'I'm handling this case,' he said. 'Leave it to me.'

He folded the paper and slipped it into his pocket. Despite Nebe's orders to investigate such subversive acts, Hugo had no intention of pursuing this. Whoever the culprit was, they deserved not only to live but also his silent respect.

He pressed the convent's bell. It had taken three phone calls to secure this meeting, each delayed by the sisters blaming the demands of feeding the displaced and maintaining their prayer schedules. Hugo had waited patiently; Gestapo-style intimidation wasn't his way. Now, just before sunset, he was finally admitted.

The sky was tinged with hues of fire as Sister Anna opened the door. Her cheerful face framed by her white coif caught him off guard.

'Come in,' she said warmly.

She was petite, but her demeanour radiated an energy that suggested she knew how to navigate life in a nation that would gladly eliminate nuns and priests. Many members of the clergy had challenged the Führer; many had paid the price in the camps.

'This way.' Sister Anna gestured down a shadowy hallway. Cool and tranquil, the corridor exuded an unexpected peace. 'The boys are temporarily housed on the ground floor,' she explained. 'St Joseph's was bombed, so we're sheltering the Jesuits along with orphans. Do you know much about our order?'

Hugo shrugged. He disliked appearing to be unprepared but had no expertise in religious orders.

'Saint Teresa founded us,' she continued without waiting for his answer. 'We practise poverty, but above all, love for all people. *All* people.'

Her stance was unambiguous. Encased in that dark habit was a core of vivid, unyielding courage. Hugo knew such a declaration could cost her dearly if the Gestapo heard it. Yet some people valued justice and moral principles more than life itself, and Hugo envied them.

He thought of von Galen, the 'Lion of Münster'. The

bishop had roared against Nazi confiscation of church property, violent expulsions of clergy, and especially Aktion T4, the programme to eliminate people with disabilities – people like Hugo. Von Galen's sermons had been secretly distributed throughout Germany, dropped like confetti by Allied planes. Reading them, Hugo had felt indebted to the priest for saying what he himself never dared.

'How quiet you are,' Sister Anna remarked as she unlocked gates that led to another section of the convent. 'Did I say something wrong?'

'No, Sister Anna, you said everything right.'

They passed a small cloister garden where other nuns worked, gathering the day's yield in the fading light.

'We Carmelites make the finest preserves!' Sister Anna knocked on a door overlooking the garden. 'I'll give you a jar afterwards.'

'Thank you,' Hugo replied, struck again by her genuine kindness. It wasn't a bribe, he could tell. It was simply the joy of giving.

'Here we are.' Sister Anna opened the door. 'Don't tire him out too much. He's been vomiting for days and has a fever.'

The room was dim and smelled of stale air mixed with the untouched soup on a nearby desk. Sparse and simple, the space was a monk's cell. A freshly laundered Hitler Youth uniform hung neatly on the wall.

Dieter lay in bed. Hugo opened the shutters to let in some light.

'Sorry to wake you,' he said.

'Don't worry,' Dieter mumbled, rubbing his temples and eyes. 'I feel better now. Can't wait to get out of here.'

Sitting up, Dieter revealed a face shaped by sharp Italian

features – his jaw and full lips were inherited from his father, while his blue eyes and blond hair clearly came from his mother. The blend of two heritages had crafted a strikingly handsome boy.

'Did they tell you why I'm here?' Hugo asked.

'Sister Anna said it's about Dr Weidt.'

'You know he's dead.'

'Yes.'

'I'm here because of the fight you had with him.'

'That old story again . . .' Dieter slumped back against the pillows, his sweat-dampened hair falling over his forehead. 'The Hitler Youth never tired of scolding me for it. But I was just defending my mother and our home. Dr Weidt was a kind man; I didn't expect him to treat us like that just because I've got Italian blood.'

'It was his wife, not him, who insisted on the eviction.'

'That witch.'

'Mind your language, Dieter.'

The boy took a deep breath. Someone like him likely hadn't had an easy time in the Hitler Youth. Or maybe his defiant temperament earned him respect. 'Blood and Honour' was their motto, and Hitler wanted his youth brutal, tyrannical, and fearless.

'How do you like the Hitlerjugend?' Hugo probed.

'It's fine,' Dieter shrugged. 'I'm part of the rubble-clearing division. I like helping rebuild. Makes me feel useful.'

'They'll call you to the front soon.'

'I know.'

'Your father died at the front, right?'

Dieter opened his bedside drawer and pulled out a medal, handing it to Hugo. The Iron Cross was engraved with the words, 'The German People Thank Their Brave Soldiers'.

The reverse bore a map of the Battle of Kiev, detailing the staggering losses: 665,000 prisoners, 885 armoured fighting vehicles, 5 Soviet armies, and 3,718 cannons.

Hugo couldn't help but think of the numbers scrawled in Dr Weidt's notebook. He pulled out the slip of paper but saw no match.

'Have you seen this note before?' he asked.

'No.' Dieter shook his head. 'Should I have?'

'Not necessarily.' Hugo tucked it away, returned the medal, and dragged a chair over to sit down. 'Let's take this one step at a time. Your father died in battle, and Weidt was kind to you and your mother, renting you an apartment. After Italy's armistice, he wanted you out. You resisted, hit him, got arrested . . . and your mother? What happened to her?'

Hugo already knew the answer but wanted to hear it from the boy.

'She . . .' Dieter's voice faltered. 'My mother died of a heart attack that same day.'

'Because of the Weidt family?'

'What are you implying?' Dieter stood, his tall frame imposing despite his youth. Hugo rose too, his greater age, height, and authority making Dieter step back.

'Relax,' Hugo said. 'I just want to understand. You visited Dr Weidt often. Did you have an eye condition?'

'No, I went just to talk. At the hospital, so his wife wouldn't find out. Maybe I just needed a father. Do you have kids?'

'One.'

'Are they in the HJ?'

'Too young.'

'The Jungvolk, then. What's their name?'

Hugo sidestepped the question, irritated by the boy's probing. He sat down again, steering the conversation back to his terms.

'So, you spent time with the man who caused your mother's death . . .'

'*I* caused her death,' Dieter said, his voice low and dark. 'I shouldn't have reacted so badly during the eviction. We'd have found a solution, and she'd still be alive.'

'She had a heart condition. It would've happened anyway.' Hugo paused. He saw himself in Dieter, grappling with the same guilt he had faced after his own mother's agonizing death. The instinct to leave the boy alone clashed with his duty to press on. 'So, no resentment towards the Weidts?'

'No.'

'Not even Marlene?'

'No.'

'She was a witch, though, right?'

'I was just saying . . .'

'Did you notice anything unusual about Dr Weidt in the last month? Was he worried or unwell?'

'No, he seemed calm as always.'

Hugo tapped his cane against the floor. A man writing a farewell letter in invisible ink wasn't *calm as always*. Weidt had known danger was imminent. Still, no fifteen-year-old could orchestrate a murder staged as suicide. Dieter likely wasn't directly involved but his constant presence at the hospital remained a puzzle piece worth examining. And then those numbers, concealed in the diary on the very same day that Weidt had received him in his office . . .

Hugo looked around for evidence that could tell him

more about just who Dieter Costa really was. He noticed a Bible and a violin in the corner.

'Do you play?' he asked.

'No, it's a friend's. She plays. I play the piano.'

'And where's this friend now?'

'She's gone now. Emigrated, I think.'

'Mm-hmm.' Hugo knew that those who had emigrated in time had been far-sighted families. Far-sighted Jews, above all, but also communists, homosexuals, Sinti, and Roma. He squinted to focus on the name carved into the wood. The violin bore the name *Duda*, an old Romani name. He chose not to press further.

'What about the Bible? Do you read it, or is it just a decoration?'

'Of course I read it. It has all the answers.'

So. A Hitler Youth recruit with a Romani friend's violin and a devotion to Scripture. Dieter Costa was anything but simple. Not a typical member of the Hitler Youth. Quite the opposite, really.

Dieter must have noticed that Hugo's gaze had shifted back to the uniform.

'Were you in the HJ too?' he asked.

What did young Dieter want to know? Whether *he* was a die-hard Nazi? Whether, besides a Party membership card, he also carried the fanaticism of those people?

'Back in my day, enrolment wasn't mandatory,' Hugo replied curtly. 'Here, however, I'm the one asking the questions. Where were you on the twenty-third of this month?' he asked.

'In bed with a fever,' Dieter replied. 'The nuns can confirm it.'

'I see,' Hugo said. For now, he had nothing more to

extract. He would have to trust the nuns – by definition, they couldn't lie.

'Get well soon,' he added, heading for the door. 'We'll meet again.'

Chapter 31

Berlin, Nikolaiviertel

When he saw her standing at the door, Gioele hesitated, unsure whether to step forward or retreat. Adele looked even more beautiful without the rigid nurse's uniform. She had been one of the few, along with Bethany, to treat him like a human being in Block 10 at Auschwitz. But she carried with her the lingering scent of medicine, blood, snow, and ash. She was bringing all of it into Hugo's home, a house that had been his refuge.

'Hello, little one . . .'

She stood still in the doorway, her voice as soft and bright as ever. He remembered how Betsy Angel, the most ruthless of the nurses, had sneered at her: *friend of the Jews.*

Gioele took a step forward, and before he realized it, he was wrapped in her embrace. She was warm – his mother's kind of warmth. Her slow, steady breathing felt like a gentle lullaby.

'How are you?' Adele pulled a chocolate bar from her handbag. Even in the camp, whenever possible, she had hidden candies and sweets to give secretly to him and the other children.

'I'm fine.'

'I hope Herr Fischer is treating you well.'

'Hugo's good,' Gioele replied, taking the chocolate. He broke off a piece and tasted it, but his stomach was too knotted to enjoy it. He couldn't ignore the question he'd been longing to ask.

How are my parents and my brother?

He knew he couldn't ask, not while she was still standing in the doorway. He waited as she removed her coat, as Edmund gallantly invited her into the dining room, and as Hugo came rushing from the kitchen, brushing his dishevelled hair from his forehead, a dish towel slung over his shoulder.

Gioele noticed immediately how Hugo looked at her. And he didn't miss how she blushed and straightened her posture when she saw him.

'What do you think?' Edmund whispered into his ear.

'They like each other,' Gioele whispered back.

Edmund was right – people revealed far more about themselves in silence than they did with words. You just had to watch, pay attention to their movements, their tones. Maybe, Gioele thought, he really was on his way to becoming a skilled mentalist.

Hugo disappeared into the kitchen again and returned with a stew and some potatoes. It was a rich meal for such lean times, and he had even opened one of the last bottles of wine. A clear sign that he and Edmund were onto something.

'I even have some homemade jam to go with the meat,' Hugo said, placing a jar at the centre of the table. 'The nuns made it.'

'And since when do you frequent nuns?' Edmund teased.

'Don't start. It's a long story.'

Gioele sat down, trying to figure out the best moment to ask his question. Not at the beginning of the meal, which passed in laughter and jokes. The mood turned more sombre when the adults began discussing the war – the Russians, who must have liberated Belarus by now, though no official reports confirmed it. Still, Hugo insisted, if you knew basic geography and followed the cities mentioned on the radio, it wasn't hard to track the German retreat.

It was Edmund who shifted the conversation, addressing the nurse. Gioele was grateful.

'It must be hell there – in that camp in Poland, I mean.'

'Papa . . .' Hugo shot him a sharp look and set his fork down.

'What? I just asked a question . . .'

'Don't worry,' Adele reassured them. 'There's no reason not to talk about it. People speak far too little of it as it is. It's one of the ugliest places on earth, Herr Fischer, believe me. If only Germans weren't taken in by Goebbels' idiotic propaganda . . .'

'Luckily, you got out,' Edmund said, sipping his wine. 'And luckily, so did Gioele.'

'Adele . . .' Gioele finally broke in, seizing the moment. 'How are my parents and my brother?'

Edmund set his glass down abruptly, almost spilling it

on the tablecloth. Outside, street noises filtered in – people bustling around outdoor soup kitchens, cars honking as they navigated through the rubble-strewn streets. Inside, there was only silence. Gioele knew that wasn't a good sign.

'Let's go and prepare the coffee substitute,' Hugo suggested, motioning to Edmund.

Gioele realized they were doing this deliberately, leaving only him and Adele at the table to talk.

'Well?' he pressed when they were alone.

'Your brother was very unwell when I was transferred . . .' Adele reached out, placing her hand gently over his. He didn't like the long pause she took before continuing. 'I have no news of him or your parents. I'm sorry.'

'But they'll be okay, won't they?'

'You've seen what happens in that camp . . . I'd be lying if I told you they're fine. But you, now – you're here. You're safe. And if your parents don't make it, you have a duty to survive, to preserve their memory and tell the world what you saw in there.'

'Do they think I abandoned them?' Gioele wiped his tears away hastily. 'Do you think they're angry at me?'

'Don't say such nonsense. No parent could ever be angry because their child is safe. I'm certain your parents loved you very much. My father panicked every time I scraped a knee because he adored me. And he was a doctor, imagine that!'

'My father would panic too . . . But we never had a chance to get hurt, really. Two of our siblings died as babies, so Mama and Papa were always extra careful with us.'

'You see? One of their children is safe. How could they be angry at that?'

Gioele nodded, comforted. Maybe Adele was right. His

father and mother would never be sad to know he was safe. On the contrary, they would rejoice.

'Your father gave you a great gift,' Adele added. 'He raised you bilingual. I think, in his foresight, he already imagined this moment. He gave you every tool you need to survive. Don't waste it.'

'I won't.'

Gioele closed his eyes and promised God and himself that he would survive, no matter what. He would do everything in his power to live through the war and find them when it was all over.

Chapter 32

'Why didn't you tell him the truth?' Adele focused her gaze on him as she stood by the window, her figure backlit, her expression hardened with irritation, arms crossed.

Hugo poured brandy into the glasses. He shut the door to the living room, leaving Gioele in Edmund's care.

'You didn't tell him the truth, either.'

'Of course not.' Adele spread her arms in exasperation. 'Did you expect me to do it for you?'

He handed her a glass and took a long sip from his own, as if to extinguish the fire rising in his chest.

'No, and I'm glad you didn't. If there's one thing worth preserving in these times, it's hope. I can't bear the burden of giving him this kind of pain. He's a child who's been deported, tortured . . . How can I tell him his mother died the day she arrived, in the gas chambers, his father succumbed to starvation, and his brother was butchered by Dr Mengele's experiments?'

Hugo realized his voice had risen. Adele pressed her lips to the rim of her glass but didn't drink.

'You're right, but someday, he might throw it back in your face.'

'One step at a time. We don't even know if we'll be alive tomorrow.'

Adele finally sipped the brandy, her gaze fixed on the grey panorama outside the window. 'I brought you something,' she murmured, seemingly eager to change the subject.

She reached into her bag and pulled out some documents. 'What's this?' Hugo flipped through them quickly.

'The original autopsy reports for the Weidt couple and Basilius Brecht.'

Adele placed a record on the gramophone and set it spinning. Music filled the room as she sat next to him on the couch. She drained her glass and handed it back to him. 'Fill it up again, because what you're about to read is pretty hot stuff.'

'How did you . . .? Did anyone see you?'

'I spoke with Dr Keller. I promised him no one would ever find out, and he assured me of the same. He's a man of integrity, someone who truly respects his craft. By the way, I also met Dr Schmidt, and I can't say I got the best impression of him. Though, apparently, I left quite an impression on him – he invited me to dinner.'

'And you accepted?' Hugo felt a sting of something he couldn't quite name.

'I deflected. I thought it might be useful to keep him in good standing.'

'Good.'

Hugo scanned Keller's report. As he'd suspected, it was different from the one signed solely by Schmidt. The first surprise confirmed his hunch: the bullet had not exited the skull, remaining lodged inside after likely hitting the floor.

A second shot had struck Dr Weidt in the chest. There were two bullets fired at him.

'So Weidt didn't kill himself,' he muttered.

'He was murdered.' Adele nodded. 'As for Marlene, she did have a laceration on the back of her head and a gunshot wound to the chest. She lost a lot of blood, though the head injury only caused a mild concussion.'

'Whereas Brecht . . .' Hugo flipped through the pages of the second report. 'Brecht died by drowning, and there's no way to distinguish injuries caused by the river's current from potential signs of a struggle or self-defence. No marks on his neck or wrists . . .'

Hugo exhaled deeply and slapped the reports onto the table. He refilled his glass and drained it in one go, as if needing the alcohol to dull the edge of his thoughts.

'What are you thinking?' Adele straightened the papers.

'These reports say nothing.'

'To me, they say quite a lot,' she countered.

'What would you know? You're just a nurse.'

The words left his mouth before he could stop them. Adele stared at him, first in astonishment, then in anger.

'I'm sorry,' Hugo blurted, reaching for her hand. She pulled it back.

'That was truly petty, and not like you.'

'I didn't mean it . . . I apologize. I'm just very tense.'

'I'll let it slide this time, but if it happens again, Herr Fischer, you won't see me again. I have no need of anyone who speaks to me like that.'

'Please forgive me.'

'Now, what's missing from these reports?'

'A ballistic analysis . . .' Hugo tried to steady himself. The strength and determination in Adele made her the most fascinating person he'd encountered in a long time. He didn't want to risk alienating her because of his frayed nerves. Clearing his throat, he continued, 'We don't know if all the bullets came from the same gun or if there were two weapons. Without a ballistic examination, we're groping in the dark. And the fingerprints – whose prints were on Weidt's gun? Schmidt's report says they were Benedict's and partly his son Klaus's, who apparently handled the weapon. But Keller's report doesn't mention the gun at all.'

'The bullets and the gun have probably been disposed of.'

'Likely.'

'See? Even us nurses know how to put two and two together.'

'I've already apologized. Don't keep throwing it in my face . . .'

'I enjoy watching you squirm.' Adele laughed. The record on the gramophone reached its end and continued spinning soundlessly.

'Didn't you see me squirm enough in Auschwitz?' Hugo leaned forward, resting his elbows on his knees, and looked at her from under the lock of hair that had fallen over his forehead.

She brushed it back in a gesture far too intimate. 'There's something about your personality that I really like,' she said.

'What's that?'

'We're not sufficiently close for me to tell you, Herr Fischer. One step at a time.'

The hum of the spinning disc became insistent. Hugo got up to stop the gramophone, grateful for the distraction. He looked out of the window at the devastation left by the bombs. Was it even permissible to love in a world where everything could be lost in an instant?

'By the way, I found a breadcrumb.' He turned back to the case, pulling himself away from his thoughts.

'Like Hansel and Gretel?'

'Exactly.' Hugo took out a slip of paper from his briefcase, the one with the string of numbers. He handed it to her.

'What's this?'

'I'm not sure . . . I thought it might be money Weidt owed someone, or dates, or numbers tied to the war. I believe it was given to him by a boy who visited often.'

'It's a *cipher*,' Adele murmured, her green eyes widening with realization, reflecting the golden light of late afternoon. 'Remember the messages the Auschwitz prisoners used to exchange? It's a coded message.'

A spark of electricity jolted through Hugo. How had he not realized this before? Of course, it was a cipher. He lit a cigarette, grabbed a pen and paper, and wrote out the numbers. He massaged his temples, thinking hard. Perhaps he knew the method. It looked like the same system used by the Red Orchestra, the resistance network that had communicated with the British and Soviets for years.

'Maybe I can decode it,' he said, feeling a strange feverish energy. Otto Weidt had been right: this work made him feel alive. The harder it was, the more he loved it. He drew a grid on the paper, numbering the rows horizontally and vertically, then filled in the alphabet. 'It's a Polybius square,' he explained. 'Each letter corresponds to two numbers.'

'So, the boy was a courier . . .'

'Yes, I think he delivered these notes to Weidt.' Hugo tried decoding the message, but the result was nonsense. 'They used a cipher key . . .'

'A key?'

'A word that converts into numbers, which are then subtracted from each letter's code. I'll need time to figure it out.'

'It could be any word.'

'I can make some guesses.' Hugo stubbed out his cigarette. 'But maybe we should drop this entirely and forget about it.'

'Are you afraid?'

'Yes.'

'If you think that's the best course, then let it go,' Adele said, placing her hand over his. 'You should prioritize your health and Gioele's safety.'

'I just don't know what the best course is any more.' Hugo gazed at the sky, now growing darker. 'Let me walk you home.'

Chapter 33

Wilhelmplatz, once dominated by the imposing Hotel Kaiserhof, now looked like a model that some petulant child had jumped up and down upon. The square's trees were uprooted, and piles of rubble had formed into small mounds. The hotel's rooms, once frequented by German nobility, were destroyed in the fires, and the golden sign at the entrance had fallen. Miraculously, the adjacent underground station had survived, its semi-circular entrance still facing the street.

'Thank you for a pleasant day,' Hugo said as they reached Adele's building. 'And thank you for the reports.'

'Thank *you*.' Adele smiled, pushing the bicycle she had ridden to Nikolaiviertel. The summer breeze tousled her hair slightly, mingling the scent of linden trees with her own. He found her irresistible. 'I'm certain you'll decipher those codes.'

'I'm afraid you have too much faith in me,' Hugo said, removing his hat and wiping the sweat from his neck.

'I think you're the one who lacks faith in yourself.'

Adele gave him a playful tap on the chest before disappearing behind the wrought-iron door. Hugo lingered briefly, staring at the entrance. What continued to surprise him was his ability to feel anything at all despite the destruction surrounding him. Perhaps this was humanity's most admirable quality – their relentless search for life's beauty even as everything else crumbled. Wasn't that what he had learned at Auschwitz? Berto, Bethany, the Jewish pathologist who had helped him with Dr Braun's autopsy, and even Adele – all had shown him that hope truly was the last thing to die.

Turning back, he headed home. Even the shattered neighbourhood looked different now. Nothing was beyond rebuilding. They would raise the city again, brick by brick, if only Hitler fell, taking with him those who had dragged them into the abyss. Nothing was truly lost. They would teach the young to appreciate beauty once more and re-open Germany's doors to those who'd been forced to flee.

As he passed the castle, a shadow behind him snapped him out of his daydream. Hugo had the distinct impression he was being followed by a dark Mercedes crawling along at walking pace. Quickening his steps, he leaned on his cane. The car stopped at the small square in front of the Berliner Schloss, its shadowy blue form looming in the evening light. Hugo followed the footprint of the palace, heading for the bridge over the Spree, watching the car reverse as he crossed.

When he reached home, the feeling of being followed gnawed at his stomach. His lungs struggled for air again, matching the tension in his nerves. Next time he saw Meyer, he wouldn't be able to deny that the shortness of breath was more than just physical.

Hanging his hat by the door, he removed his jacket, now comfortably in shirtsleeves.

Outside, the evening deepened towards curfew.

Peeking in on Gioele, he found the boy fast asleep in his small bed. Seeing him safe and still under the covers settled Hugo's nerves, especially after the unpleasant sensation of having been followed by the car. Was this what a father felt, seeing their child safe and secure?

Closing the door, he knocked on Edmund's door. His father was sitting up in bed, the newspaper spread across his legs. His glasses had slid down his nose, and he was snoring with his mouth wide open. Hugo feigned a cough, jolting him awake. Edmund fumbled clumsily for his glasses.

'Back already? I thought you'd spend the night with her.'

'No, Papa.'

'At least get a kiss out of it? Get your hands somewhere interesting?'

'Papa . . .' Hugo laughed, sitting at the bedside. 'This newspaper – is it from that print shop you're helping out at?'

'Helping is a strong word,' Edmund said, rubbing his eyes and cleaning his glasses with his nightshirt. 'Widow Volker doesn't pay me. I do it to keep myself busy.'

'You're not doing it for the widow?'

'I think she might like me, actually.'

Hugo laughed again, returning the paper. 'I've got work tonight,' he said, closing the door halfway.

'At least get some rest,' Edmund called after him.

'The golden rule, Papa. Cases should be solved within three days; it's already been five. You know the saying, don't you?'

'After three days, even a guest stinks?'

'Goodnight, Papa.'

Hugo shut the door. As much as his father joked, the timeline was critical. The probability of solving a case dropped sharply with every passing day – and too many days had already gone by.

He went to the kitchen, where he sat down at the table cluttered with candles. Lighting them one by one, he covered the window with cardboard. Laying out the slip of numbers and the Polybius cipher grid, he started thinking. *All* he needed now was the key.

He tried the name engraved on the violin – Duda. Who was this girl who filled Dieter's eyes with such melancholy? Working silently under the flickering candlelight, his calculations yielded nothing. He tried the names of Benedict Weidt's children, Klaus and Klara, but they didn't fit. Next, terms related to ophthalmology: eye, pupil, cornea. Again, nothing comprehensible emerged. It was like navigating a storm in open uncharted waters.

Late into the night, the candles burned almost to their wicks. One flame sputtered out entirely.

'There's no answer,' he muttered, resting his forehead on the table. *No answers.* What had that boy said? *The answers are all in the . . .*

'Bible,' he whispered, aligning letters to the grid.

1224.

1212.

2411.

The sum was 4847 – the numeric key.

Subtracting the key from the numbers on the slip, letters began to emerge.

'It works!'

The decoded message appeared before him: *'Children are safe.'*

What did it mean? Who were these children? Were they Klara and Klaus, the Weidt children?

Though far from solving the case, it was a clue – one of Adele's breadcrumbs. He was sure of one thing: if the cipher key was *Bible,* the message likely originated from St Teresa.

Hugo stood, extinguishing the candles and pulling down the cardboard. The room's air, thick from burning wax, rushed out with a breeze. He lit a cigarette, inhaling deeply with a sense of satisfaction.

'One step at a time,' he murmured.

For a moment, he lingered in that liminal space between night and day – a fleeting interval he cherished. This was a world on pause, where few woke and fewer still kept watch, an ephemeral, dreamlike realm of blurred edges and soft outlines.

Crushing out his cigarette in the ashtray, Hugo headed for the bathroom, determined to freshen up.

The creak of a floorboard stopped him cold.

He stepped back. The board groaned again. That sound, for some reason, unsettled him. Tapping the spot with his cane, he knelt and prised up one of the wooden planks. Beneath it, he found an envelope.

Inside were five ration cards, likely belonging to deceased individuals – a simple but deadly trick for obtaining extra food illegally. A trick punishable by hanging.

'Edmund . . .' he sighed.

Before he could dwell on it, the air raid sirens shattered the dawn with their piercing wails. Almost immediately, explosions tore through the sky, their deafening roar rattling even the blood in his veins.

Chapter 34

28 June 1944

Berlin, Wilhelmplatz

Adele lit the fire under the kettle. The house she had inherited from her late aunt was small but cosy, despite the windows that had been blown out and patched with cardboard. A faint staleness lingered in the air, now mingled with the dust wafting in from outside. The living room was brightened by several oil paintings, hinting that her aunt had either been an artist or, at the very least, a passionate admirer of art.

'Sorry for coming unannounced,' Hugo said, taking the cup of ersatz coffee she handed him. He took a sip and immediately burned his tongue.

'Careful!' Adele laughed. 'I'm on duty in an hour, so I don't have much time. I don't even know what situation I'll walk into today at the Charité . . .'

'Everything's gone around Friedrichstraße station – Central Hotel, Continental . . . all of it,' Hugo said.

'Good God . . .' Adele pressed her fingers to her lips. 'So many injured, I imagine.'

'Yeah. It's a disaster.'

'Judging by the bags under your eyes, I'd say you didn't sleep at all – not even before the air raid woke us up.'

'I didn't. I was up all night.'

Adele leaned against the windowsill. 'You cracked it, didn't you?'

Hugo took another tentative sip, more to buy time and keep her guessing than out of any real need.

'Do I need to beg?' she teased, her foot tapping impatiently. 'Or don't you trust me?'

The smile faded from Hugo's face. Suspicion was easy to indulge in these days, but that question stung. How many steps back would he have to take to truly see Adele for who she was?

'You're joking, right?' she asked, her tone dipping into disbelief. Her eyes darkened. 'That was a joke, Hugo . . . If you want to shut me out of this, fine. But you *can* trust me.'

'Forgive me,' Hugo said, his lips tingling with regret as he set down the cup.

He took a hesitant step back. Adele stood with her arms crossed, her slight frame almost childlike, but her face bore the weight of everything she'd witnessed in the camps. She was a fighter, a dissident, a dreamer. She had saved lives, collaborated with the Auschwitz Resistance, smuggled medicine, paper, pens, even cameras to prisoners documenting Nazi atrocities. If he couldn't trust her, who could he trust?

You're an idiot, he scolded himself.

This time, he stepped forward and stopped thinking altogether. It was liberating – no calculations, no second-guessing. For once, he acted on instinct. He leaned in and kissed her. Adele didn't resist. Her lips were warm, faintly flavoured with ersatz coffee. Better than Pervitin or morphine. Nothing could wake him and calm him at the same time like this.

When he pulled back, her eyes fluttered open.

They stayed like that, breath mingling, until a shared laugh broke the tension.

'Am I asking for a slap?' Hugo joked.

'No . . .' Adele grabbed his tie and kissed him again. 'But I do need to hurry – I've got to be at the Charité in half an hour!'

'I'll walk you there. We can talk on the way.' Hugo held up his notebook, where he had written the decoded phrase. 'Here's what I found.'

'*"Children safe"*,' Adele read aloud, shaking her head. 'What does that mean?'

'Everything and nothing. It tells us Weidt was genuinely worried about something. He knew he might die, so a month ago, he secured his children's safety and gave his cousin that note written in invisible ink. I think there were other messages like this one, but they must have been destroyed after use. This one was meant to be a safeguard, a reminder of a promise someone made to him.'

'Sounds plausible.' Adele pulled on her coat and grabbed her bag. She adjusted her hair in the mirror, added a touch of red lipstick that made her porcelain skin glow, and wrapped a silk scarf around her nose and mouth to guard against the lingering smoke and dust outside. 'What's next?'

'I want to talk to the Weidt children again,' Hugo said as they stepped into Wilhelmplatz, where ash still fell like snow. 'It's been a few days; they should be more willing to open up.'

'They've been placed in Otto's care, did you know that?'

'So much the better. That man might undo some of the damage their mother inflicted on them.' Hugo offered his hand to help her navigate the rubble spilling into the street. 'That kid, Dieter Costa, is . . . odd. I think he knows something but is too scared to talk. He seemed to be gauging *how close* I was to the Nazis, which can only mean one thing: he's terrified of the Gestapo.'

Adele linked arms with him, and they walked together through the bomb-scarred haze towards the shadow of the Charité. It felt new to him, walking like this, arm in arm. He'd always avoided deep connections, opting for fleeting encounters that demanded no commitments or questions about his limp, his headaches, his bouts of exhaustion. But Adele knew it all. In Auschwitz's suffocating, ash-scented snow, it had been natural to confide in her.

'No other breadcrumbs?' she asked.

'A former comedian who now works at the Hoff Circus visited Weidt more often than necessary. It's such a small lead it's probably meaningless. Truthfully, I doubt I'll ever solve this case.'

'Don't lose hope – Hansel and Gretel made it home in the end.'

'Let's be honest: they didn't get home thanks to breadcrumbs.' Hugo leaned in to kiss her. 'And before they did, they ended up in the witch's cage. I'm just wondering where my cage is.'

'You really are just a cock-eyed optimist, aren't you, Fischer?'

Chapter 35

The window of his room overlooked the dusty street, facing the few buildings in the neighbourhood that still stood alongside theirs. Gioele thought this was fortunate: why would the British bomb a district that had already been destroyed? Yet fear gripped him every time the air raid sirens wailed, with their mournful, menacing sound. They would have to get up suddenly, turn off the water and gas, fling open the windows, grab what they could, and dash down the stairs with their hearts pounding.

Edmund had mentioned how some people had been boiled alive when hot water pipes burst in basements. So, every time they sheltered there, Gioele would fix his gaze on the pipes, praying everything would be okay. He hated the filthy, damp smell of those hideaways where he had to conceal himself *twice over*: speaking as little as possible, lest his accent betray him, and keeping the number on his arm covered with a bandage.

He leaned out of the window. Berlin was a hostile city, but Bologna had been hostile, too.

He could barely remember the day when the Grand Council of Fascism decided things had to change. He was only four years old then, but his father spoke of that day as the greatest betrayal Italy had ever suffered.

Bologna had always been a smiling city, its warm red hues, narrow alleys, and porticoes offering safety from the rain. His father often recounted how, in its golden days, the university had welcomed Jewish students from countries that had expelled them. At one point, the Alma Mater hosted seven hundred Jewish students. A kosher canteen was opened, and the newcomers were embraced within the Fascist University Group, where they even formed a Zionist branch.

Then everything had fallen apart.

Books, articles, and caricatures about Jews began to circulate. His father's eyes would burn with anger and then dim with disappointment as he spoke of it: no one protested against the defamation campaign, no one said a word – not even his university colleagues. Everyone feared being seen as out of step, afraid of saying the wrong thing.

'Everyone tends their own little garden,' his father would say. 'What a disgrace.'

When the racial laws came, the university expelled its Jewish students and professors. His father lost his chair, and all of it happened in silence. The apathetic, his father claimed, were the true ruin of the world: they could make a difference, but they chose to hide instead.

Gioele pulled himself away from the window and returned to the table, bending over his drawing with the few pencils Edmund had managed to scrounge. The paper came from the leaflets Hugo picked up off the streets – Nazi propaganda turned over to reveal blank backs. But the sheet

Gioele was working on now was the one he had found during his first outing with Edmund to Otto Weidt's factory. On it was scrawled: *'Free yourselves from the Nazi yoke! Free yourselves from Nazi violence!'*

Gioele thought it was the most fitting paper to use as he sketched his mother's face, emerging in strokes of black graphite. He paused and stared at it. Tears welled up as he realized it wasn't really her.

The ringing of the doorbell broke his reverie.

Gioele froze.

Edmund and Hugo always used their keys to come in, and the doorbell hadn't rung once in six months. He tried to calm his racing heart, reminding himself of what to do: the rule was, if he was alone and someone came, he had to stay silent and hide in the wardrobe.

Gioele slid back his chair carefully, avoiding the scrape of its legs, and crept into the hallway instead of hiding. The wooden floorboards creaked beneath his steps. The bell rang again, and he nearly bolted, but his body kept moving towards the door. Pressing his ear against the wood, he listened.

'Is anyone home?' A bright, youthful male voice called out.

Gioele held his breath, his hands turning cold. He saw a shadow move under the door's crack before the visitor slipped a postcard through the slot. The sound of retreating footsteps followed.

Gioele waited a few seconds, then picked up the card.

It read: 'Bastian Fischer.'

The name made his head spin.

'In response to your early application to the *Deutsches Jungvolk* of the Hitler Youth . . .' His voice faltered. The saliva in his mouth felt like a hard lump impossible to swallow. 'Report to your local headquarters . . .'

His lower lip quivered. He understood what this meant. Edmund had explained what the Hitler Youth was – it was like the Balilla in Italy. He would end up among other German boys who hated him and wanted him dead. They'd see the tattoo, and for him, Hugo, and Edmund, it would all be over.

'What do I do . . .' he whispered.

He sat cross-legged on the floor, clutching the card. There was only one thing to do. It was time to ensure everyone's safety.

Springing to his feet, Gioele darted along the hallway, heading for the kitchen. The lingering smell of food was comforting, making him feel momentarily safe, aiding his resolve. He remembered reading somewhere that kitchens had this effect – linked to humanity's survival instinct and the life-giving role of food.

Gioele turned the gas knob, lighting the stove with a match. His hand shook as he opened the drawer, retrieving the cold handle of a large knife. The chill of the blade sent a shiver down his spine. Holding it over the flame, he waited.

It was the right thing to do. Hugo and Edmund should have thought of it months ago instead of risking so much for him.

During the air raids, as they dashed down to the shelters, Gioele noticed Hugo always checking the tightness of his bandage. But who would believe in a wound that never healed? No one would question a burn, though. Fires raged during the bombings, and Edmund had once helped extinguish a blaze in the building across the street. Gioele remembered the commotion – people passing water buckets as Edmund burned his hand on a falling beam. No one would doubt a burn. *Logical conclusion*, as Edmund would say.

When Gioele pressed the scorching blade to his tattoo, the stench of charred flesh hit him before the pain. He recoiled, dropping the knife. It clattered to the floor, leaving only a red mark on his skin. The tattoo remained.

Tears filled his eyes, but he tried again. This time, he pulled back even before the blade touched his arm. A sob rose in his throat.

The front door unlocked with a jangle of keys. Gioele heard footsteps.

Hugo appeared in the kitchen doorway, hat in hand. He sniffed the air, set down his hat on a shelf, and asked, 'What's going on?'

Gioele burst into tears. The salty taste in his mouth was unbearable, worse than the sting of the scald.

'We have to get rid of it, Hugo . . .' he sobbed.

'What?'

'The tattoo! You do it – I'm too scared!'

Hugo grabbed his arm, his widened eyes taking in what Gioele had done.

'You need to get rid of it!' Gioele insisted.

'Have you lost your mind? You could've seriously hurt yourself!'

'Please. I want it gone. We're not safe . . .'

Gioele shoved the card at him. Hugo read it, his face turning pale as his lips compressed.

'When did this arrive?'

'Just now . . . I didn't answer. They slid it under the door.' Gioele's panic surged as he saw Hugo's alarm. 'It's over, isn't it? They'll find out about me?'

'They won't. Nobody will find out,' Hugo said, though his voice wavered.

'Are you sure?'

'Yes. But you're right – we need to get rid of the tattoo, just in case.'

Gioele shut his eyes, extending his arm. His body shook uncontrollably, but he resolved not to be a coward. Auschwitz had been worse, he told himself. The tattoo itself had hurt. As had the nurses' beatings. Perhaps he was growing up, and that's why he was afraid. Adults are bigger scaredy-cats than children.

Hugo touched his face gently, and Gioele felt the man's breath quicken. He heard the hiss of the stove and squeezed his eyes shut tighter, retreating into the darkness.

'Don't scream,' Hugo warned. 'It'll hurt at first, but then it'll be over. Bite your shirt.'

Gioele obeyed, clutching the fabric in his teeth. He wouldn't let fear consume him. He had no doubts about what they were doing, and he was certain Hugo didn't either. This was going to be a liberation for him as well.

He swallowed hard. His heart was pounding louder than the anti-aircraft guns.

'Damn it . . .' Hugo muttered, pausing. It was the first time Gioele had heard him curse in his presence. 'There has to be another way . . .'

Gioele opened his eyes to see Hugo holding the heated blade, shaking his head.

'I can't do it,' Hugo said, dropping the knife. 'I can't do this to you. A burn could get infected – it's too dangerous . . .'

'You promised to protect me!' Gioele sobbed.

'Exactly.'

'Then do it! Remove it!'

'Gioele . . .'

'Protect me!'

Hugo scrubbed his face with his hands, then rubbed his palms together nervously. The silence in which he had barricaded himself only plunged Gioele into a state of despair where he felt utterly powerless.

At last, he picked up the knife and reheated it. This time, he didn't stop. The blade seared Gioele's skin, and the smell of burning flesh filled the room.

But it wasn't the pain that made Gioele faint. It was the realization that he had smelled that odour before – at Auschwitz.

Chapter 36

'It's going to end badly, you know . . .' Edmund gazed at him over his gold-rimmed glasses, seated at the kitchen table, hands wrapped around a mug of cold ersatz coffee. 'We're already dead.'

'The tattoo isn't visible any more.' Hugo took a sip. 'It's a serious burn.'

'It's not the tattoo that's the problem.'

'I know.'

The midday light filled the room, casting it into a liminal space where everything seemed to float. It was so bright it washed out every detail. Gioele was asleep, worn out by the fever that followed the burn and the fear. They had treated him, then sat there in the small kitchen, trying to decide what to do next. Protecting that child was becoming an unbearable weight, a task he wasn't sure he could carry out. When he had seen him faint, his small eyes rolled back, his face gone pale amid the stench of burnt flesh they both knew too well, he had imagined him dead.

His body grotesquely discarded in a crematorium, piled among the other corpses. The feeling of powerlessness had consumed him.

'The first thing they'll do is request records from Munich's registry office about Bastian Fischer's mother,' Edmund pressed. 'And they'll discover there is no mother. There's no Bastian Fischer. And then there's the circumcision . . . He's Jewish, surely circumcised. What if they notice?'

'I need to find out who performs the medical examination for the Jungvolk enlistment.'

'We need to make him disappear. I know some people who could hide him.'

'Are you insane? And what do we tell the Jungvolk? That I've lost my son? They'd figure it out immediately.'

'Then we'll go into hiding too.'

Silence descended again. The kitchen tap dripped steadily, marking time as it passed – time that inevitably brought them closer to disaster.

'If you didn't sign him up for the Jungvolk, who did?' Edmund murmured. 'Someone who knows?'

'I don't think so. If they did, the Gestapo would've come straight away.'

Hugo couldn't help but think of Dieter Costa and his persistent questions about his son. Could it have been him who requested the enrolment? Was he really that cunning? He had Italian blood, that much was clear, but how could he have known about Gioele's heritage?

'So, what do we do?' Edmund folded his arms.

'I don't know, Papa. Give me a few hours to think it through . . . I need to get my head straight. I'm not thinking clearly right now.'

Hugo felt crushed under the weight of it all. His eyes burned. His temples throbbed so intensely he feared they might burst. What he needed was darkness and morphine. Instead, he stood and left the house.

Chapter 37

'I need your help.'

Hugo felt sweat trickling down his neck and his heart racing. His entire body was on the verge of total collapse.

'What happened?' Otto Weidt reached for the pitcher of water on the table and poured a glass. 'Drink this first – you sound too shaken.'

'I need something stronger.'

The man opened the liquor cabinet, uncorked the remnants of a bottle of cognac, and handed it to him. Hugo took a swig directly from the bottle, but it did little to calm his nerves. He explained to Otto about the postcard from the Jungvolk, how he hadn't submitted any application for early enrolment, and how someone else must have done it on his behalf.

'Someone who wants to slow down my investigation – or worse, get me into serious trouble.' Hugo paused, sensing that Weidt, despite being blind, seemed to scrutinize him deeply.

'Your son's real name is Gioele, isn't it?'

Hearing that name from a stranger's lips felt like a gun-shot at close range. Hugo flinched, and his chair scraped loudly across the floor. He had only mentioned the name Bastian – how could anyone know the truth? Adele, per-haps? The thought of her betraying him made his blood run cold.

'How do you . . .?'

Otto Weidt smiled serenely from the other side of the modest kitchen table. Everything in the house, connected to the disused factory, was simple and practical – just like him.

'Your father brought him to me a few days ago,' Weidt said.

'My father?'

Hugo couldn't believe his ears. Rage quickly replaced his confusion. Not only had his father hidden illegal ration cards at home, but he'd also paraded an endangered Jewish child around Berlin, in broad daylight, amidst Nazi patrols raiding basements and attics. It was selfish recklessness, the kind he had come to expect from Edmund, who had always put others in danger without a second thought.

Hugo clenched his fists, his frustration bubbling over. He wanted to slam the table, to shout, to let out the helpless fury boiling inside him. But he didn't. Otto Weidt, calm and steady, seemed to perceive his inner turmoil, even though he couldn't see it.

'Don't blame dear Edmund,' Otto said, shaking his head. There was a familiarity in how he said the name, hinting at an old friendship. 'Sometimes he's careless, yes, but I'll tell you what was on his mind: he wanted to make that boy feel *alive*. He loves him like only a grandfather could and doesn't want to see him wither away, hiding like a rat.'

'Well, that boy is now in danger.'

'What can I do to help resolve this?'

'Adele told me you're . . . skilled at bribing the Gestapo. I wondered if your network extends to the Jungvolk as well.'

Otto Weidt fell into a long silence. Only the rhythmic tapping of his cane suggested he was weighing options. He stood, counted his steps, and stopped before lifting a floorboard. From underneath, he retrieved a notebook. So, that's where Edmund must have learned the trick.

The man returned to the table and ran his fingers over the raised dots on the pages.

'I assume handing Gioele over to me to hide isn't one of your options,' Otto remarked, his tone neutral.

'Now that the HJ knows he exists, the Gestapo would intervene immediately.'

'Very well.' Weidt stopped at a particular page, his fingers halting. Hugo realized it must be a list of individuals who could be bribed for various reasons. 'I have a contact. I'll speak with Dr Bachmann, who handles the medical examinations for the Jungvolk. I'll arrange for the evaluation to be brief and superficial.'

'Bachmann. Can I trust him?'

'Among Nazis?' Weidt chuckled. 'No. But I promise to do everything in my power to make sure it goes smoothly. However, you must watch your back. Someone wants to keep an eye on your son by bringing him into the Jungvolk, but their real interest is monitoring you.'

'Keeping my son close to watch me?'

'I don't know what trouble my cousin got himself into, but someone out there is worried enough to think that keeping an eye on Gioele is the only way to keep tabs on you. I doubt this person suspects Gioele's heritage, or they would have already alerted the Gestapo.'

Hugo rubbed his face. Finally, the picture was coming into focus.

'I'm relieving you of your duties, Herr Fischer,' Otto Weidt said, closing the notebook and rising from the table. 'I believe I've inadvertently dragged you into something far too dangerous.'

'I'm already in it.' Hugo stood as well. 'And I decide how and when to step away. I want to speak to your nephew and niece. One at a time, if that's possible.'

Otto Weidt nodded and led him towards the stairs to the upper floor of the house.

Chapter 38

Klara's bedroom was small and bare, much like the rest of the house. Perhaps this was due to Otto Weidt's blindness, which necessitated clear, open spaces rather than decoration. Still, the girl had managed to add some colour to the room. A red Party flag adorned the wall, and her bed was made with pillowcases and sheets embroidered with black swastikas.

She was wearing the Jungmädel uniform: a blue skirt, white blouse, and scarf secured with wooden rings. Sitting at the edge of her bed, hands clasped on her knees, she looked uneasy.

'Do you remember me?' Hugo pulled out the chair from her desk and sat. She nodded silently. 'How are you?'

'Sometimes good, sometimes bad.'

'Did you embroider those sheets? You're very skilled.'

'Thank you,' Klara replied, smoothing her braids in a nervous gesture. 'You're here to talk about my parents again, aren't you?'

'Yes,' Hugo admitted, his eyes scanning the room. On a

shelf, schoolbooks and back issues of *Das Deutsche Mädel*, the magazine for German girls, were neatly stacked. Next to a wedding photo of Marlene and Benedict on the desk sat a small metal box and a vial of adrenaline. 'But first, I'd like to talk about you. You said you're sometimes unwell.'

'I miss my parents,' she whispered. 'My group leaders call my father a degenerate. It hurts a lot.'

'People are quick to judge without understanding. You shouldn't let it get to you.'

'My father was a good man,' Klara said, hiding her face as silent tears fell. Her quiet dignity made Hugo want to reach out and console her.

'Of course he was,' Hugo reassured her. 'I'm investigating to find out the truth. I promise I'll prove he was no murderer.'

He almost regretted the promise. Benedict Weidt might not have been a killer, but both he and his wife might have been involved in something equally damning.

'What do you do in your Jungmädel group?' Hugo changed the subject to put her at ease. He needed her calm if he hoped to piece together the events surrounding her parents' deaths.

'We do athletics, hold meetings at the Party house, and go on hikes,' Klara said, wiping her eyes. 'We sing a lot and collect donations for the war effort.'

'I've made donations too,' Hugo said, hesitating as the memory surfaced. He had given something he cherished – not for the Führer, but for the soldiers sent to die like cattle. 'I donated my mother's skis for the boys on the Russian front.'

'That's very honourable.'

'Thank you. What else do you learn in your group? Do

they teach you embroidery?' Hugo gestured towards the swastikas on her sheets.

'Yes. They teach us to be good mothers, to be strong and healthy so Germany will also be strong and healthy. There's nothing more important than loving and serving the Führer. We must do what he wants because he is Germany's redeemer.'

She recited the mantra perfectly but without enthusiasm. In this, she seemed more like her father than her mother.

'What's the adrenaline for?' Hugo pointed to the vial next to the photo.

'My asthma. I guess I'm not as strong and healthy as the Führer would like.'

'But you're a wonderful girl,' Hugo said sincerely. Despite her fragile appearance, Klara seemed capable and self-aware. Leaning forward, he sought her gaze. 'That night, you said you heard only one gunshot.'

'Yes.'

Her answer was firm, yet Keller's unofficial report indicated three shots.

'You went downstairs to see what had happened. What did you find?'

'My mother was lying on the floor, and so was my father . . . there was so much blood. Klaus was already there.'

'Klaus got there before you?'

'Yes . . .'

'Why didn't you tell me before?'

'Klaus was so frightened. I didn't want anyone questioning him.'

'Where was the gun? In your father's hand?'

'Klaus had picked it up, and I screamed at him to drop it.'

'But you told me earlier that no one touched anything.'

'I know, and I'm ashamed. I just wanted everyone to leave my brother alone.'

Even Nebe had confirmed that Klaus had handled the weapon, complicating the ballistics analysis. Hugo refused to believe the boy had shot his parents. He needed to hear Klaus's account.

'Thank you for your honesty, Klara. I'll talk to your brother and promise to uncover the truth.'

'Thank you, Herr Fischer. My father would have said you're a good man.'

Klaus's room was a shrine to Nazism. Otto Weidt, being blind, was fortunate not to see it: swastika flags, photographs of the Führer, and banners decorated the walls. A portrait of Hitler, styled as the saviour of the Fatherland, was framed with a candle burning reverently beneath it.

Hugo thanked his thirty-six years of experience. While he had sympathized with Hitler early on, his fully formed adult perspective allowed him to step back when the situation spiralled. Boys raised in the Hitlerjugend had no such chance. The State decided what they read, watched, sang, thought, and hated.

Klaus greeted Hugo with a smile. He barely resembled the terrified, silent child Hugo had seen the morning his parents were found dead.

'Heil Hitler, sir!' Klaus said enthusiastically.

'You look well,' Hugo said, bowing slightly to meet the boy's gaze. His lively eyes reminded him of Gioele, and he was relieved to see Klaus no longer appeared lost and frightened. 'You seem very happy.'

'I am! This morning, we found out that Klara and I were

selected for an excursion organized by the Jesuits and the Hitler Youth!'

'The Jesuits? The Church can't organize trips.'

'It's part of the reconciliation programme between religious institutions and the State, sir.' Klaus delivered the explanation with a zeal that would have pleased the Führer himself. 'We're going to Mount Brocken. Have you heard of it? They say you can see a ghost there! Some say it's God, but the Hitler Youth say it's Hitler himself.'

'I don't think it's either,' Hugo replied, raising a finger to trace the outline of a mountain in the air. 'The Brocken Spectre appears when the sun shines from a low angle behind a climber looking into the mist. The light casts the climber's shadow onto the fog.'

'But they say the ghost moves!' Klaus argued, clearly frustrated.

'Of course, because of shifts in the fog,' Hugo said, tousling the boy's hair. He suspected all this energy masked a deeper pain. His next question confirmed it.

'Sit down, Klaus. I need to ask about your parents.'

The boy's face went pale, his eyes turned glassy, and his posture sagged.

'Klara says you were the first to see them.'

'Yes . . . that's true.'

'Did the gunshot wake you?'

'No.' Klaus hesitated before taking a deep breath. 'It was the quarrelling.'

Hugo's pulse quickened. Here was the breakthrough he needed. He rested the cane and sat on the edge of the cot, inviting the boy to do the same. Klaus complied. He had thin legs sticking out from under his shorts and scraped knees, just like all boys his age.

'What were they arguing about?'

'I don't know. I couldn't understand. Then there was a gunshot . . . I got scared and stayed at the top of the stairs. Then there was a loud crash . . .'

'What kind of crash?'

'Like something heavy falling.'

'Are you sure you heard only one shot?'

'Yes . . .'

'And then?'

'I went downstairs.'

'And you picked up the gun.'

'No!' Klaus's eyes brimmed with tears.

'Don't lie to me,' Hugo warned. 'Your sister already told me.'

'Yes,' Klaus stammered in response, visibly uncomfortable for having done something he shouldn't and for lying to an adult

'Did you take it from your father's hand?'

'No, it was on the floor, between him and my mother.'

'Don't lie again.'

'I swear on the Führer.'

Hugo instinctively glanced at the image of Hitler on the nightstand, lit by the flickering candle. One gunshot, a loud noise, the gun far from Benedict. What the devil had happened in that house? What had happened after the children ran for help? Could the killer have stayed hidden and completed their work?

'Did you see your father's face when you went downstairs?' Hugo asked, trying to pin down the suspicions he was trying to flesh out.

Klaus nodded.

'Was anything strange?'

'His eyes were wide open, and there was so much blood in his mouth!' Klaus sobbed, abandoning his perfect Hitler Youth demeanour.

Hugo had his answer. Neither Klara nor Klaus mentioned their father's face being partially destroyed by a shot to the temple – a gruesome detail impossible to overlook unless it happened later. Unless there was some form of psychological erasure, the shot to Benedict's head had come after the children fled, meaning the killer had stayed behind to cover their tracks.

'I'm sorry to make you remember these awful things.' Hugo wrapped an arm around Klaus's shoulders as the boy cried into his chest.

Klaus and Gioele were just children, forced into lives they hadn't chosen. One hidden away, the other indoctrinated. Neither of them was truly free – they were both trapped.

Chapter 39

Kiev, 28 September 1941

A Day Before the Massacre

The city is in constant turmoil. The Russians have hidden Molotov cocktails in the buildings, and the heat from the fires makes them explode, feeding more blazes and collapses. We've had to blow up other structures to contain the flames. The result is a vast desolation – a grey wasteland of ruins swarming with thousands of refugees fleeing for their lives.

Obergruppenführer Jeckeln enters the command post at four in the afternoon.

Hans looks at me but says nothing. He doesn't need to. He doesn't even need to tell me that he was right.

'Tomorrow, you will have the honour of serving greater Germany alongside my men from Einsatzgruppe C,' the Obergruppenführer announces.

They always start like this, with a bit of moral blackmail

that makes you feel like an ungrateful traitor if the thought of disobedience even crosses your mind. By now, I know our superiors well enough.

'You are not obliged to do what I'm asking of you,' he continues. He offers free will, like God. 'I will explain what we will do. Afterwards, anyone who does not feel up to it may leave the room. No punishment will be given to those who choose not to participate.'

We all stand at attention, hands at our sides, heads held high.

He has our full attention.

'Tomorrow, we will carry out a cleansing. Jews, Gypsies, communists, and mental asylum patients. This world has no need for asocial elements; it needs better people to build a better society. Our surveyors have identified a ravine near the Jewish cemetery – that is where we will gather them. Nearby, there is a railway line that will help us organize supplies and transport the confiscated personal belongings. It will not be an easy task, nor a short one. I want to be honest with you. If anyone does not feel capable, they may leave the room.'

Now, all I hear is my own breathing.

I'm afraid to make too much noise, afraid to draw Jeckeln's gaze. I want to leave the room, but no one moves. Not a single step. It would take just one person – I am certain. One man to step out, and many would follow, including me. But no one wants to be the first. *I* don't want to be the first.

'Well then,' Jeckeln exclaims with satisfaction. 'You are all true Germans.'

And there it is – the final phrase that snuffs out even the faintest spark of courage. We are true Germans. Now, anyone who steps back will no longer be one. I remain motionless. I must do what is required. Yet my hand rises on its own.

'Speak,' Jeckeln commands.

'Herr Obergruppenführer . . .' I murmur, my voice barely audible. 'Tomorrow is Yom Kippur . . .'

'The Day of Atonement,' he echoes, his voice sharp. 'Isn't it all so damn fitting?'

Chapter 40

29 June 1944

Berlin, Mitte

'The Jungvolk?' Adele quickened her pace. Hugo detected a certain unease in her voice. 'What do you mean, the Jungvolk?'

She had fallen silent when, standing on the threshold of the Charité, he had told her about Gioele. Now she was walking briskly, as if this were the prelude to further trouble she might need to escape. Hugo found himself also speeding up – not only to keep pace, but because the memory of the Mercedes that had followed him home suddenly weighed heavily on his thoughts.

'Sorry . . .' Adele slowed when she realized he was struggling to keep up. 'I just feel uneasy. Would you mind if we ate at my place instead of the restaurant?'

Hugo caught her gaze. Her eyes had darkened to a stormy green. What was she afraid of? Was it for Gioele, or for herself?

'What's going on?' Hugo grabbed her arm, a foreboding feeling welling up inside him.

'Nothing . . .' Adele looked away.

Hugo didn't want secrets between them – not with her. He couldn't bear the thought of being betrayed by the one person he trusted.

'Adele, please,' he whispered. 'What's wrong?'

'It's just . . .' Adele glanced around nervously. 'Yesterday, a car followed me home.'

'A black Mercedes?'

'How do you know?'

'It followed me, too.'

'I didn't want to worry you.' Adele shrugged. 'But then you mentioned Gioele, and I was terrified it was my fault – that I'd done something . . .'

'Your fault?' Hugo squinted as though trying to sharpen his focus on what she wasn't saying. 'Why would it be your fault?'

'They were following me . . . I thought it might be the Gestapo, because of the documents I took from Ravensbrück . . .'

'It's not that,' he reassured her, though there was little comfort to be found in their predicament. 'They were following you because they saw you with me. They want Gioele in the Jungvolk to keep tabs on me. They're watching me.'

'Because of the Weidt case?'

'I'm afraid so.'

Hugo took her hand as they walked toward the Brandenburg Gate. They stopped outside a beer hall on Unter den Linden. He went in, ordered two pale beers, and came out with the paper bag in one hand. He waved it playfully under her nose, but Adele didn't seem interested in the light-hearted gesture.

'What will you do about Gioele?' she pressed, leaning against the beer hall's window.

'I'll do nothing. We'll go to the enrolment exam.'

'That's suicide!' Adele grabbed his jacket.

'Otto Weidt promised me that a doctor he knows well would conduct the exam. He gave me his word.'

'Do you trust him?'

'What other choice do I have?'

Adele remained solemn, her lips thinning with tension. Hugo bent to kiss her, and she melted into the warmth of the gesture.

'You, who've taken so many risks, now fear for me and Gioele?' he teased.

'I don't care if I'm the one at risk.' Adele didn't share his humour. 'But I won't let anything happen to the people I care about.'

Hugo intertwined his fingers with hers as they walked silently home. The summer wind was warm. It would have been pleasant if it hadn't carried the acrid smell of dust and blood. Yet by her side, for a moment, he felt as though he were walking through the old, magnificent Berlin. He imagined dining in one of the opulent restaurants on Kurfürstendamm, then dancing the night away at Clärchens Ballhaus, losing themselves in champagne and dazzling lights. If only there were no war. If only the Nazis hadn't dismantled every dance hall to install Party offices.

But there was a war, and they had to survive.

They had to settle for a modest dining room, two Berlin pale ales, black bread, and a bit of butter. That was their supper in Adele's tiny apartment, which to Hugo felt like the only place in the world that mattered.

'To your health,' he said as they sat down at her table.

They clinked their beer bottles together. The Berliner Weiße refreshed him from the oppressive summer heat wafting through the window frames, still bare of glass.

'I suppose you'll drop the Weidt case now,' Adele said, taking small, deliberate sips of her beer.

'I don't know.'

'What do you mean, *you don't know*? It's becoming seriously dangerous . . .'

'The day I joined the National Socialist Party, I felt cornered.' Hugo leaned back in his chair, his gaze drifting out the window to the bleak view of the crumbled square. 'You want to keep working with the Kripo? Get the Party card. You want to keep your job? Conform and pretend. Well, you know what? I'm tired of being a coward, standing with my back to the wall. I want to choose what to do and what not to do.'

'That I understand.' Adele spread butter on two slices of bread with slow, precise movements that reminded him of his mother. 'But it's dangerous . . .'

'So are the bombs.'

'You know what I mean.' Adele sighed. 'What else have you learned about the Weidts?'

'I found the biggest breadcrumb.' Hugo ran his fingers over the tabletop, brushing the actual breadcrumbs into his palm and popping them into his mouth, the way he had as a child. 'When the Weidt children found their parents' bodies, the pistol wasn't in Benedict's hand, and his face was still intact.'

'What does that mean?'

'He hadn't been shot in the head yet. Someone finished the job after the kids ran away. Someone who was hiding in the house. Klaus heard an argument . . . The Weidts were arguing with someone.'

'How can you find that someone?' Adele handed him the bread.

'I don't know. The trail ends here, and I'm left in the deep dark woods.'

'Careful, Fischer. Fairy tales are banned by the Führer.'

'Listen to her . . . You're the one who brought up Hansel and Gretel!'

They laughed, a bitter edge lingering despite the sweetness of the beer. Hugo drained his bottle. The faint buzz of alcohol made him swing between a fleeting sense of ease and a sharp surge of anxiety. No matter how he tried, he couldn't shake the thoughts of the Mercedes and the looming Jungvolk exam. He wished for another beer to toast his impending downfall. At least he could march towards the gallows intoxicated.

Adele stood and ran a hand over the dusty gramophone.

'I'm not even sure it works.' She rummaged through a box of records and pulled one out. 'Let's see what my aunt used to listen to.'

The record spun, and Debussy's *Clair de Lune* floated into the room.

Adele approached him and gently took his cane.

'I need that,' Hugo protested.

'No, you don't. Shall we bet?'

Adele took his hands and placed them on her waist, letting him steady himself on her. 'When we said goodbye at Auschwitz, you promised to take me dancing,' she reminded him.

'It's true, I'm unforgivable . . . But there aren't many dance halls left.'

'Who said we need a dance hall?'

They danced, as they had at Solahütte, but this time Hugo didn't need to run away. The world was falling apart. He himself was in pieces. Yet, in that slow dance, everything seemed to find its place. The ruins of Berlin lifted and settled back together. The cathedral, the Rotes Rathaus, the Kaiser-Wilhelm rose from the dust, grain by grain. The shattered glass of Jewish shop windows reassembled, pristine once again. Time rewound, spinning backwards.

When the music ended, Hugo realized it was all an illusion.

But for a few minutes, it was enough.

Chapter 41

30 June 1944

Berlin, Corner of Torstraße and Prenzlauer Allee

The three red flags atop the Reichsjugendführung gleamed in the morning sun. The building housing the leadership of the Hitler Youth loomed grey, imposing, almost suffocating. Its façade, lined with hundreds of windows, showcased the vastness of what had once been the Kaufhaus Jonaß department store, now confiscated and 'Aryanized'.

Gioele gripped his hand tightly.

That morning, Hugo had woken him early, prepared a more substantial breakfast than usual, and drawn him a warm bath. As always, he waited outside the bathroom while Gioele undressed and dried himself. Ever since he had been locked in Auschwitz's showers, narrowly avoiding the gas chambers, the act of being naked in a bathroom brought him to tears. Hugo waited patiently, but it broke his heart. At those moments, he imagined himself in the gas chambers, naked, pressed against others, terrified. He had witnessed the horrors of the camp first-hand, but what German would ever believe such tales?

Neither he nor Gioele had spoken about the Jungvolk visit, not even on their way to the building. Now, standing before the hundred-windowed structure that seemed to watch them, they couldn't move. It was Gioele who took the initiative.

'Let's just get it over with,' he said. 'We have to face it.'

He tugged at Hugo's hand. Hugo allowed himself to be led, wondering if Gioele's demeanour was courage or ignorance. Inside, they navigated the labyrinthine ground-floor corridors, searching for the registration offices. Once they found the right room, Hugo knelt beside him, resting a hand on his shoulder. He looked him squarely in the eyes, as he had on the day he saved him.

'It's going to be fine,' he said, unsure if he was reassuring the boy or himself. 'Otto Weidt gave me his word, and I trust him. Don't look scared. We're just playing a game, all right?'

'We're playing Nazis?'

'Yes, we're playing Nazis.'

Hugo knocked. A voice from behind the door invited them to enter.

'Heil Hitler!' The doctor, seated at his desk, delivered the greeting without looking up from his papers. His head was bent over the folders, round glasses perched on his nose, and pen darting over the pages. Behind him, a portrait of the Führer loomed. 'Name?'

'Hugo Fischer,' he said, his breath faltering.

'Ah, yes, you.' Finally, the doctor looked up and smiled warmly. He must have recognized Hugo's name, which was a good sign. Otto Weidt had done his part. 'Pleased to meet you, I am Dr Gruber.'

'Gruber?' Hugo felt the blood drain from his face, his grip tightening on his cane. 'Wasn't it supposed to be Bachmann?'

'Bachmann suffered a heart attack at dawn.'

Hugo's heart raced. He was certain he would meet the same fate as Bachmann, and perhaps it was for the best: a heart attack would spare him the gallows or a firing squad.

'I've heard of you,' the doctor continued, standing now. 'There's so much talk of you and your cases.' Beneath his lab coat, Hugo noticed the uniform. He was SS. That grey uniform and the polished leather boots filled Hugo with dread like never before. 'When I saw your name, I was curious to meet you. And this must be?'

Hugo closed his eyes, vertigo washing over him.

'Heil Hitler!' Gioele shouted, catching Hugo off guard.

'That's what this nation needs,' said the doctor approvingly. 'Well done. Were you the one who requested early enrolment?'

'Yes, sir.'

'Congratulations, Mr Fischer. You've raised a true patriot.' The doctor retrieved a form from his desk. 'We contacted Bavaria for records on Bastian's mother, but the registry office was bombed, and many documents were lost. So, I need to ask if you're aware of any hereditary illnesses on the mother's side.'

'No hereditary illnesses,' Hugo replied, resisting the urge to rub his face.

'And you . . .' The doctor glanced at Hugo's leg and opened a file. He read aloud, 'Poliomyelitis. A real misfortune, but no hereditary illnesses in the family, which is good. May I have your son's ID and photo for his registration?'

Hugo handed them over. Dr Gruber noted the details and confirmed everything was in order.

'All right, Bastian,' the doctor announced. 'Now your father will wait outside, and we'll proceed with the examination. Then, you'll be a true citizen. Blood and honour! Undress and stand by that wall.'

'He has to undress?' Hugo felt his lungs collapse.

'Of course. You wait outside; I'll take care of him.'

'But—'

'Mr Fischer, if you continue treating him like a child, he'll never grow into a real man.'

The doctor gestured towards the exit. Hugo closed the door behind him and slumped into a corridor chair. He wished he were already dead, buried under cold earth, free of nerve endings, pain, and fear. Instead, he was alive and facing the end.

Ten steps. That's how far he was from the examination room door.

He stared at the wooden frame, taking in what little air his chest could hold. His lungs seemed to collapse further. He gripped his cane's handle, wiping sweat from his brow.

Time dragged unbearably. It felt like floating in a void. When the door finally opened, the sound shattered his bubble of dread. The doctor stood in the doorway, adjusting his glasses. His icy eyes said everything.

'Mr Fischer, we have a problem.'

Hugo remained frozen in his chair. A problem? Just one? He decided he might as well die on his feet, so he stood and approached the man.

'I . . .' he whispered.

'Your son's genitalia . . .'

'I know.'

'Come and see. I don't think you understand the gravity of the situation.' The doctor ushered him in. Hugo thought he had probably already alerted the Gestapo, who would soon storm the room. 'Your son is perfect,' the doctor continued. 'Broad forehead, narrow nose, symmetrical lips, slender build. And his eyes – works of art that would make even the Führer blush, and he's an excellent painter. But . . .'

The doctor leaned over Gioele, who lay naked on the examination table. For a moment, Hugo saw him as one of the corpses he dealt with daily. He shook off the thought, another creeping in: the doctor seemed too calm.

'Varicocele.' The doctor gently held one of Gioele's testicles, pointing to a bluish vein. 'It must be monitored. It could affect fertility, and we can't afford that. I recommend consulting a specialist soon. Otherwise, he's the perfect Aryan, a Type One Aryan. Just like you. The apple doesn't fall far from the tree, does it?'

Hugo had to suppress a laugh threatening to erupt from his core.

Gioele – a Jew – had been classified not only as Aryan but as a Type One Aryan: the purest of the pure.

'You can get dressed,' the doctor said, returning to his desk to finalize the Jungvolk membership. He stamped it firmly and signed with a flourish. 'Welcome to Hitler's Youth, Bastian.'

Outside, the sun illuminated the streets and the victory gardens lining the roads. Sitting on a bench, Hugo and Gioele remained silent, disbelieving. Finally, Hugo burst into a fit of liberating laughter, and Gioele joined him. They couldn't stop, their laughter flowing uncontrollably. Hugo had to wipe away tears. Who could say what efforts it had cost Gioele to vanquish his fears and undress in front of a Nazi?

'An Aryan masterpiece!' Hugo gasped for breath. 'Why aren't you circumcised?'

'I told you, two of my brothers died from it. The Talmud says a child shouldn't be circumcised if two siblings have died because of it.'

'I'd take you to the synagogue to pray, but the building's gone. And I don't have a God to thank.' Hugo held Gioele's hand, unable to contain his joy. 'Let's celebrate at the circus.'

'Can we?'

'We can do anything now. You're a Jungvolk member. A perfect Aryan, didn't you hear? If only Hitler knew, that bastard . . .'

Hugo slipped Bastian Fischer's ID and membership card into his pocket. The sun warming his skin was comforting and reassuring. He had never felt so alive.

Chapter 42

As they exited the S-Bahn station, Mitte revealed its wounded beauty. The buildings still standing towered over the waters of the Spree that flowed beneath its bridges, embracing the castle, the narrow streets of Fischerkietz, and Museum Island.

Hugo and Gioele strolled along the riverbank, walking together under the trees whose shade softened the summer sun. After crossing a small bridge, the Hoff Circus dome came into view, its bold lettering proudly announcing its presence. The stationary circus had withstood not only the winter air raids but also Albert Speer's architectural ambitions, which had levelled so many other structures to transform the heart of the Reich into Hitler's vision: austere, monumental, and immovable.

Speer certainly had his work cut out for him now, Hugo thought, as they left behind the grey dustiness of the neighbourhood and entered the retro grandeur of the Hoff Circus.

'Two tickets for the three o'clock show,' Hugo requested from the ticket booth attendant. His gaze lingered on a colourful poster featuring the former comedian Walther

Rumer, now billed as 'The Man Who Survived Lions'. To Hugo, however, Rumer was the man who visited Benedict Weidt for weekly check-ups.

'I'm so excited!' Gioele exclaimed as they made their way through the dimly lit corridor lined with aged wooden planks that carried the scents of antiquity and wild animals.

After passing through the heavy red curtains, they emerged into the circular arena. Thousands of velvet-upholstered seats rippled in waves of deep crimson, framed by marble columns and golden eagles. The opulence harkened back to Prussian grandeur. Gioele pushed ahead, eager to find their seats. Once seated, Hugo couldn't help but feel guilty for mixing leisure with work once again. He was there to question Walther Rumer, and he knew it.

As the lights dimmed, Gioele quivered with anticipation.

The spotlight illuminated Frau Hoff, the circus's new director after her father's recent passing. She appeared dressed entirely in radiant white, a striking contrast to the Reich banners hanging in the background. She led a similarly white horse, which followed her every command with poised elegance.

Hugo found himself smiling in the shadowed audience. Everything was just as he remembered. He glanced down at Gioele, seeing a reflection of himself as a boy with thin, gangly legs beneath his shorts – legs that, back then, had both functioned perfectly. His mother had always dressed up when taking him to the Hoff Circus, which she considered as refined an experience as the theatre or opera. For a moment, he thought he glimpsed her ghost: elegant, hair pinned in a neat bun, her long, graceful neck and straight posture honed by years of competitive skiing.

'Ladies and gentlemen,' the master of ceremonies announced in his formal coat and tails, 'prepare to witness the spectacular performance of Trude and Walther, the Man Who Survived Lions!'

Hugo leaned forward, his eyes narrowing as he focused on the man entering the safety cage. Beneath his formal suit, Walther Rumer proudly displayed an arm amputated just below the shoulder. A young woman dressed in a Marlene Dietrich-inspired outfit accompanied him, her sharp gaze echoing the iconic star. The lions, at the crack of the whip, behaved like obedient house cats. As a child, Hugo had been mesmerized by this act. Now, however, one question preoccupied him: how many tranquillizers had those animals been given?

He watched Gioele applaud with childlike wonder and almost pitied himself for no longer being capable of awe.

'Did you enjoy it?' he asked as the lights gradually came back on.

'Yes.' Gioele's eyes, for the first time since Hugo had met him, sparkled with joy. They seemed to capture and reflect every ray of light. In their radiant green, Hugo could see the tiny brown fleck in the left iris, like an open doorway to a soul that, miraculously, had emerged unscathed from Auschwitz's horrors.

Hugo ruffled Gioele's hair, drawing a pout from the boy.

'Now, let's go talk to the Man Who Survived Lions.'

'You're going to ask for an autograph?' Gioele smoothed his hair and followed Hugo through the rows of seats.

'No. This is more of a work conversation, but I promise it'll be quick. However, I need you to do me a favour.'

'Okay. What do you need?'

'I need you to sketch everything you see in Rumer's caravan.'

Chapter 43

The artistes' offices were in the rear courtyard of the circus, housed in the caravans used for travelling shows across Europe. The circular courtyard, bordered by a colonnade of red stone, also contained animal enclosures.

'See that elephant alone in its cage?' Hugo pointed at a massive pachyderm standing apart from the rest. 'It might be one of the zoo animals. They say the Hoff Circus rescued one, but I'm not sure if it's true. Others say a woman keeps it in her house.'

'You can't keep an elephant in a house!' Gioele shook his head in disbelief.

Hugo could never forget the night the zoo was destroyed. More than 700 bombers reduced Berlin to ashes in fifteen minutes – a night etched into his memory. That evening, fire rained down on the zoo. Elephants, monkeys, and predators burned alive as the inferno raged, while firefighters stood helpless with water mains destroyed by bombs. The RAF returned the following night to finish the job, demolishing the aquarium. The next morning, Budapester

Straße was littered with crocodile carcasses, flung far by the explosions.

'And there's our man . . .' Hugo gestured toward Walther Rumer, who, now dressed in a shirt with his braces down, was smoking a cigarette on the steps of his caravan.

He gave Hugo a nod. Rumer squinted, trying to recognize him.

'We don't know each other, Mr Rumer,' Hugo said, stepping closer. He revealed the Kriminalpolizei badge, making his intentions clear. Yet the 'man who survived lions' remained impassive – no change in his expression, no hint of surprise, except for the courtesy of standing up.

'What can I do for you, Herr . . .?'

'Fischer. I need to ask you a few questions regarding a case I'm working on.'

'Franz!' Rumer called out to a stable boy raking a nearby empty cage. 'Two glasses of rum!'

The boy nodded hastily and dashed off, his urgency suggesting a fear of the lion survivor – a reputation that seemed to precede him. Rumer invited Hugo into his small, austere caravan. He sat at a compact table in the back, motioning for Hugo to join him.

'Do you have a pencil and some paper?' Gioele asked.

'What for?' Rumer looked at him, puzzled.

'I think he wants to draw,' Hugo said as he sat down. 'So much the better. That way, he won't disturb us while we talk.'

Rumer handed Gioele a few blank-backed flyers and rummaged through a small shelf. He pushed aside a couple of books, a photograph, and several small bottles of adrenaline. Hugo wondered if, beyond sedating the big cats, the circus relied on the substance to supplement its meagre meat rations.

'Here it is!' Rumer exclaimed, holding up a fountain pen and handing it to Gioele.

Meanwhile, the stable boy returned with a tray holding two glasses of rum. Hugo took a cautious sniff. The aroma of cocoa and tobacco filled his senses. One sip confirmed it was an exceptional vintage. Why waste such quality on him? Rumer's composure before the Kripo badge had been remarkable, but offering this premium rum hinted that he had something to hide.

'Excellent,' Hugo said after savouring the drink. 'I won't waste your time, Mr Rumer, so let's skip the formalities. Did you know Benedict Weidt?'

'Of course. He was my ophthalmologist.'

'You visited his office often?' Hugo glanced at Gioele, who was deeply engrossed in his sketching, his tongue sticking out slightly in concentration.

'In recent months, yes,' Rumer admitted with a sigh. 'I suffer from glaucoma. But why are you asking?'

'I suspect Weidt didn't commit suicide.'

'What do you mean?'

For the first time, Rumer's impassive demeanour faltered. Hugo took a moment to study him. His dark, penetrating eyes suggested he was telling the truth.

'I believe Dr Weidt was caught up in something dangerous,' Hugo clarified, 'and that someone killed him.'

'Killed him? Him and his wife?' Rumer lit a cigarette, tapping the filter on the table as if trying to jog his thoughts. 'Why assume it was him in trouble and not her? She might've made enemies among the Gypsies.'

'Are you joking?' Hugo leaned closer, lowering his voice to keep Gioele from overhearing. 'There aren't any Roma or Sinti left in Germany. They've all been sent to Poland,

and they're not there on holiday. If there are any left in Germany, they're in hiding. I doubt those poor souls are in any position to exact revenge, even if they would have every reason.'

Their eyes locked in silence. Hugo realized he had said too much. Even such a small slip could bring the Gestapo knocking at his door. But Rumer's reaction was one of quiet understanding, not reproach. He nodded and looked at Hugo oddly, as if in agreement.

'Let me be clear,' Hugo pressed on. 'Do you know of anything that might have endangered Benedict Weidt? Did he seem frightened or anxious recently?'

'No. I assure you, if I had noticed anything unusual, I'd tell you. I respected Benedict. He was the only one who could save my vision. But he was his usual self – professional and approachable. He never discussed private matters. I'm sorry, but I can't help you.'

Hugo signalled to Gioele, who carefully gathered his drawings and returned the pen. There wasn't much more to ask, except to satisfy a personal curiosity.

'Did you really survive the lions?'

'This?' Rumer raised his stump of an arm and laughed – a hearty, infectious laugh befitting his comedic past. 'No, that's a story the Hoff lady and I cooked up to fortify my legend. This is courtesy of the Bolsheviks – a landmine.'

'I'm sorry to hear that.'

'Don't be. These days, everyone's lost something – whether a limb or their soul. I know which I'd prefer.'

'So do I.'

Hugo tipped his hat. They left Rumer in the dim light of his caravan, smoking the cigarette that he'd been holding all that while.

As they passed the animal enclosures, Gioele stopped to peer into each one. Hugo felt satisfied with the exchange – Rumer seemed genuine, just another figure who'd crossed paths with Weidt.

Near the elephants' pen, Hugo slowed. It took him a moment to recognize Dieter Costa in his Hitlerjugend uniform.

'Wait here,' Hugo instructed Gioele.

He marched towards Dieter and grabbed him by the collar, pinning him against the elephants' cage. Despite his lame leg, Hugo hadn't forgotten how to handle someone. But as he realized he was manhandling a teenager, his grip slackened.

Dieter's eyes widened. 'You again! Are you insane?'

'That's my son over there,' Hugo growled, nodding towards Gioele, who was tossing hay into the horses' stalls. 'He's now a Jungvolk member, enrolled a year early. Does that mean anything to you?'

'A *pimpf*?' Dieter asked, confused.

'Yes, a *pimpf*. You don't know anything about someone who signed him up without my consent, right?'

'Sir, could you be a little more explicit? Because I really have no idea what you're talking about,' Dieter stammered.

'Fine. I'll be clear, then,' Hugo leaned towards him menacingly. 'Someone enrolled my son in the Jungvolk after our meeting at St Teresa's, and I believe you know who.'

'I swear to you, sir. I have no idea what you're talking about . . .'

'Everything all right?' The sharp but gentle voice of Frau Hoff interrupted. She stood a short distance away, her hands in her pockets, observing them closely. 'What's going on?'

'Nothing,' Hugo replied, adjusting his jacket. 'I mistook this boy for someone else. My apologies.'

'I thought you were arguing . . .'

'No,' Hugo assured her, smiling at Dieter. 'Right?'

'No, Frau Hoff, it's all fine,' Dieter confirmed.

'I hope you enjoyed the show,' she said, her tone suggesting Hugo had overstayed his welcome.

'It was excellent, just as I remembered.'

'I'm glad to hear it. You caught us just in time; we leave for the tour in five days.'

'I'm impressed nothing stops you – not even the war.'

'Nothing stops us,' she replied with a wry smile.

Hugo called for Gioele, and they left the circus grounds, walking along the damp, algae-scented banks of the river Spree.

'What's a *pimpf*?' Gioele asked, pulling off his shoes and socks to dip his feet into the water.

'A little one,' Hugo replied, watching him from above.

'But it doesn't mean "little one", does it?'

'No, it doesn't. It's the sound of a fart.' Hugo chuckled. 'That's what we call the youngest in the Hitlerjugend – *pimpfe*.'

Gioele shot him a sceptical look, then burst into laughter.

Behind their moment of levity, a question nagged at Hugo, as it had been since they'd left the circus: what were Dieter Costa and Walther Rumer – two of Weidt's most frequent contacts in the last month – doing in the same place?

Chapter 44

Babi Yar, 30 September 1941

A Few Hours Before the Massacre

The sky is molten lead this morning.

Better this way. If God exists, He won't be able to witness what we're about to do.

At dawn, those still in the city reported seeing the Jews leaving their homes at the designated hour, in the pale light of the early morning. They pulled their children out of bed and loaded them onto carts, their faces still heavy with sleep. They moved in orderly silence through the damp twilight air, and no one resisted. There was no need for force.

I wonder why. A moment later, the answer comes: even I wasn't coerced, and yet here I am, following orders.

Hans says they'll all come, truly believing they're being evacuated. Perhaps to Palestine, or even Germany. No one suspects what awaits them here, by the banquet tables we've set up outside the cemetery.

A thick fog blankets the horizon in a milky veil, making it seem as though they won't come after all. But fog doesn't erase things. Suddenly, they appear – an orderly stream emerging from the far end of the road, passing through the cemetery gates.

I force myself not to look them in the eyes. They file into the narrow road, flanked by soldiers from the Wehrmacht and Ukrainian policemen. They pass the tables, where translators are giving instructions. They're told to leave their documents, money, jewellery, family photos – everything they're carrying. Who knows what lies the translators are telling them, because they nod, taking items from their bags, handing over house keys, and, in the case of children, their only toys.

When they're asked to undress, that's when the murmuring starts. It's scattered and uneasy. They ask questions, trying to understand why they must strip in the cold.

A man glances back, but the Wehrmacht stands behind him, and our police cordons flank him on both sides. There's no escape; he's walked into a funnel with no way out.

It's so cold. That's all I can think as I watch them undress. They're left in their underclothes, whipped by the wind, smacked by the leaves endlessly falling from the trees. The children begin to cry, trembling, clutching at their mothers' legs.

A shiver runs through me. The autumn chill glides over my neck like a caress from death itself.

The man from earlier continues looking around, his feverish eyes darting. Our gazes meet, and I can only shake my head to confirm the truth: no, there is no evacuation, no transfer, no promised land. No salvation.

What a grand lie life is.

The man makes a sudden move towards the woods. The bare trees seem to stretch out like skeletal arms, ready to embrace his desperate flight. For a moment, I imagine him swallowed up in the safety of those branches, carried far away, free.

But instead, he's struck down from behind by the butt of a rifle, then battered by the boots of a comrade who beats him until his temple bleeds. Not even a bullet is wasted to kill him.

This is enough to quash any further protests.

Our superiors give the order, and the first group of Jews begins their march towards the ravine at Babi Yar, escorted by the Sonderkommando under Standartenführer Blobel. Soon, the rising wind will carry the sound of gunfire and the cries of despair back to us.

Chapter 45

3 July 1944

Berlin, Jungvolk Headquarters

'Your uniform, Bastian.'

The supervisor handed him the outfit: black shorts, a brown shirt, and a scarf to tie around his neck. Gioele hurried to put it on. There was no mirror to check himself, but the emblem on his arm was clearly visible, and that alone was enough to tighten his stomach: it was a rune the supervisor had called 'Sieg'. He had one, while the SS had two. He had seen that symbol hundreds of times at Auschwitz.

Gioele joined the other children waiting in an orderly line in the courtyard.

That morning, Edmund had argued with Hugo. He had said that sending a lamb among wolves would be a mistake because no Jewish survivor of a concentration camp could endure being surrounded by their tormentors. For Hugo, however, there was no turning back: skipping the Jungvolk after enrolment was like deserting the army.

Gioele had reassured them both, but now, among the hundreds of faces and banners, he wondered if he would burst into tears or truly prove he had some guts.

'That's not how you do it.' A blond boy standing next to him, hair almost the colour of a lemon, grabbed his scarf and adjusted the knot. 'We need to be impeccable Nazis.'

'Thanks.' Gioele studied him nervously. The boy seemed about a year older than him, judging by his height. He had a lively face, but something in his eyes carried a chill, as if behind the blue hid the colours of pain and sadness.

'I'm Bastian,' Gioele introduced himself.

'I'm Klaus.'

The drumroll silenced them – loud, powerful, it filled the entire courtyard.

The crowd of cheerful children began to sing as the supervisors directed them in pairs towards the military trucks waiting outside. Klaus sang too. In fact, Gioele noticed, he was shouting as if Hitler could hear him from his headquarters.

'Adolf Hitler is the redeemer, our hero!' Klaus sang. 'For Hitler we live! For Hitler we die!'

They were loaded into the truck. Gioele found a corner seat and watched the ruined streets of Berlin speeding by. The jolts of the vehicle reminded him of another truck he had ridden in, this one filled with corpses. It was the truck that went around Auschwitz to collect the dead and take them to the crematoria at Birkenau. He had hidden in it to search for his parents. Looking at these jubilant boys, he thought none of them had ever done anything like that. They pretended to be strong and tough, but they had no idea what it really meant.

'Is this your first time?' Klaus asked.

'Yes,' Gioele answered curtly.

The military truck took a while to leave Berlin and reach what Klaus said was Grunewald, the city's largest forest. They parked in a clearing, and each was assigned a task. Gioele and Klaus were told to set up the camp kitchen. The canopy of trees tempered the summer heat, and birds chirped incessantly, though the laughter of the Jungvolk boys was louder than anything else. As they prepared the fire pit, Gioele couldn't help but wonder why all the Jews had to be expelled from Germany. Why couldn't they have shared moments like this, as they were doing with him now?

As they pulled bowls out of the sacks, Klaus kept bombarding him with chatter, never leaving him alone. He explained how the older boys in the Hitler Youth had more fun than them, the Jungvolk pups. They trained like real soldiers with gliders, boats, and weapons, and if they were lucky, they stopped digging through rubble at sixteen and were sent to fight in the real war.

'War isn't something good,' Gioele contradicted him.

'War is the most sacred of things!' Klaus's eyes widened.

The supervisors called them back to order when they had finished their task.

They spent the entire afternoon playing war games, and Gioele had to admit it was fun. They ran through the woods in teams, crouched in the underbrush and behind bushes, then erupted in wild cries when they charged to snatch the armband from the enemy. It was exhilarating, an exploration of unknown places. He was no longer confined within four walls.

'I got it! I got it!' Gioele stopped, raising his fist in the air after managing to grab the armband that sealed his team's victory.

He brandished it like a trophy. When his teammates swarmed around him, cheering, he felt like shouting with joy. He was electric, powerful. But when they stripped down and jumped into the crystal-clear lake in their underwear, splashing everywhere, an enormous sense of guilt devoured him, and the electricity vanished.

He was having fun.

How could he be having fun while his parents and brother were still trapped in that horrible prison? He, a Jew, was enjoying himself with Aryans who adored Hitler and wanted to erase every Jew from the face of the earth. A wave of nausea rose in him at the thought of the euphoria he had felt moments earlier. Klaus noticed and swam over to him.

'What's wrong?' That boy wouldn't leave him alone. For some reason, he kept seeking him out. 'One moment you're happy, and the next you're sad. You're strange. How'd you get that?'

Gioele lowered his gaze to the healing burn.

'With a hot knife,' he replied, 'to erase the tattoo from a concentration camp.'

'What's a concentration camp?'

'A place where they lock up Jews.'

'Like a ghetto? And why were you there?'

'Because I'm a Jew.'

Klaus burst out laughing, splashing him with water and letting out a wild yell. He jumped on Gioele's shoulders, holding on tightly, almost dragging him under the water's surface.

'You're such a donkey, Bastian!'

That evening, when the sun had set, they lit a spruce bonfire in the clearing. They sat in a circle under the starry sky.

They sang, ate, then sang and danced some more. The older boys shared anecdotes about Hitler, Göring, and Himmler, glorifying the lives of soldiers at the front. Afterwards, they made them shout into the wild night, proclaiming they would become soldiers too. They howled at the moon like wolves.

'Stand up!' The leader's voice resonated in the warm breeze from the flames. 'Under the gaze of the stars, let us repeat our oath together!'

'I swear to dedicate my life to Hitler!' The chorus of voices shattered against the dark shadows of the conifers, flooding the night. 'I am ready to sacrifice my life for Hitler! To die for him!'

Before the dying fire, now reduced to a pulsing ember, they waited for midnight, energized by the fervour of their oaths but exhausted by the day spent in the open air. Gioele lay on the grass. The deep, dark sky was different from Auschwitz's – black and dotted with stars. In the camp, it had been impossible to see them because of the floodlights that lit the perimeter like day. These boys had no idea what death truly was, he thought.

'What are you thinking about?' Klaus flopped down beside him.

'No one here has ever seen someone die . . .' Gioele continued to stare at the stars.

'That's not true.' Klaus shrugged. 'Many lost relatives under the bombs.'

'I've seen corpses up close.'

'So have I.'

'I've seen people die!' Gioele's voice grew heated as if this were a contest. He thought of the woman shot by an SS officer at the shower doors.

'I've seen someone die too.' Klaus's voice became a whisper. Gioele turned to look at him. Beneath his lemon-coloured hair, the boy seemed less bold. 'I found my mother and father in the living room. Someone had shot my father. My mother . . . she was alive, breathing, bleeding from her head, and I was too scared to tell anyone. I think she died because I didn't speak up . . .'

'I'm sorry . . .'

'I didn't even tell my sister. Only you.'

Gioele reached out, seeking contact. They lay there, staring at the sky. He didn't know if they were enemies meant to hate each other or just two new friends in a world trying to pit them against each other.

Chapter 46

Berlin, Jungvolk Headquarters

Hugo questioned Gioele silently from a distance. Gioele could tell he hadn't slept; his tired eyes betrayed him. They had turned a duller grey, like tarnished silver, and Gioele was tempted to polish them as his mother used to polish their tableware. He wanted to bring back their shine because he knew Hugo hadn't slept because of him.

Jumping down from the truck, Gioele ran to meet him and hugged him.

'How did it go?' Hugo whispered.

'Good.'

'How are you?'

'I had fun.'

'You . . . had *fun*?'

'Yes, really!'

Hugo's eyes, restless and feverish, studied him. Gioele

had never seen eyes so animated, so different from the empty stares of the German guards at the camp, who acted as if he and the other prisoners were invisible.

'I made a friend,' he added, trying to reassure him.

'I'm glad . . .' Hugo seemed like he wanted to say more, but his jaw tightened. In the end, he smiled and tapped his cane on the ground, pointing towards the underground. 'Want to come with me to help with something?'

'Is it work?'

'It's work.'

The place Hugo took him was far from Berlin. Gioele still carried the fatigue of the outing and the lingering shame of not only pretending to be a German but even enjoying the company of the other boys. He almost fell asleep against the train window as the woods outside rushed by in a blur of deep green.

'We're about to do something a little bit illegal,' Hugo said when they arrived at the station.

The small town seemed lovely, nestled in greenery, with a lake visible in the distance. Gioele extracted a promise from Hugo that they would go for a swim later. The house where they stopped was a two-storey, white wooden structure – elegant and inviting. Gioele wished he could live there.

Hugo entered the garden, and Gioele followed. They skirted around to the back, avoiding anyone on the street. Hugo slipped off his jacket, wrapped it around his elbow, and, with a sharp motion, shattered one of the windows. The crash of glass falling in large shards onto the ground silenced the birds in the oak tree nearby.

'You did something bad,' Gioele exclaimed.

'Well, yes . . .' Hugo shook his jacket free of glass fragments and put it back on. 'Forget what you just saw and
never do anything like it.'

They climbed through the window and found themselves in a house that smelled stale. It wasn't just the scent
of a space left unventilated for days, but of a home that had
ceased to be lived in. Hugo led the way, placing his briefcase on a table and pulling out paper and pencils.

'You'll need to draw,' he instructed.

'Draw the room?'

'The room, and whatever else I tell you to.'

Gioele had helped Hugo once before – at Auschwitz.
He had drawn the body of Dr Braun and what Hugo had
called 'the crime scene'.

Sitting cross-legged on the floor, Gioele began sketching. Morning light flooded the room, cascading through the
large central window that had no trees to block it. Everything was sharply defined and bathed in sunlight. He started with the staircase leading upstairs and the large mirror
leaning against the wall. He outlined the fireplace, the two
sofas, and the armchair, as well as the square-based column
and the carpet. It seemed stained – was it blood? As he carefully drew the details of the paintings on the walls, Hugo
began instructing him to add specifics.

'Draw a marble figurine lying here,' Hugo said, tapping
a spot on the paper. 'A woman reclining with a man. Place
the pistol here on the floor between them.'

Gioele obeyed, pouring his effort into making the work
precise, hoping it would bring Hugo some peace. He sensed
that Hugo was as worried about the Jungvolk outing as he
was about what had happened to the man and woman in
this house.

'Let me see.' Hugo took the drawing and analysed it. The corners of his lips lifted slightly as he nodded. 'This is another piece of proof that Benedict Weidt could not have killed himself!'

Chapter 47

There are things the eyes don't see until reality is simplified.

Hugo knew this well; that's why he was beginning to think Gioele's drawings should officially become part of his work. He studied the sketch of the room. Something essential, which he hadn't noticed himself, stood out in Gioele's depiction: the family photographs adorning the walls.

He moved closer to the photos. In one, Benedict Weidt was captured sitting at his desk, surrounded by books and paperwork, as befitted a scholar. He wore a military uniform and held a fountain pen in his hand – the left hand, to be precise.

'How does a left-handed man shoot himself in the right temple? Benedict was left-handed. If he'd wanted to shoot himself, it would've been in the left temple, not the right. This is definitive proof he didn't commit suicide.'

Gioele approached the photos, squinting to get a better look. His finger pointed to the Weidts' son. 'That's Klaus,' he exclaimed.

'Yes . . .' Hugo felt the muscles in his back tighten. 'How do you know that?'

'He was with me on the trip. We became friends. He told me his mum wasn't dead yet when he found her.'

Hugo felt his mouth go dry. Three things mattered in his line of work: shrewdness, science, and . . . luck. Sometimes, if fortune didn't intervene, shrewdness and science weren't enough. And somehow, fate always found a way to meddle, as if the dead themselves were trying to help. As if death were seeking to restore order to what it had disrupted.

'She was alive?' Hugo stared into Gioele's eyes, needing confirmation of what he'd just heard.

'Yes.' Gioele shrugged. 'He said there was a lot of blood under her head, but she was breathing. He was too scared to say anything. You know fear can paralyse you, right?'

'I know.'

'One time, I read that when faced with danger, there are three options: fight, flee, or freeze.'

'Most people freeze. How do you think the Nazis have kept us Germans in check?' Hugo crouched to Gioele's level, seeking eye contact. 'Do you believe Klaus told you the truth?'

'Yes.' Gioele swayed his head from side to side. 'I think he did.'

Hugo straightened up and moved to the centre of the large rug that dominated the room, between the sofas and the fireplace. He took a few steps back and noticed his shoe catching on a fold in the fabric – a poorly mounted floorboard, perhaps. If he tripped, he'd likely hit his head on the edge of the low, square column where Benedict had grabbed the statuette he'd used to strike Marlene.

He imagined Benedict and Marlene arguing with

someone – perhaps Marlene's lover? Could Brecht have been their killer, choosing suicide after the police confronted him at his office? Too simplistic. What if the fight had been only between Benedict and Marlene?

Marlene fires a shot, hitting Benedict in the chest. She drops the gun, steps backwards, trips, and hits her head against the column, dislodging the statuette. Yet this still didn't explain the third person – someone who had fired two more shots: one into Marlene's chest and another into Benedict's temple.

A glint of light made him instinctively turn towards the window. Across the street, he noticed a dark Mercedes parked in front of the gate. The creeping feeling of being followed again triggered the second reaction Gioele had called 'flight'.

'It's getting late,' Hugo said abruptly. He grabbed the drawings and stuffed them haphazardly into his briefcase. He'd examine them more thoroughly at home.

'You promised we'd swim in the lake,' Gioele protested.

'I know.' Hugo squeezed his shoulder and gestured out the window. 'Do you see that car out there?'

'Yes . . .'

'I think it's been following me for a few days. It's better not to take any chances.'

'Okay.'

Chapter 48

'Marlene was still alive?' Adele's eyes widened as she stared at him over the rim of her delicate porcelain cup. 'Are you certain?'

'Gioele is certain.'

Hugo lit a cigarette, his movements steady despite the nervous energy that coursed through him. The terrace at the Adlon was crowded, and he felt the weight of too many eyes around them. Was someone watching them even here? He left his coffee unfinished, risking its warmth fading, and gestured for Adele to move with him to a more secluded spot by the fountain.

'I think Marlene hit her head when she stumbled,' he murmured. 'As much force as you can put into a blow, it's usually the head that gives way, not the weapon. That statuette was broken clean in two – I remember it clearly. She lost her balance and slammed into the column, and the statuette fell.'

'She was scared of something . . .'

'Or someone,' Hugo corrected, his voice low. 'Maybe the

same person who shot her while she was defenceless, after the children ran to the neighbours. The same person who staged Benedict's suicide. Those are my only certainties for now. And that damned black Mercedes was still parked outside the Weidt house. I couldn't get the plate this time either.'

Adele pressed her lips together. When fear flickered across her features, it made her seem younger, almost child-like, despite the fine lines starting to form at the corners of her eyes. He found her irresistible in the way she held multiple versions of herself in her expression – a woman wise beyond her years, yet with a fragility that hinted at the girl she used to be.

'Who do you think is following you?'

'I don't know,' Hugo admitted. 'All I know is that at this point, I have to choose: fight, flee, or freeze.'

'What?'

'Never mind,' he muttered. A warm breeze carried the mingled scents of blossoming trees and the ever-present tang of ash that clung to Berlin like a stubborn ghost. Hugo placed his hands on Adele's hips, drawing her closer. Without a care for the curious gazes from nearby tables, he kissed her. There was no time for modesty, not when the world was crumbling around them.

'Don't be afraid. Trust me. It's going to be okay.'

'I've seen too much to believe that anything ever really turns out okay,' Adele replied, her smile tinged with bitterness. 'But let's promise to get through this with as few broken bones as possible, all right?'

'I promise.'

Chapter 49

Berlin, Nikolaiviertel

'Look at this tragedy.' Edmund shoved the newspaper under his nose as Hugo and Gioele were having breakfast.

Hugo skimmed it distractedly. When the alarm bells in his mind started ringing louder, he put down his cup of ersatz coffee and grabbed the paper with both hands. His focus landed on a short article buried amidst the war propaganda: a military truck carrying Hitler Youth and Jungvolk boys had exploded due to an unexploded bomb, likely triggered by a wild animal. No survivors. Just bodies charred by the flames. The vehicle, which had just left Berlin headed for Mount Brocken, caught fire, trapping the boys in the blaze.

'A horrible way to die,' Edmund commented. 'Burned alive.'

Hugo shot a quick glance at Gioele. Among those boys

must have been Klaus and Klara. It had been a trip organized in cooperation with the Jesuits, the first sanctioned
in years. An event like this would only further strain the
already precarious and repressive relationship with the
Church, even though the bomb was an Allied remnant.
'*Children are safe,*' the note delivered to Weidt had said.
Something had gone terribly wrong.

'I have to go out.' Hugo stood up from the table. He
needed to know whether the Weidt children were alive or
not – and whether the incident had truly been an accident.
He filled a glass of water at the kitchen sink, his gaze falling
on the floor where the ration cards were hidden. 'I think the
Gestapo is following me,' he announced.

'The Gestapo? What have you done now?' His father's
voice tensed.

'It might be related to the Weidt case.' Hugo swallowed a
Pervitin tablet, staring into the drain. He wondered whether the amphetamines were truly helping him stave off the
fatigue and pain of multiple sclerosis – or if they were just
a way to run from danger. 'Have you done anything that
could have put us at risk?' he asked, already certain his
father wouldn't answer directly.

Edmund shook his head. Clever, Hugo thought. If he
didn't respond verbally, there was no way to accuse him of
lying. Hugo was certain his shadowing wasn't about ration
cards, but it was worth making his father understand that
this issue needed monitoring – and resolving – sooner rather than later.

'Papa, is there a safe place for you and Gioele to go if
anything happens to me?'

'What could happen to you?' Edmund's voice grew
anxious.

'Nothing, Papa. But is there a safe place?'

'Yes.'

'Where?'

'The Volkers' print shop.'

'Good. If the time ever comes, you and Gioele will go there.'

Otto Weidt himself answered the door.

It was unnecessary to ask if his grandchildren had been on the truck headed to Mount Brocken. He had likely spent the entire morning crying, from eyes that no longer saw the world, his gaunt cheeks now dry.

He invited Hugo inside. They sat at the table in silence until Otto finally spoke.

'Herr Fischer, I do not believe this was some chance accident.'

Those words rang loudly because Hugo didn't believe it was either. Someone had promised Benedict his children's safety, only to renege on that promise. Those children had been murdered – just like their parents – along with other children whose only fault was to have been their travelling companions.

'Mr Weidt, I think your cousin had powerful enemies,' Hugo said, choosing his words carefully but failing to soften the blow. 'I don't know whose toes Benedict stepped on, but those enemies sought revenge against his very lineage. They wanted the entire family wiped out.'

'I am aware of that.' Otto sighed. 'You are officially relieved of your duties.'

'I'm so sorry . . . May I at least ask who organized the trip?'

'Arthur Welder. It was the first time the Church was

allowed to organize a youth event with the Hitler Youth. The supervising officer planned to demonstrate how the ghost of Mount Brocken was God to the Church and Hitler to the Nazis – and how, ultimately, the Führer and God could be considered the same thing. Arrant rubbish.'

Those words sounded out of place coming from a man like Otto Weidt, but Hugo couldn't agree more. Arrant rubbish. The demented Nazi educational programme within the Hitler Youth had only degenerated over the years, though the veil was beginning to lift. Hitler had promised his boys they'd be part of a dream, but instead, they'd found themselves in a nightmare. The transition from playing war to real war had been a short one.

'Is Arthur Welder a priest?' Hugo asked.

'Yes. A Jesuit.'

'Where can I find him?'

'His church was destroyed. He's at St Teresa's now.'

'Well, of course . . .' Hugo barely stifled a bitter laugh.

He said his goodbyes, leaving the grieving man alone with his sorrow. Hugo hadn't been able to do much to comfort him. In truth, guilt gnawed at him. He felt as though he had failed. He had waded through a quagmire, helplessly bogged down, while the clock ticked down on Klaus and Klara's fateful encounter with death. If he had been able to identify the true culprit behind the Weidt murders sooner, perhaps he could have saved those children's lives.

Now, he had to decide whether to fight, flee, or freeze – or perform an autopsy.

Chapter 50

'An autopsy?' Adele whispered.

Hugo pulled her into a quieter corner of the hallway. An orderly pushing a medicine trolley passed by, casting a curious glance in their direction, as if trying to gauge whether he was harassing her. Satisfied that everything was in order, the orderly moved on, the wheels of the trolley squeaking as they rolled across the floor.

'Yes, an autopsy,' Hugo muttered. 'I just need one of the bodies to figure out what happened on that truck.'

'And how do you plan to do that?'

'This is where you come in . . . Dr Schmidt is on duty today, you remember him? The one who did the fake autopsy for the Weidt case. You said he was impressed by you . . .'

'You want me to distract him?'

'Well, not with *all* your charms . . .'

'Herr Fischer, my charms are my medical skills. What did you think I meant?'

Hugo chuckled. Another nurse passed by, casting them a fleeting look that carried a hint of melancholy, likely mourning someone who hadn't returned from the front. Berlin was full of such gazes. 'So, what's the plan?' he asked as the nurse disappeared down the corridor.

'Give me an hour or so. Some traditional "charms" will take a little preparation. Wait for me in the atrium.'

Adele appeared at the hospital's entrance less than two hours later, her expression triumphant.

'Let's go,' she said, brushing past him briskly. 'I don't know how long it'll take Schmidt to call in a replacement.'

'So what happened?' Hugo asked, falling in step as they descended the stairs towards the morgue.

'He seemed delighted with my invitation for coffee,' Adele said with a smirk. 'Right now, he should be in his bathroom. The laxative I slipped him is . . . very powerful.'

'Poor man.' Hugo laughed, scanning the wall for the morgue keys hanging in their usual place.

He unlocked the door and flipped on the lights, which flickered to life one by one, illuminating the gleaming tiled floor. The smell hit them immediately – so acrid and nause-ating that it seemed to cling to their skin rather than merely their nostrils. Adele and Hugo exchanged a glance, unspo-ken understanding passing between them. It was the same smell as Auschwitz – burnt flesh, decay, and despair.

'Let's make this quick.' Hugo covered his nose with his arm. 'We don't have much time.'

He picked up a clipboard that Schmidt had left on one of the gurneys. The list detailed the victims, likely compiled by the trip organizers. Scanning it, Hugo recognized at least half the surnames.

He pulled back the shrouds on a couple of the bodies. Most were clearly teenagers, their charred clothing clinging to skeletal forms. Their faces were unrecognizable, even to their parents, most likely.

'Look at this,' Hugo said, pointing to their feet. 'Not a trace of shoes left – not even fragments.'

'Burnt in the flames?' Adele asked.

'It was just a truck fire, not a bonfire. They weren't exposed to the heat long enough for this . . .' Hugo trailed off, frowning.

He dragged one of the gurneys out of the morgue, heading down the corridor towards the autopsy room, walking in silence. Once inside, Adele threw open the windows, letting in fresh air. The chirping of birds failed to dispel the sterile, morbid atmosphere. Beneath the formaldehyde, the faint but inescapable scent of death lingered over the steel tables and sinks.

'What do you expect to find?' Adele asked, her voice muffled by both hands pressed over her nose.

'Anything.' Hugo snapped on a pair of gloves. 'Every corpse has something to say. Come and help me.'

Together, they lifted the body bag onto the dissection table. Hugo switched on the overhead lamp, its clinical light starkly illuminating the scorched tissues that were all that remained of a fourteen-year-old boy. He grabbed a scalpel and made a swift incision down the torso all the way to the crotch. It didn't have to be a perfect job, just an efficient one.

'Do we have time, do you think?' Adele asked, shooting a glance out the glass doors.

'No time for a traditional autopsy,' he muttered, separating the ribs. 'I need to focus on the organs that would be most seriously affected by flame.'

He removed the lungs, rinsed them in the sink, and

placed them on a tray for examination. The scalpel's tip paused mid-cut as realization dawned. He knew what he was observing, or actually, what he *wasn't* observing. He'd been ready for a great many answers, but not that one.

'What the hell . . .'

'What's wrong?' Adele hurried to his side.

'The lungs – there's *no* sign of smoke or burns.'

'But they inhaled scalding air . . .'

'Exactly. There should be burns or charring.' Hugo tapped the metal sink in frustration. 'These lungs are pristine – aside from traces of a recent bout with pneumonia.'

'So they were already dead when they were burned . . .' Adele's voice was barely audible. She looked between the dissected lung and the corpse. 'Hugo, what's going on?'

'I don't know. Let's clean this up. I need time to think.'

'But if it wasn't the fire that killed them, what did?' Adele pressed.

'There are no stab wounds, no gunshot marks . . .' Hugo realized that he had no plausible explanation. 'I'd need to dissect them all, and we don't have the time. All I know is this boy didn't die in that fire.'

Chapter 51

'Learn the route,' exclaimed Edmund, his finger pointing towards the sky. 'We'll call it "The Road to Salvation".'

Gioele looked around, trying to memorize as many landmarks as possible, but Berlin's streets all looked the same to him – grey, littered with towering piles of rubble. He did, however, recognize the spot where the river divided the neighbourhood, the bridge beneath which boats passed, the grand church with the shattered dome, and the long avenue adorned with fluttering flags.

When they arrived at the Volker print shop, Edmund placed his hands on Gioele's shoulders and whispered in his ear, 'If anything happens to me or Hugo, this is where you'll come. Now, you're about to see something you must never speak of to anyone, but it will show you why you can trust Frya. Understood?'

'All right,' Gioele nodded.

The basement of the Volker print shop was small but impeccably organized. Unlike most basements, it didn't reek of dampness but carried the scent of paper. Three walls were lined with shelves reaching up to the ceiling, filled with stacked sheets of paper, newspapers, books, and documents. Gioele had never seen so many in one place.

Frya stood with her arms crossed under the single hanging lamp, its light accentuating the wrinkles on her face, giving her a more imposing air than he remembered.

'So, you're Gioele, not Bastian,' she said with a raised eyebrow. 'Can I trust you?'

'Of course you can trust him,' Edmund replied with a laugh. 'I'm vouching for him.'

'I wasn't asking you. I was asking him,' Frya shot back, her gaze steady.

'Yes,' Gioele answered confidently, eager to win the trust of this woman, sensing that there was something mysterious and important hidden here. 'You know my real name, so you know I'm Jewish. We're even. You won't tell, and neither will I.'

'Edmund!' Frya let out a sharp, clear laugh. 'You didn't tell me he was so sharp. All right, Gioele. I'll show you my secret – *our* secret from now on. But you must never, *ever* speak of it to anyone.'

She reached for a specific spot on the bookshelf and gave it a firm pull. A section of the shelf swung away, revealing a hidden door – old, worn, and dark. As Frya unlocked it with a key she wore around her neck, Gioele stretched to peer through the growing gap, curiosity burning in him. Whatever lay beyond had to be of great value.

When the door fully opened, Gioele let out a breath he hadn't realized he was holding. 'Wow!' he exclaimed.

The secret of the basement wasn't a treasure trove of riches. It was people – men, women, and children.

Edmund entered first, unloading the false-bottomed sack he carried and distributing the meagre food he'd managed to scrounge. Gioele followed tentatively. The room was packed with books, stacked against walls and across the floor. There were cots, blankets, a table, and even a small area behind a drape serving as a bathroom. It was like a house, and these were its inhabitants.

Gioele spotted a familiar hairstyle on an older man, whose white beard connected seamlessly with his sideburns. Something about the man felt instantly familial, and Gioele found himself rushing towards him.

'Shalom!' Gioele greeted warmly.

'Shalom, young friend,' replied the man, smiling. He patted the space beside him, inviting Gioele to sit on a pile of blankets while he ate his meagre portion. 'Welcome. This is the safest place on earth. You're lucky.'

'I'm not staying,' Gioele admitted, accepting a piece of bread from the man and taking a bite. 'I have a fake document. A German one.'

'A German document . . .' The old man chewed slowly. 'Never renounce God, not even to save your life. Our connection to Him is the foundation of our being. It is He who guides and protects us.'

Gioele swallowed his bite with difficulty. The man's words struck a chord – hadn't he just renounced God by hiding among the Jungvolk? He lowered his gaze, unable to meet the man's eyes as he went on talking.

'I am Israel,' the man introduced himself.

'I'm Gioele.'

'Are you from Berlin?'

'No, I'm Italian.'

'You speak our language well. How did you end up here?'

'A German saved me from Auschwitz.'

'*Auschwitz?*'

Gioele focused on the crumbs scattered across the blanket. 'It's like a prison,' he explained haltingly. 'A place where people are . . . killed. People like us.'

'So, it's true . . .' Israel's face darkened. 'The death camps. That's really where they take us. I never imagined I'd live to see such cruelty and madness in humankind.'

Cruelty and madness – those words encapsulated Auschwitz perfectly. Gioele felt the familiar darkness and fear creeping in again. His family's faceless forms reappeared in his mind, pointing accusatory fingers at him.

'Take heart, boy,' Israel consoled him gently. 'The Torah is our guide.' He gestured towards a nearby bookshelf. 'Frya saved a copy. Go and look; this may be the only place where you'll get to read it.'

Gioele stood and brushed the crumbs from his shorts. He walked over to the bookshelves and began scanning the spines. There were so many – some charred, others water-stained, and a few that looked like they'd survived a storm.

'These are Frau Volker's collection,' said a kind voice behind him. 'She rescued them from Nazi bonfires and Allied bombs alike.'

Gioele turned to see a strikingly beautiful girl, her arms crossed over her chest like a schoolteacher. Her long, dark hair framed a face dominated by deep, coal-black eyes that seemed to see through him.

'I'm Duda. And you?'

'I'm Gioele,' he answered, trailing a finger along the spines of the books. 'Why are these novels hidden with you?'

'Because they're forbidden. Just like me, you, Herr Israel, and everyone else here. We share the same fate – they want to burn us all.'

Gioele remembered Hugo's story. Among these books, there might be a copy of *The Magic Mountain*. It would be amazing to find it for him.

'How long have you been here?' he asked Duda.

'A year, I think . . .'

'A year? You haven't left in a year? Really?'

'Yes.' Duda sighed. 'But one day, I'll dance among the elephants again. You'll see.'

'Among the elephants?' Gioele's jaw dropped.

Duda smiled, tousling his hair. She began to twirl and dance in the cramped space, a vision of grace and hope. Everyone watched her, mesmerized, their expressions filled with yearning for freedom.

Chapter 52

The piercing scream of the air raid alarm forced him to set down his cup and turn off the gramophone. This was how the Allies said good morning.

Hugo went through the motions he had learned to perform calmly, following an automatic mental checklist. He turned off the gas, shut the water valve, and opened all the windows.

'I'll grab blankets and supplies,' Edmund called from the kitchen. 'Gioele, the water canister!'

Hugo grabbed his briefcase, opened the door, and waited for Gioele to go ahead of him down the stairs to the basement, where the building's residents were already gathering. They entered one by one and shut the door behind them. Sitting on the benches, Hugo cursed himself for not having gone to the bathroom first. He'd have to hold it for a while.

'Here.' Edmund unscrewed a flask, and Hugo recognized the smell of brandy.

'Papa . . . it's eight in the morning.'

'Sorry. I forgot I had a son who treats his body like a temple.' Edmund took a sip and stifled a laugh.

Hugo ignored the jab about Pervitin and morphine and let it slide. He wasn't about to start an argument in the middle of an enemy attack, and certainly not in front of the others. He opened his briefcase and pulled out his notebook, flipping through it carefully in search of names, details, and patterns. It was a good way to pass the time down there, even as he anticipated another remark from his father, which came right on cue.

'Don't you think criminologists border on obsession and mania in their work? Which are both basically the same traits . . .'

'. . . as you'll find in most criminals. I know,' Hugo finished for him.

He took out Gioele's drawings and tried to block out Edmund. He studied the drawings of the Weidts' living room, then the one of Walther Rumer's caravan. He scrutinized the two drawings repeatedly, finding no noteworthy details until he noticed the common thread – an element connecting seemingly unrelated people.

'What's this?' Hugo pointed to the painting in the caravan.

'I don't know.' Gioele, sitting beside him, shrugged.

'I mean . . . did you add this symbol to the painting, or was it really there?'

'It was really there.'

'And it's the same as in Benedict Weidt's painting . . .'

Hugo examined the painting of an eye that dominated

the Weidts' living room. He remembered it well – a dark oil painting that was seemingly all-seeing. But what he hadn't noticed before was the symbol drawn within the pupil: the 'IHS' trigram enclosed in a sunburst, along with a cross and the three nails of the Passion. The emblem of the Jesuits.

'I hadn't noticed that,' he remarked.

'Of course not.' Gioele grinned mischievously. 'It's drawn in the same black as the pupil, but in slight relief, so that it can only be seen if you look closely from a certain angle.'

'Elementary, my dear Watson,' Hugo laughed.

The linking thread, then, was faint but visible, and it led to whoever had organized the excursion to Mount Brocken: as it happened, the Jesuits. First, however, he would need to learn more about all the chess pieces on the board.

The air raid siren had been a false alarm, as had so often happened that past month. No bombs had fallen, though there were rumours that the flak towers had shot down at least two aircraft. Life resumed as if nothing had happened. The streets filled with people again as soon as the all-clear sounded, and everyone returned to their business.

Lukas Eder sat across from him at the small café table, blowing on his cup of hot ersatz coffee. Despite the Orpo uniform that gave him an overly serious appearance, his expression was boyish.

'I'm really glad to see you again,' Lukas said, sipping the beverage which by now must have cooled down to his satisfaction. 'I imagine we're not just here to chat . . .'

'Not quite.' Hugo slid a slip of paper across the table with the name of former comedian Walther Rumer. 'I need your help again.'

'Whatever you need, Herr Fischer.'

'Can you do some research on this man?'

'I'll do my best, and I'll be discreet.' Lukas slipped the note into his pocket and lit a cigarette, scanning the street outside the café window. He smiled at two girls who were admiring themselves in the glass reflection. 'May I ask why you need it?'

'Would it surprise you if I said it's for the Weidt case?'

'Not at all . . . I had a feeling you were the kind of person who doesn't give up. Have you discovered anything new?'

'Not much, but I can't tell you anything. Officially, this investigation doesn't exist.'

'No, indeed . . . And I doubt Nebe would be pleased.'

'You talk about him as if you know him well.'

'I know him by reputation. I crossed paths with him once, at the front. Is there anything else you need, Herr Fischer?'

'Not for now.' Hugo finished his coffee substitute, staring at the grounds thickening in the cup. 'Do you really want to become a criminologist?'

'Yes.' Lukas's smile was sincere, though tinged with a melancholy Hugo recognized well. There must be some deep, personal reason driving him down this path.

'Why?'

'It's personal . . .' Lukas hesitated. 'I've dealt with death at the front, and I think I'd feel better working in a field where I can restore justice and order.'

'Deaths at the front aren't the kind of deaths criminologists investigate.' Hugo knew he was treading risky ground – one ambiguous phrase to the wrong person could spell trouble – but he couldn't hold back. 'Deaths at the front are the responsibility of those who decided to go to war. Actually, no . . . let me correct that. I'd say they're a collective responsibility because, whether we like it or not, we're all part of this great machinery.'

Lukas stared at him with his one eye, which was glistening as clear as water. On the wall near their table, the Führer's portrait seemed to be watching them intently.

In the long silence that followed, Hugo studied him. At first, he had struggled to understand Lukas – too many shadows, only one eye to look into. But now, he felt certain he was beginning to understand. In that silence, the old adage rang true: *'Silence gives consent.'* Lukas Eder was someone with regrets like his own. Someone very much like him.

'I'll let you know about Walther Rumer as soon as possible,' the policeman said, at last.

Chapter 53

'It's you again.' Sister Anna's expression was more annoyed than surprised. She stood at the door with her hands on her hips. 'Are you going to leave that poor boy alone or not?'

'I'm not here for Costa.' Hugo struggled to keep his tone neutral. 'I'm here to speak with Father Arthur.'

'You can confess during the scheduled times, before Holy Mass.'

Hugo pulled his Kripo badge from his pocket. The nun didn't seem impressed. Two dimples appeared on her round cheeks.

'Oh, so you're not here as a believer. Well, that badge means nothing. Where's your letter of authorization? And what do you need to speak with him about?'

Hugo had already figured out that Sister Anna was a powerhouse packed into five feet of physical stature. Perhaps she was taking the matter personally – after all, you couldn't just walk into the House of the Lord whenever you pleased simply because you worked for the Kripo. Or maybe *she* had something to hide.

'If you don't let me speak to Father Arthur, I'll have to make my visit official,' Hugo said, leaning in slightly towards her. 'I'm here unofficially, and I don't think the convent would want to attract too much attention from the Reich. Your relationship with the Party is already somewhat strained, isn't it?'

'Smooth talk is the devil's tool . . .' Sister Anna shot him a sharp look, then stepped aside to let him pass. 'At least tell me – did you enjoy the jam?'

'It was excellent, Sister Anna. Delicious.'

'Good. Praise God for His fruits.'

She escorted him past the gate to the cloister area. They entered a passage leading to another courtyard, where a man was pacing in the late afternoon light, thumbing a rosary and murmuring a silent prayer that drifted into the shadows of the colonnade.

'He's all yours,' Sister Anna said before leaving them alone.

Father Arthur stopped his prayers and approached. He pocketed the rosary and clasped his hands behind his back. 'You are . . .?'

'Hugo Fischer. I work with the Kripo. May I speak with you?'

'Of course.' The Jesuit spread his arms wide. 'God gave us words for this very purpose.'

'I need to ask you some questions about the youngsters on the trip to Mount Brocken.'

Father Arthur's expression darkened, and his forehead wrinkled like sandpaper. He motioned for Hugo to walk with him. Shadows and light alternated in the cloister, their footsteps echoing between the columns. To Hugo, it seemed as though day and night, life and death, had chosen this interplay of light and dark to encapsulate themselves in that rectangle of carved stone.

'That disaster is a tragedy that's kept me awake for days,' the Jesuit murmured. 'Those poor kids . . . It was supposed to be the first trip in which the Church was allowed to take part – a new opening. Now, every door is closed to us.'

'Have you been told what happened?'

'Only what you've read in the newspapers. A bomb exploded, the fuel caught fire, and they were trapped inside the truck.'

'God certainly has a strange way of protecting His faithful . . .'

Father Arthur stopped. He didn't seem offended, but his expression was that of someone preparing to admonish a child. Hugo braced himself for a sermon.

'You say that because you rely solely on reason and won't look beyond. The pursuit of truth requires not just intelligence, but also humility and faith.'

'In my line of work, reason is everything.'

'Really?' Father Arthur resumed walking. 'Faith is the bridge between what we can understand and what lies beyond our comprehension.'

'I've never reached the truth through faith.'

'Haven't you? But when you trust your intuition, isn't that *faith*, after all?'

However stimulating it might have been to talk to the man, Hugo realized he was straying from the main reason he was there. The Jesuit was skilfully steering him into a conversation that could last hours and ultimately reveal nothing. Hugo decided not to waste any more time.

'Did you know Dr Benedict Weidt?'

'Was he a member of my church? I usually remember everyone . . .'

'He was the father of two children who died in the explosion.'

'I'm deeply sorry, but the participants were chosen by lottery.'

'Do you know Walther Rumer?'

'The comedian? A shame about that joke he made about the Nazis – it cost him his career.'

'He got off easy. It could have cost him his life. Do you know him personally?'

'Look, Herr Fischer . . .' Father Arthur exhaled deeply and clasped his hands in prayer. 'I don't know why you're asking me these questions. I don't know these people. Could you explain what's happening?'

'Both Dr Weidt and Rumer own or owned paintings featuring the Jesuit symbol,' Hugo replied. 'Weidt was murdered not long ago, and Rumer was one of the last people he saw regularly. Now Weidt's children are dead too. Don't you find all these coincidences very strange?'

'I see.' Father Arthur clasped his hands behind his back. 'So, because both men are connected to the Jesuits through their personal faith, you think . . . What, exactly? Are you accusing me of something?'

'I don't believe it was an accident.'

'Life is sacred.' The Jesuit shook his head, his features hardening. 'You have a duty to investigate what happened. I, however, ask you to have faith: I would never soil my hands with someone's death. I would sooner put my head in a noose than be complicit in the death of an innocent. So I ask again: what are you accusing me of? Involvement in the deaths of those youngsters? Truly?'

'Let me apologize if I offended you.' Hugo tried to commit to a momentary act of faith, though he certainly didn't believe in coincidence. The presence of Dieter Costa in this same convent – Dieter, who had carried coded messages to Benedict – couldn't possibly be mere chance. 'I'm not here to accuse you of anything, but to ask if someone might have used the trip as an opportunity to kill those children . . . for personal revenge, let's say.'

'Everyone knew about the excursion. You must understand that the Party's relationship with the Church is tense, so there was much talk about this attempt at reconciliation. I can't guarantee of course that no one chose to exploit the situation, but I can certainly assure you that I know nothing about it if so. Before speaking with you, I hadn't even considered the possibility of a crime. Is there anything else you need?'

'No, not for now.'

Hugo extended his hand. In response, the Jesuit placed the rosary in his palm.

'This is for you. You seem like a good person. Have more faith.'

'I . . .'

Hugo examined the wooden beads and the carefully carved cross. He was about to return the gift – after Auschwitz, he no longer believed in anything – but he was struck by the gaze of Sister Anna, who was crossing the cloister with a basket in her hands. Returning a gift was the height of rudeness, so Hugo slipped the rosary into his pocket.

'You're a bit nosy, but no one should be denied jam,' the nun said as she approached. She rummaged in the basket, pulled out a jar of preserves, and handed it to him.

Hugo chuckled. A rosary and a jar of jam.

He might be leaving without answers, but not entirely empty-handed.

Chapter 54

Leaving St Teresa's felt like stepping into another world. Hugo left behind the silence of the ecclesiastical walls to find himself on a street where the shattered stones emanated the heat they had soaked up throughout the morning. There was a flurry of activity to clear the rubble, but cars still zoomed by, skilfully dodging the heaps. At that moment, he realized the value of the convent's silence.

Across the street, Hugo spotted Dieter Costa. If he had to describe it in Father Arthur's words, this encounter was God's own will. To put in his words, however, it was just a synchronicity of events: Costa was returning as he was leaving, and that offered him a chance to talk. He would just need to avoid scaring the young man off this time.

'Costa,' he called. 'Do you remember me?'

The boy nodded from a distance and approached. 'It would be hard not to remember you, sir . . .'

'I apologize for last time. I was a little . . . abrupt.'

'I still don't understand why you were so angry with me.'

'Let's forget it, it's water under the bridge.' Hugo gestured with his cane toward Unter den Linden. 'Walk with me for a bit. I need to talk to you.'

'As you wish.' Dieter shrugged and brushed the dust off his uniform, which rose in a small grey cloud.

'Coming back from duty?'

'We cleared a lane in Fischerkiez.'

'That must've been tough.'

'No, sir.' Dieter kept his eyes ahead. 'What's tough is immediately after the bombings, when you have to pull the dead out of the rubble.'

'I know.' Hugo thought of the body of a newborn girl, forced into a water pipe by the explosion in Nikolaiviertel, her tiny frame wedged inside. Just as quickly, his mind flashed to the newborn Jewish baby trampled on the Judenrampe at Auschwitz under the relentless heel of an SS officer. That children were the real victims of adult madness was beyond question. 'Did you know that an armoured division of the Waffen-SS is made up of Hitler Youth boys? You'd better pray the war ends before you finish your training.'

'I'll do what I must for Germany, sir.'

'I don't doubt it . . .' Hugo glanced at him. 'What were you doing at the Hoff Circus?'

'I've been going there since I was little. Mr Hoff helped my mother and me while my father was at the front, and his daughter is fond of me. She's like an older sister.'

'And you also know "the man who survived lions"?'

'Yes, he's a good person.'

'Did you know he was under Benedict Weidt's medical care?'

'No, sir, I didn't.'

Hugo coughed, the dusty air again making it difficult to fully fill his lungs, which grew increasingly temperamental by evening, making his breathing laborious. 'Have you heard about the children who burned alive?' he asked, clearing his throat. 'The ones on the trip to Mount Brocken . . .'

'An awful thing.'

Dieter Costa didn't even lift his eyes. He walked briskly, staring at the ground. He wasn't an unempathetic young man – his words, the violin he kept that wasn't his, and his clear, lively eyes proved that. So if his flat, distant tone wasn't a sign of a lack of empathy, it was more likely due to his fear of giving himself away.

'And do you know anything else about this *awful thing*?'

'Only what's written in the headlines I see on the newsstands.'

'Benedict Weidt's children were among them . . .'

'I know, and I'm very sorry about that.'

'Their presence makes me suspicious.'

'A tragic act of fate, sir.'

A *tragic act of fate*. A fifteen-year-old boy, raised on bread and songs for the Führer, deliberately kept away from any form of culture that might allow him to think critically, who spoke with such eloquence . . . Either Dieter Costa had been influenced by educated adults like Father Arthur, or someone had coached him on what to say about the incident.

Hugo slowed his pace as they reached the boulevard. Unter den Linden had never looked so grey, despite the Nazi flags fluttering red like flames. It was at night, however, that Berlin truly seemed moribund. Once a riot of lights and neon signs illuminating a city that never slept, it was now plunged into the deepest darkness. A life-saving blanket of blackness, admittedly – it gave bomber pilots less power of orientation – but at times it felt too much like death.

He reflected on the fact that, even if he uncovered what had happened, it wouldn't bring the Weidt couple or those children back to life. So why did he keep pursuing this case? Solving it wouldn't restore order to the ruined Unter den Linden or the wounded Nikolaiviertel, nor would it brighten the darkness. Yet it seemed like the only thing left that could make him feel useful and alive. It had to be because of his promise.

'You know, when I was younger, I used to swing dance,' he confessed.

'But that music is forbidden . . .' Dieter frowned.

'I know. Back then, there were the Hitler Youth and the Swing Youth. I was already too old to be a real swing boy, but I loved dancing. It drained me and energized me at the same time.' Hugo smiled bitterly at the memory. That was when the first pains of multiple sclerosis began, after years of inexplicable fatigue while skiing with his mother or climbing a flight of stairs. Yet he managed to dance, to be happy – as if the disease relented at those moments. 'And then there were the Edelweiss Pirates,' he continued. 'They didn't mess around. They gave the HJ no respite. I remember raids that ended in brawls, often with injuries. One day, I found myself in the middle of an HJ raid while swing dancing with my university friends. I don't know how that boy got a gun, but in the chaos, he shot one of my classmates in the face, a young woman.'

'Did she die?' Dieter finally looked him in the eyes.

'What do you think happens when you get shot in the face? The investigation was half-hearted. No one wanted trouble with the National Socialist Party, which had just won the elections, so the case was closed.'

'Why are you telling me this?'

'To make you understand why I keep asking about Weidt and this so-called *tragic act of fate*. I have unfinished business with that girl, I owe her my best efforts. I promised myself I would always close properly any case assigned to me, that I would never let a crime go unpunished.'

Hugo omitted the most important detail of that story: the moment he had been forced to exonerate the Hitler Youth boy if he wanted to continue his studies in criminology. He had agreed to lie, and that had broken something inside him. Not even a month earlier, he had participated in a book burning, more out of a willingness to go along to get along than from any genuine enthusiasm. He hadn't grasped the significance of that seemingly banal act, which, in the Party's intentions, was meant to be *tribal*. The flames that erased and purified had consumed some people entirely, transforming them from that moment onward. For him, however, the wake-up call had been when they had forced him to lie in order to close the investigation. It was like a kick in the guts, and it had wrenched him out of the sleep of reason.

'*The sleep of reason produces monsters,*' he said aloud.

'What?' Dieter looked at him, confused.

'Nothing.' Hugo thought of Goya's painting, with its sleeping dreamer spawning an earthly hell of monstrous beasts. That was what had happened to his Germany. 'This isn't an obsession,' he continued. 'Two people are dead, and after them, their children and other innocent victims. I can't pretend everything's fine or that it's all just chance. I'm trying to set things right because there's far too much chaos around here.'

'And what if one day you encounter something that isn't meant to be set right?' Dieter looked up. His clean, handsome face clashed with the rigid Hitler Youth uniform. 'Maybe, sometimes, chaos is fine.'

'Are you trying to tell me something?'

'No, just what I said.'

Hugo let those words sink in. He felt they carried more meaning than they appeared to. He needed to let them settle if he wanted to understand them – he was certain of that. He couldn't push any further, not in a society where one word too many could cost you your life.

He stopped on the Schlossbrücke. The bridge spanned the Spree, its stark but elegant lines reflected in the calm waters below. The goddess Nike stood atop her column, her wings spread, gazing at the desolation of the ruins – beautiful and victorious. Well, *she* was, at least.

'You can head back now,' he said to the boy.

Dieter snapped a military salute and left without needing to be told twice. Hugo could feel the boy's sense of relief at being dismissed. No criminology expertise was needed to sense how uncomfortable Dieter felt in his presence. But it *would* take that expertise to understand *why*.

He headed towards Nikolaiviertel with the intention of clearing his mind for the evening. He needed a blank slate if he wanted to make sense of what little he had gathered so far. He tried to focus only on the present around him. The streets began to fill with the smell of food from open-air kitchens. He felt a vague languor. He casually greeted the women busy stoking fires with wood from trees uprooted by bombs. He cut through the castle gardens, savouring the cool shade, the scent of linden trees, and the faintly bluish hues of late afternoon.

Nikolaiviertel was an eyesore now, but it had once been a lively neighbourhood of narrow cobblestone streets and half-timbered houses. He reconstructed it in his mind as it had been before the destruction. Skirting the church, he took a narrow street. He thought he could hear footsteps overlapping his own.

He slowed. The footsteps slowed with him.

Perhaps, in the end, his story had served a purpose.

'Dieter, what is it?'

When he turned, the punch struck him square in the face. He felt his cheekbone crack. The sharp pain exploded across his face, blinding him completely.

Chapter 55

The impact with the street was so violent that Hugo couldn't get up right away, though he was lucid enough to know that lying flat on his back like that only left him vulnerable.

After the blow to his face, Hugo had lost his grip on his cane. He had wanted to wield it as a weapon, but his hold on the pommel had faltered. He had tried to dodge to one side, but his attacker had punched him again, sending him crashing to the ground.

His mother had taught him the best way to fall while skiing, to avoid injury. This time, he went down with no way to brace himself, his forehead hitting the pavement squarely. In the seconds he lay there motionless, he mused about the fact that not even his mother had been able to follow her own advice. No one knew whether she had suffered a fainting spell or if – more likely, judging from the tracks – a wild animal had crossed the path that day. She had flown straight into a tree, colliding head on with the bark. Just as he had now.

Hugo took a kick to the back and another to the side. His ribs protested with a grating sensation.

He fumbled around for a handhold to help him to his feet, groping blindly for his cane.

'You piece of shit!' someone yelled from the end of the street. 'Leave him be!'

Hugo heard the attacker's footsteps trying to escape, followed by the sound of a scuffle. He managed to make out the shape of Lukas Eder grappling with the man. The two of them tumbled to the ground, locked together like wild animals. They couldn't speak, their efforts to overpower each other punctuated by guttural grunts that made them sound more like rabid dogs than human beings.

The sound of punches echoed through the narrow street. Lukas was on top of the stranger, gaining the upper hand. He grabbed the man by the collar and threw him to one side. But the attacker was quicker. He scrambled to his feet, stumbled a couple of times, and then fled towards the Spree.

'Bastard!' Lukas muttered, rubbing his hand. He ran to Hugo and helped him to his feet. 'Are you all right?'

'I think so.' Hugo grabbed his cane. 'Thank you for stepping in.'

'Your face, Herr Fischer . . .'

'What about it?' Hugo touched his forehead, his fingers meeting torn skin. He realized his face was smeared with blood. 'Looks like I'll need stitches.'

'Should I take you to the hospital?'

'No. I'd rather go home. I have a friend who's a nurse – she'll know what to do.' Hugo loosened his tie. His shirt was stained, too. He tried to wipe it off but only managed to smear more blood on the fabric.

'I'll walk you home.' Lukas offered his arm.

'Thanks, but I'm not on my deathbed.' Hugo brushed off the help. It was already humiliating enough that he hadn't been able to fight back. He'd gone down at the first blow and hadn't managed to fight back at all. He clenched his teeth and swallowed his frustration.

When they reached his building, Hugo opened the door and motioned for the officer to follow him inside.

As he unlocked the apartment, he made sure not to make any mistakes.

'Bastian, Papa!' he called out.

The fake name was enough to put everyone on alert. Gioele appeared from his room, wearing his Jungvolk uniform. He must have just got home. Hugo felt a wave of dizziness and had to steady himself against the doorframe. Seeing Gioele in that uniform – he, who had lost his entire family to the Nazis – made Hugo feel filthy. He wondered if, one day, when Gioele was older and understood the depth of this psychological violence, he would hold it against him.

Gioele ran to him. 'Papa!' he shouted, casting a sidelong glance at the man in uniform. 'What have you done to him?'

'This is Lukas; he's a friend,' Hugo reassured him. 'He helped me.'

'What have you got yourself into this time?' Edmund arrived, flustered, from the living room, his shirt sleeves rolled up and his braces hanging down, a newspaper still in his hand.

'I felt like having a closer encounter with the street, Papa.'

'I bet you'll take a sip of brandy *now* . . .'

'Bring two glasses.' Hugo gestured for Lukas to follow him into the living room. 'And Papa, call the switchboard and ask for Adele – I'm going to need a few stitches.'

'In my day, we didn't use excuses like that to see our

girlfriends,' Edmund grumbled as he grabbed three glasses and filled them with brandy.

Hugo opened a package of Pervitin, popped a pill into his mouth, and washed it down with a gulp of the liquor, careful not to let Gioele see. He decided to savour the rest slowly, sinking into the couch. He stared at the amber liquid in his glass, then at the officer.

'What were you doing so close to my home?'

'I was looking for you,' Lukas replied.

Hugo glanced at his father, who, despite his stubbornness, caught on quickly.

'Come on, Gioele – today's lesson is on mentalism!' Edmund grabbed Gioele by the collar and led him out of the room, leaving them alone.

'Mentalism?' Lukas raised an eyebrow.

'He was an illusionist.'

'Fischer, of course, now I remember . . . I was just a kid, but my mother used to talk about him all the time!'

'Yes, he was quite famous. So, why were you looking for me?' Hugo gingerly felt the wound on his cheekbone, hoping the Pervitin would quickly dull the pain tormenting the bone.

'I did the research you asked for.' Lukas took a sip of his drink. 'Walther Rumer ran into trouble with the Gestapo over a caustic joke about National Socialism. That joke ended his career, but during the war, he distinguished himself. Silver medal and Iron Cross for losing his arm in Kiev – that's how he regained his honour.'

'When the Russians blew up half the city?'

'Exactly, sir. I'm not sure how useful that information will be to you.'

'Everything is useful.' Hugo drained the last of his

brandy. Dieter Costa's father had also fought in Kiev, and that couldn't be a coincidence. 'If you don't mind, I'd like to rest now.'

'Of course, sir.'

'Nothing else?'

'That's all for now. I'll let you know if I find anything else.'

Hugo escorted Lukas to the door. He shook his hand, lingering in the gesture. He owed him his life – or at least a less serious beating. He owed him even more, considering the silver badge Lukas wore for the eye he'd lost in battle. Blood shed for Germany.

'Can we be on a first name basis now?' Lukas asked.

'No, not yet.'

'One day we'll be partners, and I'm sure that I'll help you solve this case.'

They both laughed. The thought of having a partner didn't seem so bad to Hugo.

When the door closed, the smile faded.

That attack hadn't been some random mugging by a homeless man desperate for money. It had been a deliberate punishment. The same person must have been following him for days, tracking his movements.

It was a message: his investigation would no longer be tolerated.

Chapter 56

'Hold still.' Adele pressed her fingertips against the edges of the wound. When she pierced his flesh with the needle, Hugo silently thanked the Pervitin coursing through his veins for having dulled the pain. 'Can I ask who did this to you?'

Hugo glanced at Edmund and Gioele, who were watching the nurse as she deftly guided the thread with tweezers and tied knots, as if she were darning a sock.

'Some thug,' he lied.

Adele stared straight into his eyes. She kept stitching until the last knot was tied. 'You should've gone to the hospital,' she said, disinfecting the wound and covering it with a bandage.

'I was counting on your help.' Hugo chuckled.

But he couldn't coax a laugh from her. Adele was sharp, and she wasn't going to fall for the story of some common thug. Her eyes were troubled, darkened by the twilight spilling through the window.

'Are you staying the night, Fräulein?' Edmund interjected.

'What?'

'Look at the sky. The curfew's about to start – you wouldn't want to get in trouble with the gendarmes because of us. I'll make a quick dinner. We've got a guest room. We owe you a debt of gratitude for coming here at this hour.'

'I wouldn't want to intrude . . .' she said, hesitantly.

'My father's right; it's getting late.' Hugo looked outside. The alley where he'd been attacked was now swallowed up by evening shadows, with no streetlights to illuminate it. Whoever had attacked him likely knew about his connection to Adele. 'You'll be safer here.'

Even his father seemed to pick up on the unease in his words. Edmund gestured to Gioele and led him to the kitchen. Once they were alone, Adele moved to the window. She rested her hands on the railing and took a deep breath.

'Now will you tell me who *really* attacked you?'

'The same person who followed us in the Mercedes, I'd guess.'

'Are you sure?'

'I don't believe in coincidences.' Hugo slipped a cigarette between his lips and flicked his lighter. He took a drag. 'I let myself get caught unawares like a rank rookie.'

'Oh, this testosterone nonsense again . . .' Adele gently plucked the cigarette from his fingers. She took a drag, her lips barely brushing the filter. 'As if not being able to defend yourself for once makes you less of a man . . . You're more upset about that than about your injuries.'

'That's not true.'

'Yes, it is. You're bothered by the fact that you couldn't hit back.'

Hugo took that blow, too. It was pointless to argue with a woman who always seemed to be one step ahead of everyone. He took the cigarette back from her and leaned down to kiss her. The electric jolt that surged from the soles of his feet to the top of his head was enough to make him forget the attack. For the first time, he was grateful for the curfew that kept Berlin anaesthetized.

'Sorry to interrupt.' Edmund coughed, stifling a laugh. 'Dinner's ready.'

Chapter 57

Hugo stared at himself in the mirror under the glow of the gas lamp. The bruise on his ribs stood out, a vivid reminder of the now stabbing pain despite the methamphetamine. He hoped his ribs weren't cracked. A dose of Eukodal would've really made him feel better.

Someone knocked on the door.

Hugo quickly put his shirt back on and buttoned it up. He expected to see his father, but instead, Adele's face appeared in the doorway. She held a bottle of brandy and two glasses, nudging the door open with her hip.

'I can't sleep,' she chirped. 'Care for a little party?'

The ease with which she swept him off balance left him breathless. This time, though, his breath caught for real when he closed the door too quickly, sending a sharp jolt of pain through his side. It felt as if his rib might be about to pierce his lung.

'Did I do something wrong?' Adele froze, holding the bottle mid-air. 'I didn't mean to make you uncomfortable . . . I'll go back to my room.'

'It's not because of you.'

Hugo lifted his shirt to show her the bruise spreading across his side. The pain throbbed like a blazing flame.

'That's not a good sign . . .' Adele shook her head.

'No, it's not.'

'You should get it checked out.'

'I will. Tomorrow.'

Adele handed him the brandy. Despite the nonchalance with which she had entered the room, Hugo could sense her tension. They were alone in a room, in a house steeped in night-time stillness, and the charged excitement in the air was impossible to ignore. He could feel her desire as acutely as his own.

They clinked glasses and drank.

'I'm glad to see Gioele so contented,' Adele said, leaning against the desk. 'You're doing a good job. Oh, and Edmund is one good cook.'

'Edmund is one massive pain.'

'That's not true – he's adorable.'

'You say that because you don't have to deal with him like I do.'

Adele set down her glass and turned off the gas lamp. She went to the window and pulled away the cardboard covering it. 'Come here. Look at this.' She leaned out, and the cool night breeze tousled her hair. 'Would you ever have thought you'd see stars in Berlin?'

Hugo stepped closer and glanced down. The moon cast an eerie glow over the street, the uprooted lampposts, the shattered rooftops.

'No, Fischer, not down there.' Adele touched his chin, gently tilting his gaze upward. 'You need to learn to see things from a different perspective.'

Hugo looked at the sky. It was endless, spangled by countless tiny points of light. He spotted constellations his mother had taught him to recognize during their vacations in the Black Forest: Cygnus, Lyra, Aquila. The Northern Cross pulsated in the still of the night.

He felt Adele move closer.

She was undressing.

The light of the moon and the stars caressed her bare flesh.

Chapter 58

Adele's legs were entwined with his, barely covered by the sheet hanging off one side of the bed. He could feel her warm breath against the hollow of his neck, where she had rested her cheek.

Hugo stroked her hair. Adele took a deep breath, murmured something, then fixed him with a languid gaze.

'Maybe now we're close enough for me to tell you what I like about you,' she whispered.

'I'm all ears . . .'

'I like it when you fall.'

'What?'

Hugo wasn't sure he'd heard her right, considering how often he stumbled due to multiple sclerosis – not to mention his tumble onto the pavement that afternoon. Instinctively, he touched the stitches on his forehead.

Adele sat up and laughed.

'I didn't mean that! I meant figuratively. I don't like people who never fall because when they do, they can't get back up. But you're not afraid to fall – because you know you can pick yourself up every time.'

'Oh.' Hugo wasn't sure whether to feel flattered or exposed as a fraud. 'I think you have too high an opinion of me.'

'Maybe you're just not seeing things from the right perspective – I told you that already.'

'The right perspective . . .' Hugo felt his muscles tense. That was it, what he'd been missing: a different perspective. 'I'm hunting the murderer of the Mount Brocken children . . . But what if there wasn't any murder?'

'What?' Adele's eyes widened. 'I'm opening up about my feelings, and you're thinking about work?'

'I just had a thought.' Hugo sat up abruptly, tossed the condom into the bin, grabbed his underwear from the floor, and put it on. He pulled on his trousers and shirt, leaving the shirt unbuttoned. 'I need you to help me with something.'

'Fischer!' Adele, still naked in bed, looked at him with exasperation. 'Is this why you still don't have a steady partner despite all your very fine qualities . . .?'

'No, there's another reason.' Hugo used his cane to lean in and kiss her. He hoped she would forgive him. 'I was waiting for you to show up.'

Adele grabbed a pillow and hurled it at his face. They laughed. Hugo wondered how long it had been since he'd felt this happy. He truly was happy, with her, in spite of the shadow of death that loomed over him, hissing in a whisper that he was going to die right here in Berlin one way or another – under the bombs or killed by whoever it was that wanted to stop his investigation.

One step at a time, he told himself. Right now, he needed to think.

He lit the gas lamp and sat down at the desk. Grabbing some papers, he wrote down names: Benedict, Marlene, Brecht, Walther Rumer, Dieter Costa, and Father Arthur. He added Lukas Eder and Otto Weidt, unwilling to overlook anyone connected to the case.

'Help me,' he said, handing Adele some adhesive tape. 'Stick these papers to the wall.'

'What for?'

'Just do it, and I'll explain.'

When Adele had finished, he gave her instructions on how to connect the names with strips of tape. When they were done, he stepped back, raising the lamp to illuminate the web of lines linking everyone involved.

'It looks like the underground map,' Adele joked.

'No one gets lost in the underground. This will be harder to navigate.' Hugo illuminated the tangle. A sharp pain in his ribs made him stifle a groan. 'Marlene was connected to Brecht, the director of *Ein Volk*. Brecht committed suicide, so it'd be easy to suspect he killed the Weidts.'

'Too easy by half,' Adele objected.

'Exactly. He's not the killer. Otherwise, who gave me that beating last night? No, the killer is alive and well, and maybe Brecht didn't even kill himself – he could've been drowned after being forced to write his suicide note.' Hugo moved the light to Otto Weidt's name. 'The victim's cousin, the man who hired me on a private basis.'

'You're not doubting him?' Adele shook her head.

'No. He's a good, genuine person. But he's an important piece of the puzzle because the message Benedict left him proves that Benedict already felt threatened – so much so that he worked to ensure his children would be safe. Now let's talk about Dieter Costa.' Hugo paused at the slip with

Dieter's name. 'He delivered a coded message to Benedict saying the children were safe. Dieter is connected to two names, which in turn connect back to Benedict.'

'Walther Rumer and Father Arthur,' Adele said, running her fingers along the silver tape linking the names.

'Walther Rumer was being treated by Benedict Weidt, works at the Hoff Circus that Dieter frequents, and is a devout Jesuit. Benedict was also a Jesuit – there's a painting in his home with the order's symbol. Then there's Father Arthur, who lives under the same roof as Dieter at St Teresa and was one of the organizers of the Mount Brocken trip, where Benedict's children lost their lives.' Hugo paused. Other connections intrigued him. 'Walther Rumer fought at Kiev, as did Dieter's father. One lost an arm, the other lost his life.'

'And what about him?' Adele pointed to Lukas.

'Eder has a silver badge on his uniform. I managed to glimpse the location and date: Kiev, 1941. Same as Rumer and Dieter's father.'

'Coincidence?'

'Possibly. Plenty of people were there.'

'I don't understand how you're going to untangle this mess.'

'*One step at a time.*' Hugo stepped back. 'And by look-ing at it from a different perspective, as you say.'

'I don't get it . . .'

'I assumed someone killed the kids on the Brocken trip. Let's change perspectives. No Jesuit would commit murder. What if the kids really are safe, just as Dieter's coded mes-sage to Benedict claimed?'

'But there are corpses . . .' Adele shook her head.

'Bodies of kids who didn't die in a fire. The lungs of the

victim I dissected were clean, and the bodies didn't have shoes.'

'Shoes . . .?'

'It's true that shoes burn, but in this kind of fire, remnants are usually found still on the feet – they don't disappear completely.' Hugo stared into her eyes. 'Those kids didn't have shoes. Who goes on a trip barefoot? The kids are alive, and their bodies were replaced with corpses . . .'

'They staged an accident?'

'Dieter Costa told me that sometimes chaos is better – that not every case should be solved. He knows something. And what if those kids are alive and hidden at St Teresa's? A place like that could have basements, secret rooms . . .'

Adele stood beside him, taking in the names and connections on the wall. 'Who are they protecting them from?'

'Finding that out will solve the Weidt case.' Hugo paused, taking a long breath. 'Where can you find a large number of bodies with clothes but no shoes?'

'In a concentration camp . . .' Adele's voice was barely a whisper.

'Exactly. But we need to narrow it down. Which camp?'

'Ravensbrück,' Adele answered without hesitation. 'It's outside Berlin and holds girls and boys the same age as the victims.'

'Then we'll go to Ravensbrück.'

'But after the attack, I thought . . .'

'I always get back up – you said it yourself. I'm not giving up this case.'

Chapter 59

The Moment of the Massacre

When the sun is directly overhead, they call us to relieve our comrades.

We leave the collection points and head towards the execution site. My hands tremble. I don't know what awaits me. Hans said we'll be shooting them in the back of the head so we won't have to look them in the face. I pray to God that's true. A moment later, I feel ashamed for even thinking it.

We escort the Jews towards the ravine. The path is enveloped in an eerie silence, in that forest bleached by autumn. As we get closer, the sound of gunfire becomes clearer. It's constant, one shot after another, with only a few seconds' pause in between. If my comrades have been at it for hours, it means it's not as terrible as my imagination makes it out to be. We are at war. This is war. I have nothing to reproach myself for. I am merely following orders, just as the Jews heading to their slaughter are following theirs.

The trees line the road, thin and bare.

A woman walks beside me. I catch myself staring at her childlike face, her lips drained of colour. She is very beautiful. She shivers in the cold, clad only in her undergarments. She clutches the hand of a little girl, barely two years old. The girl looks at me and smiles. I smile back, and my chest implodes; I feel my bones creaking, splintering into a thousand pale shards. Why did I return her smile, while leading her to her death?

The child gestures to her mother to pick her up, but it's me who lifts her. The Ukrainian policemen shake their heads, looking at me with disapproval, though soon I will understand it is pity – pity for the breach I have opened in my own heart with this simple yet dangerous gesture.

'I'm Anna,' the child says.

Hush, I think inwardly. I don't want to know your name. I don't want you to have a name.

But it's too late.

Her mother looks at me, frightened. She wants to take the girl from my arms but doesn't dare. I quicken my pace, pretending to trot like a horse to make the child laugh.

The mother seems to relax. 'Miryam,' she says, touching her chest.

I don't tell her my name. I don't want her to know it, to scream it when we're standing at the edge of the ravine, or to curse me forever after her death.

We reach the final sorting point. I set Anna down and leave her with her mother as the Ukrainian policemen herd them into small groups. We relieve the other soldiers, who are exhausted.

The ravine of Babi Yar suddenly opens out before me, but what hits me first is the nauseating stench of blood and who knows what else. High above, on the spur overlooking the ravine, I see Jeckeln observing the operation with the other officers, proudly pointing to something.

Below us lies a sea of bodies, piled one on top of the other in grotesque positions. They bring in the first group of thirty people. The Jews finally see what is happening in that ravine and begin to scream and kick, trying to flee. The Ukrainian policemen step in immediately, restoring order with whips and batons. They force the Jews to turn their backs to us, to descend into the ravine, and to lie on the corpses.

My hands shake. The barrel of my rifle is unsteady.

We have to shoot quickly before they try to escape again. As I fire my first shot, I scream. I see the jet of blood spurting from the back of *my* Jew's head.

Why didn't I leave when I had the chance? Why didn't I walk out of that room when they gave me the opportunity? Why did these stupid Jews listen to us?

They bring us more. My eyes burn. Miryam stands before me, holding little Anna. She looks at me with wide brown eyes. She says something I don't understand.

'Wait!' I beg my comrades to lower their weapons. 'Let her . . .'

Miryam pulls down the neckline of her camisole and bares her breast. I sense my comrades tense. She picks up the little girl, cradles her, and offers her nipple. Anna calms down. No one dares move.

Miryam nods. We can shoot now.

I can't breathe. I touch the trigger lightly. I will kill her because it's the right thing to do. I must do it – I know her name. I let out a scream, letting my superiors know that my nerves are already frayed after just two executions. The shot fires. It strikes her in the neck, and she falls like a bird with broken wings.

I stand there, breathless. As dead as she is.

We are relieved only after an hour. They lead us to the field kitchen, set up near the ravine. I don't know how I make it there, passing by all those stacked corpses, now being covered over with dirt. I don't know how I make it, considering I can't feel my legs any more.

I sit. The things around me have lost their contours. I drift in an intangible world, a world without consistency. They bring us glasses of rum and ample supplies of Pervitin. I gulp it down greedily as the sun sets, and the shooting continues methodically.

'You should patent this technique!' The voice of an officer, seated in a corner of the tent, jolts me. 'What do you think, the "Jeckeln Method"?'

Jeckeln laughs, satisfied. 'I still need to refine it. I call it the "sardine-packing method", actually.'

The other officers laugh too. The name is so fitting.

'We make them lie on top of the other corpses, then shoot them. That way, the soldiers don't have to push the bodies into the pits. These boys are on edge enough as it is – we need to look out for them.'

I feel their eyes on me. I lower my gaze.

The officer drinks and compliments him. 'I came specifically to see your technique – it's talked about so much. No offence, but I've found a method that's even more efficient and effective.'

Jeckeln's face tightens. He doesn't seem to like the direction this conversation is taking. 'More effective?'

'More efficient *and* effective,' the officer repeats, draining the rest of his rum. 'I use gas in Belarus. I just need to perfect the technique, but I'm sure you'll want to adopt it soon. You'll all want to adopt it. If you allow me, I'll demonstrate tomorrow.'

I listen as gusts of wind carry the smell of flesh and blood into the tent. Screams and gunshots still echo in the distance, and the officers' voices fade away, becoming faint and insubstantial.

The executions continue into the evening, even under the rising moon. The moon is an eye watching us from on high, judging us, peering down into the depths of that cursed ravine where Miryam and Anna and all the others of this wretched earth are endlessly shot down.

Chapter 60

15 July 1944

Ravensbrück

Rain fell relentlessly over the forest of pine and birch trees that greeted them as they stepped off the train. The sunny skies of the previous day were a distant memory, replaced by a pale shadow draped over this northern corner of Brandenburg. The rain washed out every detail. The ground exhaled a scent of graves. Hugo had expected nothing less from a place whose name carried such ominous details: the 'Ravens' Bridge'.

'I hope I've guessed correctly,' Adele said, drawing closer to Hugo under the umbrella. She couldn't avoid stepping into a puddle, splattering her trousers with mud. 'This is the only nearby camp that houses minors of both sexes, even though it's primarily a women's camp. Siemens Werke needs nimble, delicate hands.'

Hugo felt a sense of déjà vu. He spotted the car sent by

his cousin and thought back to Tristan Voigt picking him up at Auschwitz in a Kübelwagen.

'I did everything I could to help the women in this camp and their children,' Adele murmured. 'There are some women in there who are braver than you and me put together.'

'Small acts of rebellion,' Hugo recalled her words from Auschwitz.

'Small acts of rebellion, exactly.' They continued walking through the summer downpour towards the car, which was waiting for them with its engine idling. 'Small kindnesses to endure imprisonment. Some of them have even managed to sabotage Siemens by improperly assembling bolts, delaying shipments of war materiel. And the educated women hold evening lessons in the barracks. I did what I could to help, but it's not always easy with so many eyes watching, especially when you're suddenly transferred from a camp like Auschwitz . . .'

They climbed into the Kübelwagen – a tin can of a vehicle – and were driven to the gates of Ravensbrück. Its high, grim walls rose dark and imposing against the rain-soaked sky. As they passed low, elegant cottages nestled in the greenery, Hugo spotted a blonde woman cradling a baby under a porch as the rain battered the roof. She must have been the wife of an SS officer.

Inside the camp, Hugo glimpsed the lake, its waters blackened by the weather, where prisoners were pouring wheelbarrows of dust. When he noticed the smoke and the crematorium, he realized that they were dumping wheelbarrows full of ashes.

It shocked him how this no longer felt unfamiliar. He wondered whether prolonged exposure to such horrors would eventually render him as cold and unfeeling as the SS officers he had seen in action in Poland.

Fritz Ernst Fischer greeted them in the main courtyard, a dreary rectangle as dark as everything else in the camp. Hugo immediately noticed the rank of Sturmbannführer on his cousin's uniform.

'Heil Hitler!' Fritz saluted. 'Fräulein Krause, it's a pleasure to have you back.'

When it came to Hugo, Fritz dispensed with formalities, slapping him nostalgically on the back. Only then did Hugo notice that Fritz was missing an arm. He remembered his cousin from their childhood vacations at Wattenmeer or Rostock. They had spent hours collecting shells and swimming in icy waters, often joined by Fritz's Alsatian dog. That felt like another lifetime, and perhaps it was. Only Fritz's pale blue eyes remained unchanged. The rest of him, at least according to the stories Adele had told, now belonged to someone else.

'I'm sorry it took so long,' Fritz apologized. 'It took me seven days to secure those damned permits, but as Fräulein Krause knows . . . This isn't exactly an open-door facility. What do you need?'

'I need to speak with whoever's in charge of disposing of the dead,' Hugo replied.

'Follow me.'

Fritz led them through the camp. The barracks stretched out in orderly rows, monotonous and surrounded by watchtowers. They crossed a stone walkway as the rain turned the ground into a bubbling mire.

'How's Uncle?' Fritz asked.

'The same as always,' Hugo replied, glancing at a line of women walking in single file under the relentless rain. Emaciated and exhausted, they trudged back and forth from their work.

'Impressed by this place, huh?' Fritz teased. 'You should

see my experimental facility on the other side of the camp – it's fascinating. You wouldn't believe how useful these *lapines* are for the German cause.'

Hugo exchanged a look with Adele, suppressing the urge to react to the term his cousin used for the interned women he experimented on: rabbits.

'Hugo, you used to be so chatty.' Fritz frowned. 'What's wrong?'

'It's the weather,' Hugo said. 'I hate summer rain.'

'You're right . . . I prefer the bit of warmth summer brings us. Here we are.'

Fritz led them into an office, shaking off his umbrella and boots to avoid tracking mud inside. 'This is Eva, a promising trainee at the SS Helferinnen school. We're one of the best training centres around.' He gestured towards the young woman, looking at her from under his cap. 'This is my cousin. I'm leaving him in your capable hands. Now, if you'll excuse me, I have other matters to attend to. Heil Hitler!'

'Heil Hitler!' Hugo responded. Turning to Eva, with Adele beside him, he wasted no time. 'I need to know if any corpses were recently removed from this camp.'

Eva raised her eyebrows, clearly surprised by the request.

'The bodies go to the crematorium,' she said.

'I know, but I have reason to believe that some bodies were taken elsewhere – officially, of course. There must be some record of it somewhere.'

Nothing the Nazis did went unrecorded, not even the exact figures of their war crimes, which they sought to keep hidden from the population and the world.

Eva flipped slowly through a ledger.

'Maybe during my colleague's shift . . .' She ran her

finger down the page and froze. Her face went pale. 'You're absolutely right.'

'Who requested the bodies?' Adele's voice was as shocked as Eva's expression.

'They were taken to feed the big cats at a circus. This is unbelievable!' Eva laughed. 'It was a formal request, citing a meat shortage, and it was approved.'

'Was it the Hoff Circus?'

'If you already knew, why ask?'

Outside the rain had stopped, and the sky seemed to clear as Hugo and Adele walked side by side, skirting the camp's perimeter wall. From their vantage point, the barbed wire on top of the enclosure seemed to pierce the heavens.

'You were right,' Adele said, leaning on her umbrella. 'Walther Rumer is involved . . .'

'He supplied the bodies to Father Arthur. Now I'm certain the children are alive. Someone staged their deaths to protect them. I'm almost sure they're hiding at St Teresa's, and that gives me some peace.'

'What about the Weidts' deaths?'

'I'll stop here.' Hugo took a deep breath, catching the crematorium's acrid stench now that the rain had ceased. 'I've thought it over, and I believe continuing might endanger the children hidden at St Teresa's – and me. The Weidts are dead, but their children are alive, and for once, I have to leave things in chaos.'

'I agree with you,' Adele said, gripping his hand tightly.

They walked in silence toward the exit of that godforsaken place, forgotten even by God.

Chapter 61

Berlin, Pariser Platz

'Today we had a lesson about race,' Gioele remarked, kicking a fragment of plaster on the pavement and dusting the tips of his shoes.

Hugo didn't know how to respond. The calm way Gioele recounted his days with the Jungvolk unsettled him. Barely seven months ago, this same boy had been a prisoner at Auschwitz, one of Mengele's experimental 'rabbits'. Hugo understood the mechanisms of the mind, the processes people used to suppress trauma to survive. Yet he couldn't bear the idea that this child might forget completely. Was this tranquillity the result of Jungvolk indoctrination? How far could the Reich go in producing loyal, brainwashed followers?

'Let's sit for a moment,' Hugo suggested.

They settled on one of the few intact benches along the

avenue, facing the imposing Brandenburg Gate. The swastika banners hanging between its columns stained the scene with blood-red accents.

'Listen closely . . .' Hugo took a deep breath. 'The Jungvolk is just a way for you to blend in, to stay unnoticed. You don't have to believe anything they teach you. What did they say about race?'

'They said Aryans are superior to every other people.'

'And do you believe that?'

'Of course not,' Gioele replied with a small smile, and Hugo felt a wave of relief. 'Our supervisor made me stand up in front of everyone, measured me, and announced I was of the purest race. So obviously, his theories are flawed.'

'Never forget who you are. I couldn't live with myself if you did.'

'I think I've figured something out these past few days,' Gioele said, meeting Hugo's gaze with the maturity of someone far older. 'I know who I am. I'm not Aryan, and I'm not Jewish. I'm a child.'

Hugo was struck silent by the clarity of Gioele's words. He smiled and ruffled the boy's hair. Whatever happened, he had to make sure this child's essence remained intact. That was the only promise he could truly keep to Gioele's murdered family. Even though Hugo himself hadn't poured the Zyklon B crystals into the gas chambers, he felt stained by guilt. And the guilt he carried felt collective, inescapable.

A noise from further down the street brought him back to the present.

Hugo stood. He took Gioele's hand and stepped forward to get a better look at the soldiers moving into position, setting up machine guns and halting traffic.

'What's happening?' Gioele tugged at Hugo's jacket.

'Nothing good,' Hugo replied, glancing at the sky. No planes, no air raid sirens, yet the scene below was unmistakably one of preparation for battle. 'Come on, let's go.'

The headquarters of the Kriminalpolizei was a hive of activity, swarming with pale, sweating officers darting in every direction. Hugo intercepted Nebe's secretary.

'What's going on?' he asked, gripping her elbow to stop her mid-stride.

'You don't know, Herr Fischer?' she panted. 'Our Führer . . . they say he's dead!'

Hugo held his breath. He felt Gioele squeeze his hand tightly and met the boy's gaze with an unspoken warning: *show no reaction.* His stomach churned, his heart raced, but he forced his face to remain neutral. Any hint of celebration could be fatal.

'How tragic,' he managed to say. 'How did it happen?'

'It was Count von Stauffenberg!' she exclaimed. 'They say he planted a bomb at Hitler's feet! Now they're trying to stage a coup!'

Hugo took Gioele's hand and led him towards the stairs leading to the upper floors. He'd met Count von Stauffenberg once, during a party at the Adlon Hotel shortly after the officer's return from Africa. Hugo remembered the man for his striking charisma, as well as his distinctive battle injuries – in particular a mangled hand. An old mutual acquaintance, Dr Sauerbruch, had saved his life on the operating table.

'Herr Fischer!' Lukas called from the ground floor, sprinting to catch up with them.

As Hugo looked at Lukas, his gaze lingered on the black eyepatch. Another detail about the count struck him. Like

Lukas, the count had been wounded in the eye and wore an eyepatch. The voices of the Weidts' neighbours echoed in his mind, words he'd heard right after the discovery of the couple's bodies: a confused echo, hard to pin down exactly, but something he felt certain had to do with Stauffenberg.

'Herr Fischer!' Lukas's urgency snapped him back.

'Eder, what's happening?'

'There's chaos in the streets . . .' Lukas was out of breath, gesturing wildly, his tone a mix of excitement and apprehension. 'They say the conspirators have seized Bendlerstraße and will soon announce Hitler's death on the radio, along with the name of the new Reich Chancellor!'

Hugo measured his words carefully. If the rumours proved false, anything he said now could later be held against him.

'Is he *really* dead?'

'Apparently Stauffenberg claims to have seen it with his own eyes.'

Hugo caught up with Arthur Nebe as he was heading for the exit, flanked by a dense group of police officers. Someone from across the atrium shouted 'high treason!' after him, but Nebe marched on in soldierly fashion without looking back. He stopped only when he saw Hugo.

For the first time, Nebe refrained from raising his arm in the Nazi salute.

'This is the beginning of history, Fischer,' Nebe exclaimed. 'We'll be working together again soon, don't worry – this time under your rules. I have great plans for you!'

Hugo looked right into Nebe's eyes. Nebe turned on his heel and disappeared through the sunlit doorway, flanked by his platoon men. There was no further explanation. Outside, military trucks awaited. Hugo glimpsed von Helldorf and von Bismarck among the group. Clearly, the police leadership had thrown their support behind the coup.

Though every nerve in his body buzzed with anticipation, Hugo bit his tongue. The history Nebe spoke of was precariously balanced on a knife's edge, and one wrong move could send it – and them – spiralling into chaos.

'Let's go home,' he whispered to Gioele.

Chapter 62

From the living room window, they could hear tanks rolling through the city centre. Officers from the suburban military academies had taken up arms and were marching to suppress an SS uprising, as prescribed by the Valkyrie plan. Even Goebbels' ministry was under siege. Those were the only updates Hugo had managed to glean from his colleagues.

'Will these men who killed Hitler also free my parents?' Gioele stared at the street, his face taut with anxious anticipation.

Hugo stroked the boy's head, managing a smile, though he lacked the courage to give him an answer.

Edmund leaned out of the window, binoculars in hand, scanning the tanks. 'The important thing is that they've taken out that swine. We'll take care of the rest. We'll dismantle all the filth these bastards have piled up!'

'Father, watch your language . . .' Hugo lit a cigarette and tuned the radio.

As the broadcast began, the three of them fell silent,

settling on the couch. Hugo rubbed his jaw, then took a deep drag on the cigarette, though it did little to steady his nerves.

'This afternoon, an assassination attempt on the Führer's life was carried out with explosives.' The voice crackled through the speakers. Hugo's hand trembled, and cigarette ash spilled onto the carpet. His father punched the air in triumph. 'The Führer was not even injured,' the voice continued. 'He sustained only minor burns and bruises.'

Hugo's eyes widened, his chest tightening as if his heart had seized up.

'Lies!' Edmund slammed his hand against the radio. 'These bastards are lying to stall the coup. Damned porky liars, every last one of them!'

The announcer stated that Hitler would address the nation at midnight. Then the transmission ended abruptly. Hugo wanted to say something, but the words died in his throat.

'Is he really alive?' Gioele looked at them with wide, bewildered eyes.

'Of course not,' Edmund said, patting his grandson's head. 'And even if he were, there's no way he could return to Berlin in time. If those men overturn the government, it's over. Don't worry.'

'If he truly is alive, half the fence-sitters will change sides,' Hugo muttered, feeling the throbbing beginnings of a headache. For a fleeting moment, he had glimpsed a way out: the war's end, an armistice without the total collapse of Germany. But Edmund's fierce expression and Gioele's confused one forced him to rein in his anguish and adopt a pragmatic tone, immune to the temptations of despair.

'Maybe you're right. Maybe they're bluffing to buy time. Let's wait until midnight and see.'

The hours crept by with agonizing slowness, minute by minute.

Outside, the sky had darkened, and Berlin's blackout wrapped the city in an oppressive shroud. There was no sound, but Hugo doubted anyone had gone to bed. Even Gioele sat on the couch, facing the radio, his face illuminated by the faint glow of the candles. The grandfather clock struck half-past midnight.

'He's dead,' Edmund whispered, though he made no move to rise from the couch.

Hugo uncorked the brandy, pouring generous servings into their glasses. He lit another cigarette, adding to the overflowing ashtray on the table. Dr Meyer would have been furious to see how blatantly he was ignoring medical advice.

'You're right. They were bluffing.' Hope lingered in his voice, faint but stubborn. After all, the regime's only chance to thwart Valkyrie and return control to the SS was to deny Hitler's death. But how could he have survived an explosion in a concrete room? He had to be dead – there was no other explanation.

Hugo downed his brandy and rose, too restless to remain seated. The radio remained silent. The clock now read 1:00 a.m. A dry chuckle escaped him.

'Father, he's dead. He's really dead . . .'

'Told you so!' Edmund exclaimed.

But just then, the radio burst back to life, its static filling the room. None of them moved. The air seemed to thicken, pressing Hugo down into the couch.

'Fellow Germans!' The voice boomed from the speakers. Hugo's head snapped up, and a piercing whistle rang in his ears, briefly throwing off his balance. 'Tonight, I speak to you for two reasons: so that you can hear my voice and know I am safe, and so you may learn of a crime unparalleled in German history.'

'It's him.' Hugo's voice wavered, and his face paled.

'I don't think so,' Edmund replied, shaking his head.

'Papa . . . it's him.'

Hitler continued speaking, railing against the dishonourable, power-hungry officers who had dared plot against him.

'A group so unscrupulous yet irrational, criminal and foolish!' His voice seethed with anger. 'They orchestrated a conspiracy to eliminate me and, in doing so, sought to annihilate the entire German High Command. The bomb, placed by Colonel Count von Stauffenberg, exploded two metres to my right. While some of my esteemed collaborators were gravely injured – one fatally – I myself remain completely unscathed, save for minor abrasions, bruises, and burns. I see this as Providence affirming my mission to pursue the purpose of my life, as I always have. For I may confess to the nation that since the days when I moved into the Wilhelmstraße I had only one thought – to dedicate my life ever since I realized that the war could no longer be postponed. I have lived for worry, work, and worry only, and countless sleepless days and nights.'

'What now?' Gioele whispered, his fists clenched on his knees.

Hugo shook his head slowly. Things were about to get worse. Anyone who had revealed their loyalties in those tumultuous hours would pay the ultimate price.

'To restore order,' Hitler continued, 'I have appointed Reich Minister Himmler as commander of the national army. Colonel General Guderian will take his place as Chief of Staff.' Hitler went on talking and Hugo felt as if he was listening to a tape that kept reciting the same lines. 'It is my pleasure to greet you once more, my loyal comrades, for I have again been granted the privilege of escaping a fate that would have devastated the German people!'

Hugo leaned back against the couch, his gaze fixed on the ceiling. The German people had been thrust back into their nightmare, with no prospect of ever awakening from it.

Chapter 63

23 July 1944

Berlin, the Charité Hospital

'It's a disaster.' Adele, sitting on the bench, shaded her face from the sun with her hand.

The heat gripped Berlin. Summer had exploded, making everyone feverish and amplifying the sense of disorientation into which the population had sunk after the failed assassination attempt. It felt like floating in a bubble as the Gestapo ransacked offices, hunting down conspirators. Even a careless word could now arouse suspicion, and the failed coup was already becoming a bloodbath.

'What news do you have?' Adele sought his gaze.

'Very little. Arthur Nebe is at large, impossible to track down. He's compromised – everyone saw him gather his men.'

'Are you at risk too?'

'I knew nothing about the conspiracy, you can relax.'

Hugo paused. If Nebe had asked him to help, he might have accepted. He was grateful he hadn't been placed in such a compromising situation. 'Stauffenberg and his collaborators have been executed by firing squad – without so much as a trial. I think Helldorf and Bismarck of the police are also compromised . . . I'm certain I saw them with Nebe.'

'What about Stauffenberg's family?'

'All arrested, as far as I know. His wife, his children, even his parents, his in-laws, uncles, cousins, and their spouses. Hitler wants to annihilate his entire bloodline.' Hugo locked eyes with Adele. 'You're familiar with the concept of Sippenhaft, right?'

'Family responsibility,' Adele whispered.

'A family shares the responsibility for a crime or act committed by one of its members, justifying collective punishment. I think I know what Weidt was trying to protect his children from . . .'

'He was part of the conspiracy!' Adele gasped, covering her mouth. 'Now the message he left his children makes perfect sense!'

'The list of children killed in the Brocken incident had already made me suspicious,' Hugo said, rising from the bench. 'They were prominent surnames. I imagine someone decided to safeguard themselves in case the coup failed. I fear it won't take long for the Gestapo to figure out what happened. But now, I want confirmation of my suspicions. I can't rely on acts of faith alone.'

Dr Meyer furrowed his brow as soon as he heard Stauffenberg's name. He wiped the sweat from his forehead with a handkerchief, glancing nervously at the double-locked door of his office.

'Young man, you're putting me in a tight spot.'

'I just need one piece of information.'

'That's a name no one wants to be associated with these days.'

'I understand. Nothing will go outside the walls of the Charité, I promise.'

Meyer sighed and picked up the phone, dialling an internal number. He called for Sauerbruch. 'Come to my office, please,' he said.

Normally, he would have asked for the information over the phone, but paranoia must have been high even among the doctors. Stauffenberg had been cremated, and some claimed his ashes were scattered to prevent him from having even a small plot of German soil to rest on. No one wanted even the faintest connection to his name.

Sauerbruch knocked after a few minutes. Hugo opened the door, and the accordion-fold curtain rattled against the glass.

'Fischer!' the doctor exclaimed upon seeing him. 'More trouble with your lungs?'

Adele shot Hugo a worried look, but he brushed it off with one hand.

'I'm fine, no more issues,' he reassured them both. 'I'm here to learn who you worked with when you operated on Count von Stauffenberg.'

Sauerbruch offered a sheepish smile, shrugging.

'I'm not here on Kripo business,' Hugo clarified. 'You can trust me. After all, I trust you. Tell me about Stauffenberg and the surgery.'

'The bullet had entered the back of his head,' the doctor began hesitantly, then resolved to continue. 'It went through an eye and lodged in his skull. We couldn't remove it, but I saved his life. I hope this doesn't make me responsible for an assassination attempt . . .'

'No, you're safe. Don't worry.'

'And for the eye? Did you consult anyone?'

'I brought in Benedict Weidt.'

Hugo smiled. The sense of victory rejuvenated him, even as the situation remained grim.

'Thank you, Doctor.'

'Can I rest easy?' Sauerbruch loosened his collar.

'Yes, don't worry.'

The midday sun had made the heat oppressive.

Outside the Charité, Hugo suggested going to the Grunewald forest for lunch to cool off. They wandered through the greenery, far from the rubble, eating bread and cheese. The air there was cool and mild, filled with the scents of the undergrowth. They went over to sit by the lakeshore.

Adele kicked off her shoes, dipping her feet into the cool water and sighing with relief.

'How did you know?' she asked.

'About Stauffenberg and Weidt?' Hugo dug his fingers into the sand. The shimmering light on the water exuded an almost surreal peace. 'The Weidts' neighbours told me that a man who resembled Lukas Eder often visited them.' He tried to delve down to recover the exact words from his memory, assisted by the hypnotic lapping of the water. 'They said, "He looked at least ten years older, but there was a certain resemblance." Lukas, the officer who worked with me on the case, wears a black eyepatch. That's how Stauffenberg resembled him, "*in some ways*".'

'So Weidt met Stauffenberg at the Charité and joined the conspiracy . . .'

'I don't know in what capacity, but that's likely what happened.' Hugo picked up a few flat rocks and stood there, leaning on his cane. 'In January, a certain von Moltke was arrested for running a circle of dissidents. I believe there were also a few Jesuits implicated. Rumour has it Moltke's group opposed a violent overthrow.'

Hugo skipped a stone. It bounced once on the surface of the water before sinking.

'Weidt had connections to the Jesuits, as did Walther Rumer. They probably formed a circle like Moltke's, under the leadership of Father Arthur. But Weidt knew a coup needed violence to succeed.' Hugo flung another flat stone; this time, it skipped three times, making perfect arcs each skip.

Adele bit her lip and then thought out loud. 'So Weidt left the Jesuits to join Stauffenberg's more . . . realistic plan?'

'Exactly. The Jesuits wouldn't stain their hands even with Hitler's blood. But they have no problem with *saving* lives – hence the arrangement between Weidt and Father Arthur, aided by Rumer, with messages delivered by young Dieter Costa.'

'And who killed the Weidts?'

'I'm increasingly convinced that Marlene shot Benedict after discovering the conspiracy. She lived for the Party and would've done anything to forestall a coup attempt. Their son heard them arguing before the shot rang out. When he found them, Marlene had a head injury but was still alive, and the gun was lying on the floor.'

'Which means?'

'Marlene must've threatened to turn Benedict over to the Gestapo.' Hugo sat back down. 'Benedict must have tried to stop her, she fired, hitting him square in the chest. She dropped the gun in shock, stumbled, and struck her head on the low column behind her.'

'That makes some sense,' Adele mused, dipping her hands into the lake. 'Then who killed Marlene and staged the suicide?'

'I need more time to piece everything together, but I'll figure that out, too.'

'It's as if you can *see* exactly what happened . . .'

'That's true. Perhaps I do have a criminal mind after all.'

Adele splashed him with water, laughing. Hugo flinched, which only encouraged her further. Moments later, she was dragging him into the water, laughing as she kissed his neck in a wet embrace.

'It'll take forever to dry us off,' Hugo complained.

'What does it matter?' She slipped off her clothes, revealing her body in broad daylight. 'Life is so short! If we're dead tomorrow, at least you'll have skinny-dipped with me today.'

Chapter 64

25 *July 1944*

Berlin, Werderscher Markt, Headquarters of the Kripo

'No news of him.' The secretary paced back and forth from the desk to the window. She paused to look down at the fountain in the square, then began gnawing on a finger-nail – a rare lapse in composure for someone usually so precise and orderly. 'The Gestapo came yesterday.'

'Did they say anything?' Hugo approached the window.

'They asked if I knew where he was, and I was terri-fied they'd drag me to Prinz-Albrecht-Straße for question-ing . . . Did you know they've arrested Helldorf too? So many people are committing suicide . . .'

'How . . . involved are you?'

'Not at all, thank God!' She placed a trembling hand on her chest, visibly shaken. Hugo poured her a glass of water, and she drank it down in one gulp. 'I didn't know anything, Herr Fischer. I never even suspected that someone like Nebe could plot against the Führer. He must have been scared stiff by how things are going at the front . . .'

'What do you mean?'

'Herr Fischer, how well do you know Arthur Nebe?'

'Well enough. He's not a friend, just my superior.'

'I know him better than his mother ever did. I've been his secretary for over ten years. Nebe only turned against the Party he's fed off for so long because he sees the war ending badly. You have no idea the crimes he's committed. He knew that standing by Hitler would be a death sentence once the war ended.'

'We've all been complicit to some degree . . .'

'No, not like him!' Her voice quivered with rage, fists clenched at her sides. 'I just did my job – typing, answering phones, sorting mail, and enduring his jokes and those of his cronies. That man has the blood of thousands – no, tens of thousands – on his hands. Do you know what he did in Belarus with the Einsatzgruppen?'

The normally composed Frau Richter was now a torrent of anger and tears, oblivious to the risk she took by speaking so freely. It never seemed to occur to her that he might easily be an informant for the Gestapo she so feared.

'You should have seen him boast about it to his colleagues,' she said, breaking into sobs. 'He claimed that mass shootings traumatized the soldiers. The soldiers, Herr Fischer! He told us about a young soldier who was so distraught after what he'd seen and done that he gouged out his own eye with a stick!'

Hugo felt a jolt of recognition, like an electric shock. 'Really? That seems extreme . . .'

'I'm not exaggerating! Nebe was in Ukraine to observe

Jeckeln and Rasch's operations. That boy tried to blind himself, and Nebe stopped him before he could gouge out his other eye! He used to repeat the story every time he bragged about finding the final solution. He claimed that in order to keep the soldiers from going out of their minds, he'd come up with his own method: he ordered a room in a mental hospital to be sealed, with only two openings for the exhaust from the engine of a truck. He filled the room with inmates from the insane asylum. And within minutes, everyone inside was dead. Everyone! "Guess who invented the gas chamber?" he'd say, ever so smugly.' The woman paused. She sniffed and then, exhausted from her outburst, she slumped into a chair. 'But I still can't believe they're killing Jews in gas chambers. Who would do such a thing?'

'We Germans,' Hugo replied bluntly. 'I'm sorry to say it, Frau Richter, but it's all true. I've seen those gas chambers with my own eyes.'

'Then may God forgive us. When we lose this war, none of us will escape judgement.'

Hugo left Kripo headquarters with a crushing weight on his shoulders. For years, he had worked under a man he deeply respected, only to learn that Nebe was just another perverse cog in the Nazis' monstrous machinery.

He stopped in the middle of the square.

Closing his eyes, he let the sun warm his face. He thought of the soldier so desperate that he had gouged out his own eye, and then he recalled Lukas Eder's empty eye socket and the turbulent sea behind his one surviving good eye.

How had they reached such depths of depravity? One

thing was certain: they had turned Germany – and the rest of the world – into hell. And it didn't matter whether he or Frau Richter had personally operated the gas chambers. The Sippenhaft applied to them, too.

Chapter 65

Hugo slowed his pace when he saw the two men in civilian clothes standing by the front door to his building.

One of them opened his jacket, revealing the hidden Gestapo patch inside.

In the few yards that separated him from them, Hugo felt the instinct to run. Reason prevailed, however: he hadn't done anything wrong. He hadn't known about the assassination attempt in advance, and even if they arrested him for his connection to Nebe, they would have to release him after a few days due to lack of evidence.

'Are you Hugo Fischer?'

'Yes, that's me.' As he responded, he noticed the door hanging slightly ajar. They'd already searched the house. The memory of the ration cards hidden under the floorboard made him tremble. 'How may I help you?'

'You are under arrest.'

'For what?'

'From now on, we ask the questions.'

* * *

The photographer gestured for him to move slightly to the right and look directly into the lens. As the camera shutter clicked, Hugo feverishly tried to piece together who might have betrayed him. The Gestapo usually acted on tips from informants, but he felt certain he hadn't exposed himself to anyone – apart from Edmund, Gioele, and Adele. He thought of the documents Adele had smuggled out of Ravensbrück and meticulously copied to serve as testimony of what was happening in the camp. Those documents were sensitive, highly classified. Perhaps someone at the Charité had noticed and reported her. They had been seen together quite often lately.

The photographer directed him to turn his head to one side, then the other.

Or had they uncovered the truth about Gioele? The lump in his throat became unbearable at the thought.

'We're done,' the photographer announced, putting away his equipment.

A police officer grabbed Hugo to cuff his wrists.

'Please . . .' Hugo indicated his cane. 'I can't walk without this. If you cuff me, I won't be able to use it.'

The young officer put the handcuffs away and escorted him out of the room. He seemed like a kind man. Hugo wondered if all the stories he'd heard about the Gestapo were exaggerated, designed to build their fearsome reputation.

The officer opened a door and motioned for him to enter another room. The walls were bare, and there were no windows. The only light source was a single bulb casting a spectral glow over a polished steel table.

'Take a seat. Someone will be with you shortly.'

The young man closed the door behind him. Hugo sat at the table and waited. Even this waiting must be part of the Gestapo's tactics, for he couldn't silence his thoughts. Questions and doubts piled up, one on top of the other.

'Be quiet . . .' he whispered to his racing mind.

The word *quiet* sparked an idea. Klaus Weidt had heard only one gunshot. So had Klara. The neighbours, ditto. A silencer didn't make a gun completely silent, but it muffled the sound enough that, with windows shut, it wouldn't be audible in the next house. The subsequent two shots at Benedict and Marlene had likely been inflicted with a silencer. Who would have access to such an accessory?

The door creaked open, cutting off his thoughts. A Gestapo officer in civilian clothes, holding a folder, entered and sat down across from him. Two uniformed officers followed. Hugo tried not to betray his fear but wasn't sure if he'd succeeded.

'Good evening, Mr Fischer. I'm Kriminalrat Jung.' The tone of voice of the man in civilian clothing was cordial, his bright blue eyes lively, his cheek marred by a couple of scars. 'I hope for your cooperation – it will make everything faster and less *painful*.'

The jovial tone was almost too friendly, but Hugo didn't miss the emphasis on the word *painful*.

The man slid a drawing across the table. Hugo immediately recognized Gioele's handiwork, and his mouth went dry. They'd caught him. They'd either sent him back to Auschwitz or killed him on the spot. The man flipped the drawing over, and Hugo felt a strange wave of relief.

'Why did you have this leaflet in your house?'

Hugo stared at the typed page. He recognized the worn letter 'v'. It was one of the resistance flyers that someone had scattered across Mitte barely a month ago.

'My son picks up leaflets from the street to draw on the

back,' Hugo replied quickly, his confidence bolstered by the simple truth of his statement.

'He draws very nicely,' the man remarked, though the gleam in his eye suggested they were far from finished. 'And what about this?' He slid over a list of names. 'We found it in the safe at Bendlerstraße. It's the list of the government proposed for the twentieth of July.'

Hugo scanned the page. Ludwig Beck was listed as provisional Head of State; von Witzleben was named Supreme Commander of the Army, and Goerdeler was set to be the Reich's new Chancellor. Another list proposed other key figures. Among them, Arthur Nebe had noted names for a revamped police department. Hugo's name appeared next to a question mark, followed by the phrase *to be verified.*

'Your name is on the list. On the day of the coup, someone saw you rushing to the Kripo headquarters. Nebe reportedly said to you,' Jung paused, reading with emphasis: '"We'll be working together again soon, don't worry – this time under your rules." What did you know about the plot against our Führer?'

'Everything I've ever known, I learned that same day.'

'Why did Nebe want you by his side?'

'We've always worked well together.'

'And what does "this time by your rules" mean?' Jung leaned in closer. 'Do your rules pertain to a post-Nazi government? After all, you had a subversive leaflet in your house . . .'

'No, Herr Kriminalrat.' Hugo responded without hesitation, knowing hesitation could be deadly. 'I was investigating the deaths of Benedict and Marlene Weidt, but I couldn't work as I normally do because of certain bureaucratic obstacles. I had a dispute with Nebe over it and told him I wouldn't work under those conditions again.'

'I'm glad you mentioned Benedict Weidt.' Jung's smirk turned sharp. 'Weidt was a conspirator. During his trips abroad for conferences, he set up a platform for peace talks with the Allies.'

Hugo allowed himself a faint smile, hoping it wouldn't be misinterpreted. Now he understood Benedict Weidt's role in the conspiracy and knew another conspirator must have staged his suicide to prevent the plot from being exposed prematurely. The circle was tightening.

'Do you know where Arthur Nebe is hiding?'

'No.' This time, too, the answer was simple and straightforward, as he genuinely had no idea where the head of the Kriminalpolizei was hiding.

'And you claim not to know where the conspirators' children might be concealed?' Jung's subsequent pause made Hugo hold his breath. The man clearly sensed his fear. 'I'm referring to the supposed tragedy of the Mount Brocken excursion.'

'I don't understand . . . those children are dead.'

'Are you sure of that?'

'I saw the bodies.'

'Perhaps you should clear your head while you're in your cell.' Jung stood, gathering up the contents of the folder. 'I'd rather you didn't insult my intelligence. We both know those children are alive. I hope by the next time we meet, you'll do the right thing and tell me where they're hiding. For now, enjoy your stay in the lovely Plötzensee prison. Heil Hitler!'

Jung clicked his heels and exited the room. He'd left Hugo there, which must also be a part of their technique:

let him stew in uncertainty. It was another calculated tactic, designed to unsettle him with the prospect of the next interrogation, making him wonder whether it might not be smarter just to talk.

As Hugo was led out of the room, he glimpsed a woman lying on a stretcher in the hallway. She was trembling, her face smeared with blood. An SS officer threw a bucket of water on her face, making her gasp for air.

'What do you say, Frau Richter? Shall we continue the interrogation?' The SS officer's tone dripped with mockery.

When the woman turned her head, Hugo recognized her: Nebe's secretary.

Chapter 66

28 July 1944

Berlin, Plötzensee Prison

The cell where he had been confined for three days was suffocating and windowless, a burial vault whose walls bore the names of those who had once occupied it, scratched into the stone. Hugo could imagine fingernails clawing at the rough stone surface, breaking and bleeding as they left their marks. The thought made him shudder. He had followed the breadcrumbs, and now he was trapped in the witch's house.

Hugo sat on the floor and wrapped his arms around his belly, a sharp pain stabbing his side and leaving him breathless. He noticed that the door showed marks where someone's knuckles had dented the metal from inside. Someone had pounded on it in desperation, from the inside, and that, too, made him tremble and sweat.

He tried to breathe, but his lungs refused to cooperate.

This imprisonment might not have been so unbearable if it weren't for the shivers and fever wracking his body, and the endless vomiting that filled the cell with a vile stench.

He loosened the sweat-soaked collar of his shirt, which hadn't been changed in days. It dawned on him that he knew where the children of the conspirators were hidden – and it wasn't at St Teresa's. The realization made everything harder. If he were interrogated now, in the throes of withdrawal from morphine, he would betray them without even meaning to.

'Three more days,' he whispered. 'Just give me three more days . . .'

That's all it would take for the nightmare of withdrawal to pass – at least, that's what he'd heard. But when his teeth began chattering uncontrollably, he understood he was in over his head. He was an addict. He should have listened to Sauerbruch and Meyer.

The sound of the door opening crushed his last hope.

Hugo felt bile rise in his throat as he vomited yet again.

During the ride to Gestapo headquarters, the cramps in his stomach intensified.

As he stepped through the gates of Prinz-Albrecht-Straße, he realized he was in no condition to withstand an interrogation. He had cornered himself, and the Gestapo hadn't even needed to lay a hand on him to get him there.

Inside, Herr Jung was already seated at the table, composed as ever, his sharp smile welcoming him.

'I trust the accommodations were comfortable,' Jung said, his voice dripping with mock courtesy. 'I hope they allowed you to reflect on what the right thing to do might be.'

'They were fine,' Hugo replied, sinking into a chair. A wave of nausea swept over him.

'Now, where were we? Ah, yes . . .' Jung leafed through the folder before him. 'The youngsters from the Brocken incident. We've received a report from Dr Schmidt, who claims you performed an unauthorized autopsy on one of the victims. Several other witnesses saw you near the dissection room. Dr Schmidt insists that you were working on the case. Did you find anything out about it?'

'Nothing in particular.' Hugo felt a rivulet of sweat dripping down his neck. The air in the room was scalding hot. 'The youngsters died of asphyxiation and burns.'

'Schmidt says otherwise, though now he has a hard time saying anything at all.' Jung stood up and walked around the table. 'He says he doesn't know where the youngsters are, and I believe him. He's the kind of citizen who'll sing like a nightingale at the slightest violence. But he insists that when you set your mind to solving a case, you always figure it out. So let me ask you once again: do you have any idea where those children might be hiding?'

Hugo took a deep breath. 'No.'

Jung snapped his fingers, and Hugo barely had time to react before two guards grabbed him. He fell out of the chair and hit the floor hard. Kicks rained down on his back, each one stealing the air from his lungs. The sharp toe of a boot smashed into his face, splitting his lip. He felt it swell up and throb. He wallowed in the taste of his own blood. He found himself curled up on the floor, gasping for breath, like when he got hurt as a child. He thought he could hear his mother's voice.

One step at a time, Hugo.

One step at a time. He forced himself into a sitting position, choking back a scream of agony from his ribs, very likely broken. Blood and saliva dribbled from his mouth as he coughed, his head lolling.

'I don't know anything,' he croaked.

Jung grabbed him by the shirt and hauled him upright, denying Hugo the use of his cane, which he hurled to the other side of the room. Hugo clung to the table for balance and sat back down.

'We've already arrested Father Arthur Welder and Klaus Bach, the organizers of the Brocken trip,' Jung went on. 'Welder insists that he knows nothing and that the youngsters are all dead. We've searched the entire convent where he's a guest – but we've found nothing. I know the priest won't talk. He'd rather rot in Dachau. And Bach had a minor . . . accident during questioning, so now he's dead. That leaves only you. And you *will* talk. I guarantee it.'

Hugo burst out laughing, though it quickly exploded into an overwhelming eruption of coughing, spattering saliva and blood all over the file and the table.

'You find this amusing?'

Hugo wanted to say yes. They wouldn't find anything at St Teresa's because the children weren't there, that's not where Father Arthur had hidden them. In the darkness of his cell, Hugo had remembered the adrenaline vials in Walther Rumer's trailer. At first, he'd thought the former comedian was using the adrenaline to buck up the starving, weakened big cats, but then he'd remembered that Klara Weidt was taking adrenaline for her illness. Rumer was stockpiling as he awaited the arrival of his young guest. The Hoff Circus had folded up its tents the very same day as the accident, just as Frau Hoff had forewarned him.

What better way to smuggle fugitives out of Germany than with a travelling circus, dropping them off safely at another Jesuit convent?

He was certain of his suspicions. He could *feel* it. It was the act of faith Father Arthur had spoken of. Hugo wished that priest were by his side now, to give him the courage to banish all fear of pain. He slipped his hand into his trousers pocket and found the rosary that for some reason he had been carrying with him ever since the Jesuit had given it to him. He clenched it tightly.

'Where are those youngsters hiding?' Jung slammed his fists on the table. His lips turned pale. 'When we find them, they'll meet the same end as all the others! The children of those filthy traitors won't even remember their parents' names!'

He stood abruptly and punched Hugo square on the nose. Hugo's head snapped backward, his mouth filling with the metallic taste of the blood that was now dripping from his nostrils.

'And you,' the man hissed, 'will end up dangling from a piano wire like those swine!'

Hugo licked his lips. The pain of the blows was completely replacing the agony of withdrawal, and strangely, he was glad for it.

Jung regained his composure. He straightened the lapels of his jacket. He noticed he'd stained his shirt with blood and tried to clean it off with a handkerchief. When he finished, he gestured to the guard, who left and returned with a small metal box. Jung emptied its contents onto the table – a collection of drugs.

'Eukodal, Pervitin, morphine,' he said. 'You can have as much as you want if you tell me where they are. Or perhaps you prefer heroin, judging by how sick you've been these past few days? We can offer you that, too.'

Hugo felt his hands tremble, his stomach churn. Every inch of his skin screamed for the substances his body had grown dependent on. He shut his eyes and thought of Gioele's eyes. He would never go back to being the coward he had been before meeting the boy. He forced a smile that must have looked like a bloodied mask.

'Thank you, Herr Jung. I'm flattered by your high opinion of my investigative skills, but you're overestimating me. I never solved that case, just as I couldn't solve the Weidt case. You can torture me all you like, but unfortunately for you, I know nothing.'

'You've only tasted a shadow of our enhanced interrogation techniques. Think it over when you're at Plötzensee. The next time I see you, you'll be down on your knees begging me to let you tell me everything you know.' Jung paused, his slightly asymmetrical smile – twisted by the scars on his cheek – sending chills down Hugo's spine. 'Oh, and while you're at it, think about your father and your son as well.'

Hugo felt the lash of a whip across his back. Jung laughed.

'What did you think? That we wouldn't arrest them? That poor old man won't last a minute in the next interrogation. He cried at the first slap. And your son . . .' The man grimaced and gestured dismissively. 'Maybe we'll send him on a little trip to a camp. What do you say?'

'Leave my family out of this!' Hugo lunged forward, unable to contain his anger.

The guards intervened immediately, slamming his head down onto the table as Jung loomed over him like a ravenous predator.

'It's all up to you,' the man hissed in his ear. 'Talk, and nothing will happen to your loved ones. I'll give you a few days to think it over, but remember – every passing moment could be the last for a weak man like your father.'

One of the guards delivered a punch to his temple that sent his head bouncing off the table, leaving him half-unconscious. With his cheek pressed against the cold steel, Hugo felt his eyes fill with tears. The thought of his father, old and defenceless, beaten by the Gestapo, left him breathless. A profound shame overcame him for failing to protect both his father and Gioele.

Chapter 67

29 July 1944

Berlin, Plötzensee Prison

The ceiling was stained, as if a leak were slowly devouring all the plaster. Hugo felt as though he were floating, lying on the cot. He couldn't move. The pain kept him pinned down with stabbing sensations between his ribs, in his jaw, even in his skull.

The sound of the door opening made him instinctively shut his eyes. They had come to get him again, and this time, he wouldn't survive. He lay there, waiting.

He heard the door slam shut again.

'Herr Fischer! Look at the state they've left you in . . .'

Lukas's voice forced him to open his eyes slowly. He struggled to sit up so that he could look him in the eye and put an end to that objectionable display of pity.

'The next interrogation will be *enhanced*,' Hugo laughed, though he had to clutch his ribs with his hands. The clotted blood in his nostrils wouldn't let him take in enough air to soothe the pain.

'I know. That's why I'm here.' Lukas tapped the floor. Only then did Hugo notice he was holding his walking stick, the one Jung had confiscated. 'A request has been made to interrogate you using enhanced methods. You're smart enough to understand that you only emerge from that kind of interrogation either talking freely or stone cold dead. I got permission from my uncle to escort you to Gestapo headquarters.'

'Your uncle?'

'Kaltenbrunner.'

'Of course . . .' Only then did Hugo connect Lukas to Elisabeth Kaltenbrunner, née Eder, wife of the Reich Security Main Office commander. 'Is it you I have to thank for winding up in here?'

'Are you joking, Herr Fischer?' Lukas bent over to look him in the eyes. 'I'm here to get you out, because I don't want anything bad to happen to you and because I don't want you to talk under torture. Now, we're going to walk out of here, but I won't take you to Prinz-Albrecht-Straße. I'll leave you in safe hands. All you need to do is stay hidden for a few months, and someone will contact you.'

'What do you mean? Who will contact me?' Hugo was tired of half-truths. 'Why should I trust you? You've known all along why the Weidts were killed, and you offered to help with the investigation just to keep me under control. You knew it was Nebe who killed Marlene and staged Benedict's suicide.'

'How do you . . .' Lukas spread his arms.

'It took me a while, but eventually, everything fell into place. One step at a time.' Hugo tried to stand. The dizziness that blurred his vision forced him to give up. He collapsed back onto the cot and looked at the ceiling. He realized he was speaking more to himself than to Lukas. 'Benedict was part of a circle linked to the Jesuits, but then he joined Stauffenberg's group because the Jesuits would never kill Hitler; they inherently repudiated violence. Marlene found out and decided to turn him over to the Gestapo, threatening him with a gun. But a lethal gunshot went off. Terrified, she stepped back, lost her balance, and hit the back of her head. The children woke up, alerted the neighbours, and the neighbours called the police. And then came Nebe.'

Hugo stopped. Continuing cost him great effort. He only wanted to close his eyes and sleep forever. He wet his lips to muster the strength to keep talking.

'I asked myself – who else could have had a pistol with a silencer if not an SS officer? Nebe went to the crime scene himself, realizing the conspiracy was in danger. Marlene was still alive . . . I imagine that, seeing Nebe, even while disoriented, she told him about the planned attack in order to protect the Führer. Nebe shot her. Then he staged Benedict's suicide, but haste leads to carelessness: he should have considered Benedict was left-handed and that the bullet wouldn't have exited. Or perhaps he relied on Schmidt's sham autopsy to tidy everything up. At that point, given rumours about Marlene's infidelity, Nebe wanted to know who her lover was, someone she might have confided her suspicions about her husband to. That was my role – to quickly give him a lover to eliminate preemptively for security reasons, whether or not the lover knew about the plot. You, Lukas, were supposed to ensure I didn't step too far out of line . . .'

'That was my task, it's true,' Lukas nodded. 'When I

realized the kind of person you are, I was tempted to explain everything and involve you in the plot . . . but then I thought it would unnecessarily endanger you if it failed. The more you know, the worse things are for you.'

'I'm in trouble anyway.' Hugo stifled a groan from a sharp pain in his side. He forced himself to continue: 'You met Nebe in Ukraine. And in Ukraine, you also met Walther Rumer and Dieter Costa's father, who introduced you to Father Arthur and . . .'

He was about to add that it was Walther Rumer who had hidden and taken the children with him, but he stopped. He still wasn't sure whether or not Lukas knew.

'I'll confirm my first impression of you, Herr Fischer: your insight is exceptional.'

'And I still say you all overestimate me, for some reason. Now I have two questions, if you'll do me the favour of answering them. Were you the one who enrolled my son in the Jungvolk?'

Lukas shook his head. 'It was Nebe. He said he needed to verify your loyalty to Germany and to check if you were lying about something, but he never explained what.'

'Fine.' Hugo thought about that *to be verified* on the documents found in Bendlerstraße. So, Nebe harboured doubts about Gioele's identity and wanted to confirm them before offering him any role in the new government. He grabbed the cane and this time managed to stand up. 'And who ordered the attack on me outside my house?'

'Nebe again. He said you needed to be stopped because you were discovering too much too soon. I rushed to help you to make sure they didn't hurt you too badly.'

'You helped me; I won't forget that.'

'It was meant to be just a warning, but I deemed it

unnecessary and disobeyed the Gruppenführer. I hope this makes you trust me more. Everything I did was to free us from the fate the Nazis have condemned us to. I never wanted to endanger you, and if I lied, it was only to keep you out of trouble like this. You were only supposed to find a lover, and instead . . .'

'So now what's your plan?' Hugo gripped the cane tightly, resisting a wave of dizziness. He felt as if the cell walls were warping. 'I can't run. Jung has my father and my son.'

'Jung has no idea where your family is.' Lukas gripped his arm firmly. 'He lied to you. They're safe.'

Hugo felt a weight lift from his shoulders and chest, flowing down his legs and grounding him. He wanted to collapse and cry like a child. Instead, he remained standing.

'And the place where I'm going to hide you is secure,' Lukas reassured him.

'You need to tell me who these people are who are helping me.'

'You'll have to trust me. You'll know in due course.'

'A leap of faith . . . Father Arthur really trained you well, didn't he, Eder?'

Lukas laughed. Hugo tried to join in, but the pain in his chest wouldn't let him.

Chapter 68

On the way from his cell to the prison yard, Hugo felt like a dead man walking. It wasn't just the impossibility of moving without pain but the fear that, at any moment, the guards might uncover their plan – a plan that seemed reckless and hastily improvised.

Lukas showed the guards the permit issued by Kaltenbrunner, and the prison gates opened without question.

'Everything's going smoothly.' They climbed into the car, and Lukas pressed his foot down on the accelerator.

Hugo glanced at the rear-view mirror, watching the prison recede, the guards vanishing behind the gates. For the first time since his arrest, he caught sight of his reflection. They'd done a number on him, and whatever the Gestapo hadn't done to him, his withdrawal from opioids had finished off.

'If I have to go into hiding, who will take care of my father and my son?'

'We'll handle that too.' Lukas turned onto the bridge spanning the Spree river, heading in the opposite direction of Gestapo headquarters as promised.

'You said you're saving my skin to stop me from revealing where the conspirators' children are. How are you so sure I've figured it out?'

'I know because I've seen you in action.'

'And what if they arrest you? Aren't you afraid you'll talk?'

'I don't know where they are, Herr Fischer. Father Arthur never told me because he didn't trust Nebe. Frankly, I didn't trust him either. I'm fine with knowing that those kids are safe and nothing more.'

Lukas's gaze flicked between the road and the rear-view mirror.

'Everything all right?' Hugo asked.

'No. I think we're being followed.'

Hugo turned to look. Lukas was right. A dark car was trailing them, slowing down when they did and speeding up when they did, always keeping a safe distance.

'Who could it be?'

'I don't know . . .'

'I know Kaltenbrunner. He doesn't trust anyone,' Hugo said, opening the window to let in some air. The warm wind dried the sweat on his neck. 'He wants to make sure you're taking me to Prinz-Albrecht-Straße.'

Lukas didn't respond. Hugo adjusted his position in the seat. His heart started racing, pounding in his throat and suffocating him. He ran his tongue over his teeth, still tasting the faint metallic tang of blood.

The officer turned left, and the car behind them did the same, confirming their suspicions. They entered a deserted street in one of Berlin's most bombed-out districts.

'Your uncle doesn't trust you,' Hugo said, gripping the

head of his cane. 'Turn back. Take me to Gestapo headquarters – it's the only sensible thing to do.'

'That's not an option . . .' Lukas licked his lips. 'I have
agreements with my uncle.'

'Well, let me tell you, this plan is full of holes. What
were you going to tell him after dropping me off at your
so-called safe house?'

'I have a very clear plan. We're going to stage your escape. You'll have to shoot me in the leg, and then he won't
suspect a thing.'

'You young people are so naive and arrogant . . .'

'I know what I'm doing, trust me. We just need to deal
with this complication first.'

Lukas drove deeper into the ghostly neighbourhood. The
car weaved through broken streets and shattered buildings,
skeletal and grey, seemingly on the verge of collapse. He
turned off the engine. The other car pulled ahead by a few
metres but then stopped.

'Herr Fischer, can you run fast?' Lukas asked.

'Are you kidding?' Hugo raised his cane.

'But you can shoot.'

'Yes . . .'

'Can you shoot without hitting anything vital?'

'Yes.'

Lukas opened the glove compartment and handed Hugo
a Walther P38. 'Don't hesitate to shoot me and run if I tell
you to – but let's hope it doesn't come to that.'

'I . . .'

'This is no time for hesitation.'

They got out of the car in silence. The eerie, dusty landscape was oppressive. Only the creak of structures and the
crunch of debris under their shoes could be heard.

'I'm escorting a detainee,' Lukas announced, holding up his brass police buckle. His voice echoed among the ruins. 'Is there a problem?'

'You were supposed to take him to Gestapo headquarters.' The two men in plain clothes got out of the car, and one raised his pistol. 'You're under arrest for treason!'

'I have a permit from Kaltenbrunner himself,' Lukas said, waving the document.

'And what route did you think you were taking to get to Prinz-Albrecht-Straße?'

'I'm telling you: I have an agreement with Kaltenbrunner.'

'You're under arrest!'

The man fired a shot that struck the ground near Lukas's feet, sending up a cloud of dust that slowly dissipated. Hugo instinctively meant to loosen his grip on the Walther P38 hidden behind his back, preparing to drop it. But to his surprise, he found himself holding it even more firmly instead of letting it go.

'You fools!' Lukas spun around and pointed his service weapon at Hugo. 'I was supposed to pretend to take him to safety and get him to confess something very important! You've ruined our plan, and I hope you can explain this to Obergruppenführer Kaltenbrunner!'

'Lukas . . .' Hugo felt the blood drain from his head. He struggled to stay upright, but the image of Eder began to blur behind a swarm of bright spots clouding his vision.

The two men exchanged confused glances. Hugo's finger slid to the trigger. Why had Lukas given him a gun if he was betraying him?

'Now, Herr Fischer . . .' Lukas's voice was barely a whisper. His eye gleamed like a stormy sea.

Hugo mustered his strength, aimed the pistol, and

targeted a non-vital point. He lowered the barrel to the height of Lukas's thigh, avoiding the artery, and prayed he wouldn't faint.

One of the men spotted the movement and stepped forward. The explosion came like a fiery flash when he stepped on an unexploded bomb.

Chapter 69

Hugo felt the shockwave throw him backwards.

The blinding white light that followed the impact rendered him blind and deaf for what felt like an eternity. When he regained his senses, he found himself lying on the ground. A piercing whistle rang in his ears, blocking out any other sound. There were no screams, no sirens – only that long, shrill tone that seemed to press him into the dust, which slowly began to settle.

He struggled to sit up, brushing off bits of rubble. The movement wrung a scream of pain from his throat. He clutched his chest; it felt as though someone had driven a nail into it with a hammer. Breathing was almost impossible, the dust-choked air barely passing through his nostrils.

He looked around, squinting through the haze stirred up by the explosion.

The two men who had been too close to the blast were gone, their remains indistinguishable. Nearby, he spotted someone slumped in a corner and crawled towards them. As the figure came into focus, he recognized Lukas's hair, now grey with dust. Hugo turned him over but pulled his hands back sharply when he saw the gaping wound in Lukas's abdomen.

The young man's lips quivered. His hand reached out weakly, and Hugo clasped it tightly.

'It wasn't supposed to end like this,' Lukas mumbled, his words wet with blood. 'I had a plan . . .'

'I know, I know. Stay calm,' Hugo said, forcing himself to speak despite his laboured breathing.

'We're . . . we're on an informal basis now,' Lukas murmured with a weak smile.

'Yes . . .' Hugo stifled a sob with a laugh.

'I . . . I wanted . . . a free Germany.' Lukas's gaze wandered skyward. His hand trembled as it fell to the warm, gaping wound spilling his life away. 'I . . . wanted to atone for my sins . . . And you, Hugo . . . you and I . . . we would have worked well together . . .'

'We would have been a great team,' Hugo replied, gripping his hand even tighter. He felt Lukas slipping away, slowly, and with him, Hugo felt himself fading too. A crushing weight pressed down on his chest, draining the last bit of air from his lungs.

'We've done horrible things . . .' Lukas's eyes widened as if he could see something only he could understand. 'It's not just the SS; it's all of us . . . guilty . . . the police . . . the Wehrmacht . . . we killed them . . . thousands every day, women and children . . . killed and thrown into pits . . . It's so dark here . . .'

Chapter 70

Babi Yar, 1 October 1941

The Day After the Massacre

Even though it is dark now, I see them. Thirty thousand bodies crammed at the bottom of the ravine, crushed on top of one another – men and women, women and children, all together.

I pick up a sharp stick from the ground.

I grip the piece of wood tightly. A splinter burrows into my skin. Hans will call me weak. Only Ermanno would understand me, but he died with his trousers down. And Walther – he went home, minus an arm. I don't want to see any more, don't want to remember any more. I don't want to do it any more. I just want to go home too.

I drive the stick straight into my eye.

I feel the softness of the eyeball give way. It takes a second strike before the pain – a searing, unbearable pain – rips through me, forcing a scream from my throat.

I collapse to my knees. The agony consumes every nerve in my body. With my hand, I probe the result of my madness. I feel the torn flesh, the pulp where my eye used to be. I tremble.

'For God's sake, boy! What are you doing?'

A shout reaches me from behind. Someone grabs me, wrests the weapon from my hand, and holds my face tightly between theirs.

'Holy God!' the SS man hisses. 'What the hell have you done?'

I taste the blood in my mouth. It's as though I'm being suffocated by the mangled bodies of the Jews, their mutilated flesh. A retch overtakes me, and I vomit onto the grass. The acid floods my tongue and nostrils, jolting me awake.

'I didn't want to do it! I didn't want to shoot!' I stammer.

The officer – an SS man, I can tell by the gleaming rank on his collar under the moonlight – places a hand over my mouth, pressing firmly despite the blood making it slippery. 'Shut up,' he orders. His voice carries no anger, but neither does it show pity. It is calm, cold. 'If you tell anyone what happened, you'll end up in an asylum. Or worse – you'll be *eliminated*. Now listen to me.'

He pulls a handkerchief from his pocket, pours rum from a flask onto it, and presses it to my ruined eye. I scream at the burning pain. It feels like fire is eating me alive, though it is nothing compared to the punishment I deserve.

'What's your name?'

'Lukas . . . Lukas Eder . . .'

'Good, Eder. We'll say you fell while taking a piss, straight onto a sharp branch sticking out of the ground,' he continues. 'I saw it all. You can give them my name – Arthur Nebe. I'll corroborate your story.'

I nod, still dazed. My hands and feet tingle.

'You'll be fine, boy.' The officer claps a hand on my shoulder. 'Turn your anger into motivation. You'll need it, I promise you.'

I hear his voice fade into the cold air of Babi Yar.

I collapse to the ground. From the one eye I have left, I see the star-filled sky. The clouds have cleared. The stars are so bright, speckling the heavens with a beauty that seems miraculous. I am nothing more than a tiny, insignificant man, yet one who has managed to fill this ravine with thousands of corpses. We are so small, and yet so savage. So destructive.

I lie there, in this death-like state, wondering if I will ever be forgiven.

Chapter 71

Lukas tried to speak, but no words came.

Blood trickled from the corners of his mouth and nostrils like a stream. Hugo tried to hold down his trembling arms and legs, but realized it only worsened things – for both of them. Unable to stay upright any longer, he lay down beside the young man. The only way he could accompany him now was like this.

He gripped Lukas's hand tightly, refusing to let him face this alone.

He felt the last, faint shudder, then nothing more.

Hugo remained lying next to the corpse. A scream lodged in his throat, unvoiced, and the shattered buildings around them could not return even the faintest echo of his grief. With great effort, he sat up, his breathing reduced to a wheeze. He gently stroked Lukas's face, folded his hands over his chest, and adjusted the bandage over his eye. Then he removed the silver badge from Kiev. One day, he would find Lukas's mother and return it to her. He slipped it into his pocket, crawled towards his cane, and used it to drag himself to his feet.

He staggered to the car, brushed the shattered glass off the seat, and climbed in. Gripping the steering wheel, he prayed he wouldn't die right there. He needed to see Edmund and Gioele. He needed to hold Adele. Only then could Berlin claim his blood as well.

'What happened to you, sir?'

A nurse rushed to his side as Hugo stumbled into the Charité hospital and helped him into a chair in the waiting area.

'There was an explosion . . .' Hugo scanned the atrium. The space was occupied only by medical staff, yet he felt vulnerable. He could no longer tell if the pounding in his chest was fear or the aftermath of the blast.

'I'll call for a stretcher immediately!'

As soon as the nurse disappeared down a corridor, Hugo forced himself to climb the stairs to the second floor, searching for the department where Adele worked. He slowed as it dawned on him how this could endanger her. He turned to leave, but her voice stopped him in his tracks, just as it had at Auschwitz, anchoring him.

'Hugo!' Adele ran towards him, throwing herself into his arms. 'They let you go!'

His ribs screamed in protest at the pressure, but Hugo swallowed the pain. She sobbed against his chest. Those hours must have been unbearable for her.

'They didn't let me go.' His voice was barely a whisper, more air than sound.

'What have they done to you . . .' Adele looked up at him. 'They're monsters!'

'Lower your voice.' Hugo glanced around the hallway, which was mercifully empty. 'Take me to a room – it's not safe to stay here.'

Adele led him into an office, setting down the files she had been carrying. She rummaged for gauze and disinfectant, then began cleaning the blood from his face. Unbuttoning his tattered shirt, she froze, her hands suspended mid-air.

'Oh my God!' She quickly covered her mouth with her hands.

'Do I have broken bones?'

'I need to call a doctor!'

'Wait.' Hugo grabbed her wrist to stop her. 'I told you – they didn't release me. I escaped. They're looking for me. I can't stay. Where are my father and Gioele?'

Adele shook her head, then knelt in front of him. 'You need surgery!'

'I'm fine.' Hugo struggled to breathe, each inhalation shallow and laboured.

'You have shrapnel in your lung and a pneumothorax!' Adele pressed on his sternum. A faint crackling sound of trapped air met her touch. 'It's serious . . .'

'Then call Sauerbruch,' Hugo wheezed. 'Him and Meyer – no one else.'

Adele leapt to her feet, bumping the files off the desk. The papers floated to the ground like autumn leaves. Hugo felt fever ignite his temples, the oxygen leaking from his body, his brain faltering. A patient's file, detailing the birth of a child, landed on his lap. Bringing a child into this world, under the bombs and the chaos of a Germany hurtling towards its doom – what sense did it make?

As he slumped in the chair, his eyes caught the worn-out 'v' in the typewritten pages.

He tried to speak, but no words came out. The room

darkened, and it felt as though he were sliding into a crack in the floor, a black abyss that consumed him without mercy.

Chapter 72

2 August 1944
Berlin, the Charité Hospital

'You're a lucky man, young fellow.' Sauerbruch's jovial face looked down at him. 'To have the best thoracic surgeon at your disposal – if that's not good fortune, I don't know what is!'

'What happened?' Hugo glanced around the room. They were alone. Not only had the doctor saved his life, but he had also ensured his privacy.

'I repaired the punctured pleura.' Sauerbruch removed his glasses and tucked them into the pocket of his coat. 'Fortunately, it was less severe than it looked. Nurse Krause explained your delicate situation. You understand we can't keep you here long – it's too risky.'

Hugo took a deep breath. The hunger for air had passed.

'Do you have a place to go?' the doctor asked.

'Yes.'

'Good. I can arrange for you to leave in an ambulance. It won't attract attention, and you won't strain yourself too much.' Sauerbruch patted his leg lightly. 'I'm sorry, but we can't take any chances. Yesterday, some men in plain clothes were asking questions . . . I'll leave you with Fräulein Krause. I need to organize a vehicle.'

The doctor left, and Hugo glimpsed Adele beyond the doorway.

'Herr Fischer, good to see you awake,' she said softly as she closed the door.

'Fräulein Krause . . . lucky for me, I saw Sauerbruch first. If I'd seen your heavenly vision, I'd have thought I was already in Paradise.'

'Idiot.' Adele laughed. She wrapped the blood pressure cuff around his arm, inserted the stethoscope, and squeezed the bulb. 'Not bad, considering how you looked,' she commented as the needle steadied. 'You scared me this time . . .'

She bent to kiss him, and Hugo held her, savouring her scent.

'Is your typewriter missing a key?' he murmured against her lips.

'What?' She straightened abruptly.

'The "v".'

'I don't understand . . .'

'I noticed it on the reports you typed. The "v" key is worn out.'

'It's what we've got to work with.'

'We agreed to tell each other everything.'

Adele stared at him with wide eyes. Hugo realized he adored that expression. He probably adored everything about her.

'Do you have something to tell me?' he pressed. 'Something involving leaflets?'

'How do you . . .?' Adele pursed her lips and crossed her arms. 'I stopped. When that Mercedes started following me, I was too scared . . . mostly about dragging you and Gioele into it.'

'Well, I'm pretty good at getting myself into trouble.' Hugo gingerly touched the bandages on his chest. The drainage tubes were uncomfortable, but at least he was alive. He straightened his sore shoulders, eliciting a crack from his neck. The image of Lukas's death flashed through his mind. A sob lodged in his throat, unable to escape.

'What's been happening while I was gone?' he mumbled.

'They've arrested many people,' Adele said, squeezing his hand. 'They've executed them, and now they show the footage of their executions in cinemas. It's horrific. They're arresting anyone who so much as comments on it . . . And Goebbels announced the Totaler Krieg on the radio.'

The total war. They had reached the point of no return.

'They're closing non-essential shops and declaring a general mobilization,' Adele continued. 'Rumour has it they're even conscripting sixty-year-olds. I hope your father is safe.'

'Have you seen him?' Hugo swallowed, the bitterness filling his mouth. What if Jung hadn't been lying? What if Lukas had reassured him only to convince him to follow?

The door opened quietly, interrupting them. Sauerbruch entered, checking that the corridor was empty before stepping in.

'It's time,' he announced. 'You're not in the best shape to be discharged, but I can't do any more for you.'

'I understand, Herr Doktor. Thank you for everything you've done.'

'Let's remove those tubes and get you out of here.'

Sauerbruch parked the ambulance halfway to their destination. He opened the door, and the pale light of the late afternoon spilled into the vehicle.

'I'm leaving you here, son. I don't want to know where you're going. It's safer for all of us.' The doctor helped him down and handed him a small case. 'This contains all the medication you'll need for post-op recovery and for your multiple sclerosis. Fräulein Krause knows what to do.'

'Thank you.' Hugo shook his hand, holding it a moment longer than usual. He didn't know if, or when, they might meet again.

'Take care of yourself, young man.'

'I will.'

Adele took his arm, supporting him as they watched the ambulance pull away. For the first time, Hugo found the streets of his Berlin hostile. He felt betrayed by the crumbling buildings, blackened by soot, by the streetlamps that wouldn't light that evening, plunging everything into a terrible darkness.

The air raid sirens blared. People quickened their pace, seeking shelter. Hugo and Adele, however, moved slowly. After the last few days, nothing – not even an Allied bomb – could disturb them.

'Are we close?' Adele whispered.

'Yes.' Hugo pointed to the Volker signs.

Adele helped him into the print shop. A woman was busily shutting down the machines in preparation for the air raid. She turned to study them briefly before resuming her work, pulling levers and throwing open windows.

'I'm looking for Edmund Fischer,' Hugo said.

'And why would you look for him here?' The woman rolled up her sleeves and twisted her white hair into a bun. 'Go and find shelter. Hell's about to break loose.'

'I'm his son.'

The woman studied him with narrowed eyes. A nearby explosion made the walls tremble, and the lights flickered.

'All right. Come with me.'

Epilogue

Dozens of eyes turned to stare at them as they entered the shelter.

Hugo recognized the eyes of Gioele and his father. This time, the lump in his throat found a way out and transformed into liberating sobs that swept away all the darkness that had burrowed into his soul. A light illuminated that place buried in the earth – not sunlight, but a light of hope and survival.

'You're alive!' Gioele ran to embrace him, just as he had outside the showers of Auschwitz on that snowy, freezing night. 'You're alive, I knew it! I told them!'

Hugo held him tightly, ignoring the pain in his chest.

'What did they do to you?' Edmund cupped Hugo's face with his hands and hugged him with the same tenderness he had shown when Hugo was a child who'd hurt himself. 'Those beasts . . . I was so scared I wouldn't see you again. I did what you told me. I brought Gioele to a safe place. I thought they might come for us, too . . .'

'You did well, Papa,' Hugo said, gripping his father's shoulder. 'You did the right thing.'

He looked around. There were blankets, bowls, food, and water containers in the room. A line stretched from one wall to another, holding drying laundry. Piles of books filled the remaining space of the hidden room, which wasn't just an air raid shelter.

'Is this what you needed the ration cards for?' Hugo asked.

Edmund's eyes widened in mock surprise. He shrugged and curled his lips. 'I don't know what you're talking about.'

'Fine, Papa,' Hugo said with a laugh.

'Let me introduce you to everyone!' Gioele grabbed Hugo and Adele's hands, dragging them into the small crowd. 'This is Israel, and over here are Sara, Ruth, Rudolf, Hannah, Duda . . .'

'Did you say *Duda*?' Hugo scanned the room. In a corner near the bookshelf, a girl looked up from a book. She had deep, dark eyes that gleamed in the dim light.

Hugo moved to sit beside her, bending carefully to avoid pulling the stitches in his chest. Outside, the bombs boomed loudly, shaking the plaster into a fine dust. For a moment, the light flickered and went out.

'I met Dieter Costa. He still has your violin.'

Duda's eyes widened, her lips parting slightly. She quickly wiped away a tear and hugged her knees to her chest. 'Is he all right?'

'Yes. He's a remarkable young man.'

'Does he really still have my violin?'

'He keeps it beside his bed.'

Hugo noticed the flush in her cheeks and realized that Duda was in love with Dieter. The thought brought a smile to his face, and unexpectedly, a warmth spread through his chest where there should have been only pain. That young love had bloomed amid the chaos of Berlin, a city drenched in blood, between people who weren't even supposed to mingle. It was the truest defiance against Hitler's madness.

'Is he the one who helped you hide here?' Hugo asked.

Duda nodded. 'With Herr Hoff.'

'The circus Hoff?'

'Yes. He hid me in secret compartments in the caravans or the animal cages. When the SS came, he'd shout to the stable boy to bring some rum, and I knew what to do. That was the signal.'

'And what rum!' Hugo chuckled, recalling Walther Rumer offering him a bottle of excellent vintage, which had actually been the warning for the entire circus. 'Did he ever think about smuggling you out of Germany during the tours?'

'He does that with the others,' Duda said, wrapping her shawl around herself, confirming Hugo's theory about the children from the Brocken. 'But I didn't want to leave. I wanted to come back to Berlin and stay with the circus.'

'For Dieter?'

Hugo found her blushing again utterly charming. Her proud, resolute gaze and exotic features evoked the image of a queen from distant, faraway lands, yet the mere mention of that name made her tremble.

'When things got more dangerous, I had to hide here, with Frya,' she explained.

'Hugo, look!' Gioele interrupted, rushing over with a book in his hands. 'Look what I found!'

'Wow . . .' Hugo ran his hand over the scorched corner of the cover, recognizing the title.

'Open it!' Gioele bounced with excitement. 'You won't believe it!'

'All right, all right . . .'

Hugo's hands trembled as he opened the book and read the signature on the first page. He had thrown that book into the flames, destroying his own integrity in that act and becoming a cog in a terrible machine. But now the novel had risen from the fire, returning to his hands to erase his mistakes and offer him salvation.

'Why is it here?' he whispered.

'Frya saves people and books,' Duda said with a smile. 'She says they're equally important.'

'Give it to Duda!' Gioele sat cross-legged on the floor. 'She's amazing at reading for everyone!'

'Would you read to us?' Hugo handed her the book.

Duda turned the pages. Her voice silenced everyone. It was deep, melodious, resonating like a violin string. It mingled with the sound of the bombs outside and, in the end, drowned it out completely. In the beauty of those words the Nazis had tried to erase, they found a measure of peace, and Hugo knew with certainty that something – whether ideas, books, people, or even fragments of the soul – always survived the worst.

Author's Notes

While Hugo Fischer's story is fictional, many elements of this novel are true.

In its nooks and crannies, you'll recognize nurse Maria Stromberger, who rejected the logic of extermination and, at Auschwitz, saved prisoners and collaborated with the camp's resistance.

You'll recognize Solomon Perel, a young Jewish boy who disguised himself as German and joined the Hitler Youth, hiding in plain sight as the perfect Aryan.

You'll recognize the Althoff Circus and others like it, which provided protection to Jews and dissidents, smuggling them out of Germany during their tours to ensure their safety.

You'll recognize the clergy who spoke out against the Reich, risking being sent to concentration camps, and the resistance circles where many Germans fought the regime.

Lastly, you'll find Otto Weidt, the 'Schindler of Berlin', who protected his Jewish employees as long as he could and even travelled to Auschwitz to try to save one of them.

History, even in its darkest moments, is dotted with small lights that make all the difference.

Acknowledgements

I would like to thank Piergiorgio Nicolazzini for believing in me once again; Arianna Miazzo, Emanuele Malpezzi, Antonio Carminati, and Maura Solinas: nothing would be possible without you.

Thanks to Agnese Messina for medical consultation and to Francesca Trois for sharing her daily experience living with multiple sclerosis.

Special thanks to my amazing beta readers: Scilla Bonfiglioli (whom I'm grateful to also count as one of my dearest friends), François Morlupi, William Bavone, and Luciana Fredella.

My gratitude goes to all those people who, with their presence and affection, are part of my life.

To Sebastian and my children, Samuel, Elia, and Emanuele, who never cease to make me proud of them.

To my father and mother, the best parents in the world; to my aunt Maria Antonietta, my sister Fernanda, and Arturo, Andrea, Paolo, and Maria. And to Antonello, Fernanda, and Pasqualino.

To Alessandra, Marcella, Grazia, and Incoronata – friends and sisters.

To Elisa Bertini, the 'Handmaidens', Luca, Anna, and Alessandro.

To Marietta, who taught me that you can go far even in a wheelchair.

To Diego Di Dio, friend and colleague; to Franco Forte for all his lessons; and to all the former members of Collettivo 28, with whom I continue the adventure of a wonderful friendship.